Praise for Frazer Lee

"Stoker Award nominee for Best First Novel, *The Lamplighters* is a disturbing book, I mean REALLY disturbing. Unsettling and ultimately a shock to the system, but I loved it!"

—Dreadcentral.com

"The Skin Mechanic is destined to become one of the great monsters of modern horror."

—Dave Brzeski, British Fantasy Society, on *The Lamplighters*

"The Skin Mechanic is one of the darkest characters I have ever had the pleasure of reading about...(Frazer Lee) not only takes you to the edge, but he shoves you into the darkest depths of true human vanity."

—S. Siferd, Night Owl Reviews. Reviewers Top Pick, 4.75 of 5 Stars on *The Lamplighters*

"Think the mystery of *Lost* mixed with the bizarre beauty of Dario Argento and you might just be close to *The Lamplighters*."

—Pat Dreadful, Dreadful Tales

Look for these titles by
Frazer Lee

Now Available:

The Lamplighters
The Lucifer Glass

thank you John !

The Jack in the Green

Red & Green should ALWAYS be seen :)

Frazer Lee

Cheers !

SAMHAIN
PUBLISHING

Samhain Publishing, Ltd.
11821 Mason Montgomery Rd., 4B
Cincinnati, OH 45249
www.samhainpublishing.com

The Jack in the Green
Copyright © 2013 by Frazer Lee
Print ISBN: 978-1-61921-563-4
Digital ISBN: 978-1-61921-453-8

Editing by Don D'Auria
Cover by Scott Carpenter

First Samhain Publishing, Ltd. electronic publication: October 2013
First Samhain Publishing, Ltd. print publication: October 2013

Dedication

To the green men, the green women, and all their saplings.

"Wae's me, wae's me

The acorn is not yet

Fallen from a tree

That's to grow the wood

That's to make the cradle

That's to rock the bairn

That's to grow to a man

That's to slay me."

—'Song of the Cauld Lad of Hilton' (Anon.)

Prologue

Tom's nightmare was always the same.

He was six years old again and it was Christmas Eve. Tom's breath fogged up his bedroom window then disappeared like a ghost. He tried again, but no luck—the frost clinging to the outside of the windowpane refused to melt. He wished his parents would just go to bed. He'd been kneeling here on his bed, leaning on the windowsill for what seemed like an eternity. Then he heard footsteps on the stairs.

It was his mom, there to tuck Tom into bed. He lay rigidly still, breathing heavily with his arms by his side. He felt his mother's shadow falling over him as she leaned in to kiss him softly on the head. He listened intently as she closed the door and went back downstairs to the living room. *Must be wrapping my presents right now,* he thought, his ears conjuring sounds of foil paper and sticky tape.

This was the most crucial part of Christmas Eve for Tom—waiting for Mom and Dad to come to bed. Then he had to leave it for just long enough to make sure they were asleep, without nodding off himself and missing his chance.

Tom awoke with a jolt and shivered. His bedclothes had made a bid for freedom, leaving just his pajamas to protect him. He grabbed his alarm clock, the luminous face teasing him with the time. Four o'clock a.m. Brilliant, he'd nodded off and been asleep for hours. But there was still time.

He swung his legs over the side of the bed, and ever so carefully stood up. Without a sound, he crept over to the door. *Careful now,* this was where it could all go horribly wrong. One false move and he'd wake them up. He reached out for the door handle, his arm rehearsing the exact distance he could open the door before it creaked. Slowly, slowly, he pulled the door open, slipped sideways through the gap, grabbed the outside handle and closed the door behind him with the tiniest click.

Heart beating, Tom stood on the dark landing for a few seconds, catching his breath. Satisfied he hadn't woken his folks, he padded gently across the landing towards the stairs. The soft, soundless carpet beneath his feet, he allowed his mind to wander a little. He began thinking of the prize that awaited him at the end of his mission, remembering how wonderful his presents had looked under the tree last year. They'd gleamed in their shiny wrapping paper like treasure, begging him to squeeze them. His pace quickened as he reached the foot of the stairs.

Downstairs was even chillier than his bedroom, cold seeping into the hallway through hidden nooks and crannies. Tom folded his arms around him, shivering, and snuck into the living room. It was pitch-black inside. An acrid metallic smell filled the room. What had they been wrapping in here?

Only one way to find out, thought Tom as he edged his way around the perimeter of the room, feeling along the cabinet, then the wall. Finally, he felt the Christmas tree as he brushed against it. Baubles clinked icily as he located the power cord and followed it, crawling across the floor to the power socket in the corner. He felt the cold metal pins in his hand and turning the plug right side up, inserted it into the wall. Something wet dripped on his hand just as he pressed the switch. Something heavy, and slick, slid across his head.

Tom scrambled backwards in shock. Looking up, he saw the fairy lights twinkling. But they were red, not clear, as they had been earlier today and all last week since they'd decorated the tree. He stared, mouth agape, as he realized the lights weren't red after all. Rather, it was what hung around them that gave them their crimson glow.

The Christmas tree was slicked with blood and covered in strands of flesh and hair. His mom's hair. He could pick out his dad's tattoo on a piece of bloodied skin that dangled above a bauble like a handkerchief; a mermaid rendered in fading blue ink on now-dead flesh. Drooping branches struggled beneath the weight of the innards scattered across them like red tinsel. Ruined organs steamed like butcher's offal at the hot kiss of the lights. Eyeballs hung there like baubles. He could recognize some of the pieces; a section of intestine here, a tangle of veins there.

Tom scrambled to his feet. Nausea hit him and he vomited stomach bile onto the living room rug. Turning fearfully around, he saw his parents lying lifeless on the sofa like grotesque dolls. Their bodies had been torn apart. Flesh ravaged and rib cages exposed like the hulls of broken ships.

The room spun and Tom sank to his knees, a dry scream dying in his throat.

Then he saw them. Red, burning eyes watching him from the dark black of the fireplace.

Watching him touch his presents.

Chapter One

Tom's nightmare was always the same.

And it always had the same effect. He awoke with a start, a dry scream dying in the pit of his throat. His body was slicked with sweat, his pulse pounding. Afraid to open his trembling eyelids for fear of what they might reveal, he tried to remind himself he was no longer that six-year-old boy; almost thirty years had passed since then. Still, he kept his eyelids clamped shut. Then a hot, urgent buzzing sound dared him to look. Angry red eyes glared at him in the gloom. He lashed out at them, self-defense of the half-asleep, and knocked the digital clock from the nightstand to the floor. The noise cut off as the clock-face hit the deck, the after-image of its numerals burned into his retinas: 6:15. Time for work.

Julia stirred, right beside him but leagues away. Had he cried out again during the throes of his nightmare? Had he whimpered like that child did on Christmas Eve all those years ago? A new and terrible fear lurched into his consciousness and he reached down quickly to feel the crotch of his boxers, then the sheets either side of his hips.

Dry.

At least he hadn't wet the bed again—no shameful sheets to explain this time.

"Tom?"

So she *was* awake.

Here it comes, he thought.

"You... You okay?" she asked sleepily. Her words were slurred and she sounded stoned. The meds usually knocked her out for longer, until way after he'd left for the office.

"I thought I heard... Bad dream again?"

Making a hasty exit from their bed, he tripped over the clock and its hot coal eyes glowed crimson against the floorboards.

"Gotta shower. Early start. Meeting."

He was at the door and into the en suite before she could utter another word.

If Tom's nightmare was one recurring hell, his journey to work was another. Always the same undignified crush to clamber onto the overground Caltrain, always the same surly looks from his fellow passengers as they jostled in vain to create some personal space. That morning, the smell in the carriage was a hangover from the night before; fast-food-grease smell imbued with subtle body-odor variants cut through with a sharp spice that smelled like stale vomit.

Good morning, America.

Somebody coughed and sneezed on the back of his neck, showering him with droplets of nasal mucus. Charming. He tried to crane his neck to get a look at the culprit but, still stiff as a board from his lousy night's sleep, only succeeded in straining a muscle in his neck. Wincing painfully, he tried to maneuver his free hand up and over to his shoulder to massage the spasmed muscle. Instead, he got his arm entangled in a fellow passenger's bag strap and had no choice to but to remain in bondage with the indifferent stranger until his stop. The doors yawned open and he and dozens of other travelers spewed out onto the platform like flapping fish from a net. The woman to whom he had become so attached in such a short space of time gave him a look that could curdle milk before she snatched her bag away from his arm and stormed away cursing under her breath.

Yeah, good morning, America. Have a nice day.

Tom rubbed at his shoulder, which clicked like a faulty latch, and meandered toward the exit.

The headquarters of The Consortium Inc. was just as he had left it on Friday; monolithic, cold and somehow indifferent to human life in its design, much the same as Tom's experience of working for such a large global corporation. He had worked there for six years and barely knew any of his coworkers' names, especially those in other departments. Standing by the elevators along with a group of smartly dressed drones, he basked in the slightly uncomfortable corporate silence. At the familiar *ding* of the arriving elevator car, a complex hierarchical dance played out as the workers boarded. Tom watched as the person nearest the row of polished buttons pressed for the second floor. He recognized the member of staff as Monroe from Legal. Tom's division, Risk Assessment (& Contracts), was on fifth, so he reached through the crowded elevator and almost sprained his arm to press the button marked *5*. He'd rather risk injury than actually speak to anyone, especially first thing in the morning. His hand brushed against Monroe's arm as he pushed the button.

"Sorry," Tom said, his voice barely a whisper. Monroe glanced round at Tom, who noticed the man's face looked pale and melancholy, like he was sickening for something.

"Good morning." Tom's words were a verbal reaction to the strange haunted expression on Monroe's face.

"Is...it?" Monroe muttered glumly before the doors slid shut at the sound of another *ding*. The elevator lurched skyward, as though powered by the collective sighs of the workforce.

Ding.

Second floor. The Sales people got out in their droves; they owned the second floor. Tom's department was smaller, much smaller, and efficient enough to tick along relatively unnoticed by the company at large, and that was just the way Tom liked it. He had always been someone to shrink away from any kind of spotlight. Even when his team was instrumental in enabling a big contract, he was only too happy to let someone else (usually Team Sales) step up and take all the glory. That way he could simply blend into the crowd at the monthly and quarterly office meetings he was subjected to as part of corporate life. It was a life he didn't necessarily love, or hate, but the only one he really knew. And it offered the additional benefits package of keeping him distant from the unknown commodity that was his relationship with Julia—a once happy accident.

Ding.

Third floor, where he'd worked until the re-org sent him upstairs a couple of years ago. It had been here that he and Julia had first met at an office party organized by The Consortium Inc.'s mysterious Human Resources division. H.R. was a group of people whose sole purpose seemed to be the creation of an email newsletter that, each week, applauded the various successes of Team Sales and reminded all workers that smoking was forbidden in any of the restrooms on-site. Tom had remained at his desk, working as usual, even when the champagne corks had started popping like a cannon fire salute across the office. As it turned out, this tactical heads-down approach had become his undoing. A small group of drunken diehards from the cubicles nearby had made it their mission to get some drinks down his throat. His faced had burned with embarrassment as they'd dragged him from his swivel chair, chanting, "Shot! Shot! Shot!" Other cackling denizens of the fluorescent-lit nightmare joined in the chant and pretty soon Tom had found himself doing shot after shot of hard liquor to the cheers of his coworkers. He'd felt like a glum gladiator, forced into an arena for the amusement of a baying crowd.

When the tequila hit, he had felt numb. When the Jägermeister had been unleashed, he'd felt quite sick. It was around that point that he'd been introduced to Julia. She'd been so helpful and considerate; grabbing a wastepaper basket just in time to save what was left of his already diminished dignity. Escorting him to the bathroom, she had even procured a mouthwash sampler from her desk drawer on the way. Outside the office, the air had smelled almost as cool and refreshing as the mouthwash had tasted and, in a rare display of impulsiveness, Tom had kissed Julia. She'd reciprocated of course, being more than a little inebriated, and had continued reciprocating for the following ten months until they moved in together. Soon after their marriage she had suffered a bad fall down the stairs outside their apartment, and the miscarriage had happened.

Ding.

They were on Four. Monroe let out an audible sigh and wandered out of the elevator like a sleepwalker. As the doors slid shut behind him, Tom saw the man stop stock still in the corridor. Something about the man's gait gave Tom the chills.

Dead man walking. A fair few of them around these parts.

Ding.

Fifth floor. Tom filed his thoughts away and headed for his cubicle, prepared for the welcome drudgery of work.

Chapter Two

"Mathers wants to see you."

The dulcet Eurotrash tones belonged to Dieter, Tom's least-favorite coworker. Tom peered up at him, instantly disliking the way Dieter was leaning over the wall of his cube. He was perched there like some Aryan Eagle, his blue eyes gleaming, and a meringue of sandy-blond hair framing his arrogant face. Dieter used way too much product; the man was a walking Photoshop filter. Tom just stared, then opened an Intranet Chat window on his computer.

"Not online. He wants to see you right away. In his office."

"His office?"

Dieter smiled, a rictus grin that made the muscles in his neck twitch, making him look even more annoyingly athletic.

Tom hit *Ctrl+Alt+Delete*, locked his workstation and rose from his swivel chair. Dieter made like he was going to escort him.

"I know where it is."

Truth was, he didn't know exactly where Mathers' office was, only that it was situated somewhere on the mezzanine floor where *no one* went. He strode away, putting as much distance as humanly possible between him and Dieter, who was left standing amidst the rows of cubicles like a little boy lost. The last thing Tom needed was that creep breathing down his neck. What a guy like Dieter wouldn't give for a chance to get a glimpse of Mathers' office. What *anyone* wouldn't give for a peek behind the curtain in the Consortium's equivalent of The Emerald City of Oz. No one saw Mathers' office. No one saw Mathers for that matter, not in the flesh. Their boss was never on-campus; always making his quarterly address from some sun-kissed island or other, live via satellite like a movie star. So why the summons? Was this some inter-office practical joke? Some Team Sales jape concocted at his expense? That would perhaps be preferable to meeting Mathers. He was the fucking Chairman for Christ's sake. Of the company. All the moisture had left Tom's mouth.

Why does he want to see me? Why now?

Tom wiped at the cold sweat forming on his brow and headed for the stairs. If he took the elevator he might just throw up.

"Good to see you, McCrae, come on in, take a seat."

The ten-minute wait outside Mathers' office had done nothing to calm Tom's anxieties about being called there "urgently" out of the blue.

Urgent, my ass, he thought, *how can it be urgent when they keep you waiting nearly a quarter hour?*

He sat down, glancing around at the minimalist enclave, taking in the polished surfaces, the unused stationery sitting atop the huge mahogany desk like props on a movie set.

"Coffee?" Mathers offered.

Tom shook his head and swallowed dryly. Truth was, he could murder a coffee, but not right now, he might spill it and make an ass of himself.

"Well, I'll take one," Mathers said.

His voice boomed in the echo chamber of the near-empty room. His secretary, an efficient-looking woman wearing a trouser suit, nodded and closed the door after her.

"Scottish, isn't it?"

Tom felt the confusion spread across his face like a nosebleed on a handkerchief.

"Your name, man. McCrae?"

"Oh y-yes. Yes, sir."

"Scottish parents? Ancestors perhaps?"

Tom wished Mathers would speak at a normal volume. He felt as though he was being castigated for some crime he didn't know he'd committed.

"Perhaps. I have no idea."

"Look into it, Tom, look into it. It's an important part of the assignment I have for you."

There was a sharp series of raps at the door and Mathers' secretary entered carrying a pot of coffee and a china cup on a small silver tray. She set it down on the desk and loitered for a moment, her manner precise and practiced.

"Thank you, Eve, that will be all," Mathers said, without even looking at her.

Tom watched her leave the room. She closed the door again with barely a click, the room filling with the piquant aroma of Mathers' coffee. It smelled fresh—expensive.

"Sure you won't take some coffee?" Mathers asked.

Tom shook his head, his lips beginning to form a question.

"Passport in order, Tom?"

"Yes..."

"Good, great. Eve will book your flight, a rental car will be at the airport for you, it's quite remote where you're going. Say, is your driver's license clean too? I neglected to ask..."

"I...don't drive, sir."

"Don't?"

Mathers looked at Tom like he'd just beamed in from some distant alien planet.

"How the fuck do you get to work each morning, man?"

"Caltrain."

"Jesus God." Mathers looked gobsmacked. He stroked his chin and muttered the word under his breath like he'd never heard it before, "Caltrain."

Maybe he truly never had heard it before.

"No problem, Tom, no problem at all, we'll have someone go with you. Not a bad idea anyhow. Drive you up there, help you with the paperwork, no, not a bad idea at all."

Mathers turned his back on Tom, peering out through his smoked glass window at the atrium.

"Sir?" Tom cleared his throat, "May I ask what this is all about?"

Mathers turned from the window, frowning at Tom.

"The assignment, I mean," Tom continued.

A look of apprehension crept into Mathers' features. His eyes twinkled, then he let out a great bellow of a laugh.

"Oh! The assignment! McCrae, you must think me quite insane!"

Tom just smiled, preferring not to answer the question out loud.

"Biofuels. How are you on biofuels—up to speed?"

"I...um...my division helped out with the Amazonian deals, sir. I understand there are some plans to expand, but..."

"But?"

"Environment agencies in several territories have nixed expansion operations at the R&D stages."

"Indeed they have. I can see your finger is on the pulse, very good. But the tide is changing, and that's what I want you to help me with." Mathers paused for breath. "We are expanding into Europe and our priority as of right now is the United Kingdom. Scotland to be more precise."

"Scotland? I thought their forestry laws prevented us from..."

Tom faltered, aware that Mathers was the kind of man who liked to do the talking while others listened.

"Go on."

"Well, from expanding at all in that region of Europe. It's all too well protected—too much red tape, I thought?"

"You thought right." Mathers grinned. "Until now. The new right-wing government in London is keen, very keen in fact, to make some money in these austere times. Those plucky Brits are rushing a bill through Parliament. Vast swathes of forest available to the highest bidder. Scotland is prime real estate for our biofuels division, Tom, and we are all set to play house there if we make the right noises."

"Wow. Okay, that certainly puts a new spin on things," Tom said.

Mathers smiled and nodded, looking like the cat that could smell the cream.

"It sure does, McCrae. You have a meeting scheduled with Monroe from Legal for this afternoon."

"I do?"

"You do. Eve has the details, see her on your way out. Monroe's flight back from Scotland landed this morning. He'll fill you in on the story so far regarding contracts and so forth. Here's a copy of his preliminary report, we'll send you a PDF too; get you up to speed before you fly out."

Mathers handed Tom a spiral-bound wad of paper. Tom leafed through it and saw reams of text, charts and photographs of forests and the Highlands. The document's front page bore the author's name—Monroe. Tom recalled how sickly Monroe had looked in the elevator earlier that morning.

Jet lag would explain it for sure, thought Tom. Only at The Consortium could one be expected to commute directly into work after a long-haul flight. *Poor bastard.*

Tom's mind reeled; Mathers' directive was all so sudden and unexpected. The Chairman scrutinized Tom's face, seeming to take Tom's hesitation as uncertainty; which he remedied with a hearty slap on the shoulder packed with enough kinetic force to knock a smaller man to the floor.

"Time is of the essence, McCrae. Others will be sniffing around so we have to move fast. That's why I want you on the plane tomorrow. Meet with the local landowners, smooth things out with them *vis-a-vis* the contracts. There's bound to be a little resistance, but you have the full weight of The Consortium Inc. behind you. Get the lay of the land, Tom, sniff out the risks and market the advantages. This is what you do, what you're built for. You're our secret weapon, Tom. Clear the area for us. I'm sure you'll do an excellent job. And your name won't do any harm either—you're practically Scottish already. Look into that though, Tom, look into it right away. It's a five-hour drive to Douglass from there. As you appear to be the only man in Christendom who doesn't drive, we'll send someone along with you. Any questions?"

Tom wanted to ask so many questions, like what his name had anything to do with administrating such a huge contract. Surely Mathers couldn't have selected him on the basis that he had a vaguely Scottish-sounding name? Tom felt the Chairman's beady eyes on him. He could only think of one question, and blurted it out before the thought was fully formed in his brain.

"Um, who is Douglas?"

Mathers' jaw dropped open, giving him the appearance of a dummy without its ventriloquist. Then he sucked in a huge lungful of air, threw back his head and roared with laughter.

"Who's Douglas?! Who's Douglas?!"

His entire frame rocked with laughter as he circled the desk and slapped Tom on the shoulder with his massive hand.

"D-o-u-g-l-a-double-s," he spelled aloud, "As in Douglass Firs, McCrae! Beautiful trees, they named the whole goddamned area after them! Who's Douglas... Ha-ha! Indeed!"

Mathers' barking laughter stayed with Tom all the way to the door as he showed him out, the sound still ringing in his ears as he wandered past Eve's desk towards the elevator. Her eyes were fenced off from the outside world behind the cold lenses of her spectacles. The *clack-clack-clack* of the secretary's fingernails tapping her workstation keyboard beat out a quick-march tattoo that accompanied Tom to the elevator door. He reached out and pushed the call button, little red arrow pointing down. After a couple of minutes waiting for the car, Tom remembered Mathers' instructions to check with his secretary about the meeting with Monroe. He turned and headed back towards Eve's desk but saw that she had gone.

Great time to take a bathroom break, Eve, I'm on a clock here, he thought.

Then he heard an almighty crash, like glass exploding. It was followed by a further, more disturbing sound; shrill female screams ringing out from below the mezzanine.

Tom stepped away from Eve's desk, following the sound around the balcony leading to the stairwell to the side of Mather's office entrance. Overlooking the atrium, Tom could see several suited figures standing stock still, gawping at something on the floor below.

Gripping the handrail, Tom peered over the edge of the balcony and saw a man lying on the floor surrounded by fragments of broken glass. Further screams of horror cut through the paralysis that had gripped Tom's body in the same way his night terrors did. Without thinking why he was doing it, Tom bolted for the stairs and began his descent, taking two steps at a time to speed up his progress.

Rushing out onto the mezzanine floor, Tom broke through the line of shocked bodies gathered a few feet from the fallen man. His steps slowing, Tom already knew who he was looking at. Monroe, who he'd seen in the elevator only that morning, was flat on his back with his lifeblood pooling around his head like a sickly red question mark.

Tom knelt down next to Monroe then glanced upwards over his shoulder. More workers were peering out from a shattered fourth floor window, hands to mouths as they looked down on their fallen comrade. Monroe had almost certainly jumped, but why? The question began to form on Tom's lips, when Monroe's tortured breathing gave way to an agonized hacking cough that spattered dark blood across his chin, onto his silk tie and crisp white shirt. He gagged and choked, his legs twitching like those of a dying fly as his body made every effort to enable him to speak again. Monroe's eyes bulged, his face blotchy and red. As though he were seeing Tom for the first time, he spoke.

"He's..."

His voice had become no more than a death rattle and Tom couldn't quite make out what Monroe was saying. The lawyer was struggling to speak so hard it left Tom with no choice but to lift the man's head from the floor, cradling it in one hand while clasping Monroe's hand with the other. Leaning closer, Tom positioned his ear near to Monroe's bleeding mouth and tried to blot out the background shrieks and murmurs of his coworkers so he could hear what the dying man was trying so desperately to say.

"He's in the trees...he's..." Monroe said.

His eyes were fixed open, gazing glassily into the distance over Tom's shoulder.

"Waiting..." he murmured; then breathed his last.

On instinct, Tom glanced back in the direction of the dead lawyer's gaze. He glimpsed a few suited figures, retreating from the jagged glass of the broken window.

Back to work, show's over, folks.

A grim silence fell over the office floor and Tom stood up, almost slipping in the crimson spiral emanating from Monroe's shattered cranium. As the paramedics arrived, quietly and efficiently clearing the area, Tom retreated through the crowd and back to the stairwell like a man in a dream.

He was almost at his desk when he realized he had Monroe's blood on his hands.

Chapter Three

"Good day at the office, dear?"

That used to be Julia's little joke greeting every time she got home before him.

She didn't make jokes anymore. Or even greet him, for that matter. For a while, Tom had tried to bring jokes of his own home with him, but found he had neither the wit nor the spirit necessary to alleviate Julia's grief. So, instead of trying to conjure some humor in their home, Tom had *become* the joke. He took to wearing his tired day job zombie clothes like a jester's costume as he struggled indoors under the influence of one too many happy hour chasers and the weight of grocery bags filled with convenience meals Julia would not want to eat anyway. That behavior had gone on for several months too long. Only when he'd realized he'd gained so many pounds his gut was spilling over his belt had he seen fit to try and break the cycle. He'd successfully abstained from the alcohol for the last few weeks at least, resulting in his belt tightening up by all of two notches, but his culinary expertise had not improved any.

Closing the door to the apartment behind him quietly, Tom shrugged off his coat and hung it on the rail in the hallway before calling out to Julia and asking if she wanted any pizza. The muffled chatter of a TV talk show was the only reply.

Same as it ever was, thought Tom as he moved through his own apartment like a ghost, *pizza for one at the kitchen diner*.

He hit the counter lights in the kitchen and turned the oven on to preheat. Fishing his laptop from his workbag, Tom set to work at the kitchen table, reading through the complex legal background on the

Douglass takeover deal in Monroe's PDF document. Tom paused on a page detailing the huge acreage of fir trees in the area. Monroe had included in the document a bunch snapshot photos from his preliminary visit to Douglass, and one of them caught Tom's eye. It depicted the dark, looming shapes of tree trunks stretching as far as the eye could see—each one surrounded by swirling mist. Two trees in the foreground appeared massive; each must have been growing for a couple of centuries at least. Just looking at the scene made Tom feel chilly and unsettled somehow. He hurriedly clicked the track pad button on his laptop to navigate to the next page. There were still hundreds of stodgy pages to get through and the flight would take a good ten hours, so he felt okay about leaving the bulk of the reading until then. When the oven beeped that it was ready to incinerate his dinner, Tom put the laptop to sleep, threw his pizza into the oven and went to check on Julia.

She was in her usual position, lying sideways on the couch with the TV just a little too loud. Her old blanket lay on the floor next to her; she must have kicked it off. Tom walked over to the couch, crouched down and picked up the blanket. He enjoyed the sensation of its familiar texture and weight in his hand. The blanket had accompanied them on many a road trip during happier times long gone.

"You are such an old...risk assessor!" Julia had laughed the first time he'd packed it in the trunk with the rest of their weekend luggage. *"Packing a blanket in case we break down!"*

Tom frowned at the blanket, then at Julia. Things had been so simple then. They could take off anytime they wanted. They'd had each other; whatever befell them along the road. Not now. They had broken down, after all. Tom placed the blanket over his comatose wife and headed back to the kitchen to try and eat something, alone.

Tom awoke with a start, feeling the warm betrayal of sticky moisture around his groin. Lying on his side, facing away from Julia's sleeping form, he reached down beneath the sheets and explored his nether regions with furtive fingertips. Dismay welled up inside him on feeling the sodden sheets and mattress. He glanced at the electronic clock face bedside the bed, its LED lights flashing red fury at him. Four in the a.m. He didn't need to leave for the airport for three hours, but this setback was convincing him otherwise. Tom resigned himself to sneaking out of bed to go boil a kettle of hot water so he could dry out the damage with a hot water bottle. Julia wouldn't wake anyhow, she never did, and Tom was becoming a bit of a hand at clandestine middle-of-the-night mop-up operations. He pictured himself as a crime scene cleaner swathed head to toe in a yellow HAZMAT suit, breathing loud through his respirator as he mopped up the shame of his own piss.

We know who did it, Chief, he left DNA at the scene again, it's just a matter of time 'til we get the bastard, then he'll pay for his filth, the scum.

Tom almost laughed at his bitter little inward joke, but any such mirth was dispelled by the unexpected sensation of a hand in his crotch. The hand was small, warm, and unmistakably Julia's. Tom's breath lingered in the back of his throat as he felt Julia gently cupping his still-damp penis.

Must be stoned, thought Tom, *yeah that's it, she's doing this in her sleep, God only knows how many sedatives she swallowed tonight, must be doped like crazy...*

"Poor baby," Julia whispered.

Her breath was warm and tickly on his back, breezing through the hairs on his shoulder line like a sirocco through pampas grass. She was awake—well, awake by Julia's standards.

She can't be, thought Tom.

He couldn't remember the last time he'd seen Julia awake before he left for the office. He certainly couldn't recall the last time they'd been intimate. Her fingers closed around his penis, smoothing over its surface, tugging him gently. Tom's pulse quickened as his member stiffened almost in spite of itself.

"Poor baby."

Julia's purr sounded pitying and mocking. The strangely laconic sound made Tom's body feel somehow angry and he tore the duvet away. Turning over, away from the urine stain at the edge of the bed, he faced Julia. He could barely see her, the red glow from the digital clock making vague lava forms of her flesh. His fingers fumbled with Julia's nightdress, lifting it to expose her. He wrenched himself free from her hand and thrust himself between her legs. She was already wet for him there. He pushed against her and she arched her back, soughing in approval. They fucked for only a few moments before Tom felt the huge shuddering dismay of orgasm surge through every fiber of his being. Clenching his eyes shut tight, he could see a pinprick of hot red light in his mind's eye, like a hot coal. It was the color of hate and shame and self-disgust. His eyes leaked tears as they swallowed the hateful burning light, then his loins poured all of it into Julia. Lukewarm sperm dribbled out of him like spittle. Cold sweat covered the both of them like a sickly film. Tom's frantic, gasping breaths descended into sobs and he separated from her. Cold air crept between them and turned the clammy sweat into gooseflesh, as though Tom's very skin was alarmed by what had just happened.

"Poor...baby..."

Her ghost whisper of a voice trailed off as she turned her back on him.

Tom buried his face into his pillow. As the silent howl within him subsided, his aching body gave way to a dreadful, funereal sleep.

Chapter Four

There was nothing Tom hated more than flying overseas. The prospect of being hermetically sealed inside a metal tube at thirty thousand feet, breathing other people's recycled ablutions for ten hours was already giving him a headache.

He trudged across the polished surface of the Departures Hall, dragging his suitcase on wheels behind him, feeling that old familiar blend of dread and excruciating boredom filling his soul like a black void. Everywhere he looked he saw holidaymakers as they strolled this way and that, gazing at racks of products they didn't need. Each corner he turned offered a new and unnecessary retail opportunity, and a lengthier line of portly shopaholics to navigate his way around on the deathly inevitable trudge to the check-in desk. He became distracted by the excited chatter of a Japanese contingent, apparently overjoyed by their discovery of a concession selling Christmas cards and gifts.

In October. Not even Halloween yet. Jesus Christ, how I hate Christmas.

Lost in his vitriol, Tom almost plummeted over a hurdle-like procession of overstuffed suitcases being pulled along by their rather overstuffed owners. Tom regained his balance, apologizing aloud to no one in particular, before taking a deep breath and ploughing on through the teeming throng to find his check-in desk.

His morning had not started well. Needing someone to keep an eye on Julia while he was away, her sister Ellie had seemed the natural choice. Wishing to avoid contact with her for as long as possible, he'd left it until 6 a.m. to call her. Then, lacking the courage necessary to go head-to-head with big sis, he had chickened out and sent a text asking

Ellie to drop by and look in on her younger sister. She had called thirty minutes later, berating him for the short notice. When he'd tried the "urgent business meeting—nothing I can do" card, Ellie had all but exploded on the other end of the line.

"How dare you assume I don't have anything better to do than pick up the pieces while you go gallivanting off on some corporate jaunt," she had shouted—so loudly that he'd had to move the phone a few inches from his ear to prevent any damage.

Truth was she didn't have anything better to do after being let go from her teaching job a few weeks prior. She knew it, and she knew Tom knew it too—a fact that no doubt added to her ire. Her tirade had continued until his train had disappeared into a tunnel and he had lost his cell phone signal.

Good for nothing... Leaving her to fend for herself... Those awful meds... Your fault... had been the words ringing in his ears for the rest of his Caltrain journey.

A boarding gate announcement shook Tom from his thoughts. He glanced up and, seeing the American Airlines logo, was about to march up to the desk when he spied a familiar face in the crowd.

Christ, he thought, *I hope he didn't see me.*

But it was too late. Dieter's gleaming white teeth were already flashing their trademark sharklike grin as he made stiff little waving motions at Tom.

What the fuck is he doing here? Tom wondered as he feigned a "pleased to see you" smile at Dieter, who was racing his way.

"Leaving it until the last moment as usual?" Dieter chuckled; a sound entirely without mirth.

Tom just looked at Dieter, unable to disguise the discomfort and suspicion on his face. The man had a pink sweater draped over his shoulders, sleeves tied loosely together. He looked like he was going on a golfing vacation, but back in time, to the early '80s.

"Lucky really," Dieter continued.

"What?"

"I was just about to check in. Now they can put us together."

Oh, holy fuck.

Only now was the "coincidence" of their meeting like this at the airport dawning on Tom.

"Which flight are you on?" Tom asked.

Dieter chuckled again robotically. "Same as you of course!"

"You're going to Scotland? To Douglass? With...me?"

"Well, you wouldn't get very far without me. Mathers told me all about your little handicap."

Dieter mimed a steering wheel, adding a little push of the horn for "comic" effect.

"I'm your driver!" Dieter barked. Then, cackling, he slapped Tom hard on the shoulder. "Hey, where are you going?!"

"Forgot something," Tom muttered as he ambled away, clutching his stinging shoulder. He'd just remembered he needed to buy something—anything. With Dieter's whiny voice ringing in his ears, Tom disappeared into the crowd in search of a retail opportunity.

"Please switch off all electronic devices, including cell phones, during takeoff and landing. Keep your seat belt fastened with your seat in the upright position..."

The recorded safety announcement droned on, the chirpy female voice bestowing further wisdom upon its captive audience; where to find the emergency exits, how best to affix an oxygen mask to one's face in the event of a white-knuckle plummet into the ocean several thousand feet below, and so on. The jumbo's interior lights flickered as the engines started and Tom checked, and rechecked, his seat belt. God's cruel joke had placed him in a window seat, so he was sandwiched between the cabin wall and Dieter who, it seemed, would be unable to stop fidgeting for the entire goddamned flight. At least the on board safety announcement afforded Tom a few moments respite from his coworker's irritating stream-of-consciousness banter. The world, to Dieter, was a vacuum that had to be filled at all times with hot air. No sooner than Tom had thought the small talk was over, another yawning gust of drivel flooded from Dieter's mouth. Tom glanced at him and watched him fiddling with the switch next to a clearly nonfunctional air vent. The man must be single, either that or the cause of perhaps more than one suicide, Tom thought bitterly as he turned away from Dieter and back to the in-flight magazine he was pretending to read.

The journey through customs had been torturous, Dieter a constant companion at his side despite Tom's attempts to shake him off by visiting the bathroom, even though he didn't need to. His coworker's jocular disposition had begun to grate well before they took their seats in the Departure lounge. The shiny-toothed European cracked bad jokes and laughed uproariously every time anything in a skirt wandered within five meters of him, with Tom cowering in embarrassment nearby.

Tom had tried in vain to talk shop for a while, running through their travel itinerary while a disinterested Dieter continued eyeing up the women and attempting an ill-informed Scottish accent at the merest mention of their final destination. Eventually, in desperation, Tom had managed to dislodge his idiotic conjoined twin under the pretence that he needed to make a private phone call. Wandering through the gray-carpeted corridor outside their departure gate, Tom fantasized about ditching Dieter and heading to the nearest bar. He pictured himself knocking back a bottle of Douglass Scotch on the parking lot, his chin heavy with beard after living rough at the airport for months. Driven mad, and to drink, by his yammering coworker, Tom would wear Dieter's teeth on a necklace as an homage to his indomitable foe. Then the call to board the aircraft had boomed over the loudspeaker like the pronouncement of a death sentence and Tom had resigned himself to his fate. He hoped to God above it was going to be a short trip. Flying with Dieter was one thing, but then he had the prospect of a few days—exactly how many he wasn't sure—on assignment with the jerk.

Maybe they had contract killers in Scotland.

Look into it, McCrae, look into it, he imagined Mathers booming, *put the fool out of his misery. Both barrels, there's a good man.*

Chapter Five

Tom's dream was always the same. But this time—it was different.

There he was, standing between the Christmas tree and the fireplace. Those eyes like hot pinprick wounds piercing him from the coal black beneath the mantelpiece. Then, powerful, sinewy arms were upon him, pulling him up through the chimney flue at breakneck speed. Long bony fingers as sharp as talons clutched his wrists, their touch as cold as ice, their grip unyielding. Tom's abductor, whoever or whatever it was, wore clothes. Or at least he imagined it did, as he could feel the cuffs of its jacket brush against the skin of his hands, soft as fur. Higher they soared, through coal-black dark, up and out into the freezing shock of night, arcing high into the air as though they'd been fired from a cannon. Yellow-white clouds churned overhead like spoiled milk and, feeling air sick, Tom looked down and wished he hadn't. Droplets of blood were raining down on a thicket of fir trees below, a glistening crimson torrent of plasma coating the spiky branches of the trees. Tom felt sick and lurched—

Awake.

He was on the plane, complementary airline blanket tangled around his neck. He opened his eyes and found himself peering down at the armrest. Dieter snored next to him, loud as a train. Tom felt icy cold. Instinctively, he reached down to check the crotch of his pants. Static electricity, caused by the manmade fibers of the blanket and all the electrical gizmos on board the plane, snapped at his fingers. At least his crotch was dry as a bone, thank God. Tom sat up straight and blinked away the confusing afterimages from his dream. The deep black beyond the fireplace, the sickly sky, all that blood raining down on the branches. His stomach yawned. He felt bilious, uncomfortable and utterly perturbed by the conjurations of his subconscious. The nightmare never changed. Never, *ever.* It was always the same—until now. This had been something different, something new. For the first time, Tom felt an actual yearning for his old familiar nightmare, the same one that had jolted him awake and disturbed his sleep for as long as he could remember. His tired brain ached for the strange comfort gained from knowing what happened next, how his night terrors ended. Uncertainty terrified him most of all and, even now, he felt it closing in around him like the narrow confines of that chimneystack. Tom shivered in the air-conditioned chill of the cabin, pulled the polyester blanket around him with a crackle of static electricity, and tried not to sleep.

The empty luggage carousel clanked and whirred as a crowd of passenger spectators stood watching it intently as though visualizing their bags would make them appear quicker. Their summoning didn't appear to be working—Tom had stood at the loud metal runway of the carousel, listening to the beat of the black rubber blades clunking by for a good fifteen minutes already. A brief flurry of excitement had passed through the crowd with the appearance of a lone suitcase a few moments after the carousel had started up, but all present had quickly and silently ascertained that the bag in question was an unclaimed leftover from an earlier flight. Tom reached into his pocket and thumbed his cell phone again. He'd been putting off texting Julia since his flight had landed and, much as he'd like to continue doing so, he couldn't justify putting it off any longer. His problem, as was so often the case, was deciding what to say in his message. Tom often wished there were text message templates available for any given scenario. He seriously doubted his phone's on board suite of entreaties—"I am afraid I cannot help you with that right now" or "I am unable to make the meeting because (enter reason here)"—would cut it somehow. Neither would honesty. "Did we really have sex last night or was it a dream? I'm enjoying being on my own. Hope you and your meds are too. I'll call you in—well, I'm not sure if I will call you to be honest. Bye, Tom x."

No that wouldn't do either.

Clumsily thumbing the phone's touch screen keyboard he opted for, *FLIGHT LANDED. HOPE UR WELL. MAKE SURE U EAT SOMETHING. LOVE, T.*

He still couldn't fathom how to deactivate the caps lock function on his new phone, so those rare texts he did send always came out larger than life. He hit *Send*, then cursed under his breath that he'd forgotten to add an X at the end of his missive. Then the huge metallic mouth of the baggage claim carousel began noisily spewing forth suitcases of every size and color imaginable, affording Tom the welcome distraction of looking for his luggage.

As the parade of personal effects whizzed by, Tom felt a large, muscular form squeeze into the scant space next to him, almost pushing him onto the conveyor belt. He didn't need to look to know that it was Dieter, back from his trip to "the little boys' room" as he'd so gleefully described it. For a few moments, Tom had mercifully almost forgotten Dieter was with him at all, but now he was back with a vengeance, helping female passengers with their bags. He made a show of lifting the heaviest bags from the carousel, handing them with a winning smile to their grateful recipients. Tom had the sudden and barely controllable urge to throw himself onto the carousel.

That feeling stayed with Tom for the rest of the morning. As they shuffled their way through immigration, onto a crowded monorail and out into the stultifying microwave glow of Arrivals, Dieter had seen fit to provide a running commentary from the pages he'd torn from the in-flight magazine. The article was built around a list of *-isms*—those subtle yet oh so hilarious, in Dieter's world, differences between American and British English. Dieter, with his European background, was already familiar with the subtle variations from "bathroom" to "toilet" and "pavement" to "sidewalk". Taking great delight in showing off his linguistic prowess, Dieter's voice drowned out the background noise of machinery and people that Tom felt so desperate to lose himself in.

By the time Dieter had done the article to death and moved on to the weather, Tom had lost the will to live. The disorienting fog of jetlag was descending on Tom's addled brain after sleeping so little on the plane. He tried not to snap at Dieter, who was trying his damnedest to chat up the pretty blonde working the car rental desk. The man's appetite for attention was startling and seemingly unquenchable, but what Tom really could not fathom out was the fact that people seemed to *like* Dieter. The man was like some kind of idiot guru, beaming his vacuous grin as he saw fit to bestow a few of his sunshine rays upon another unsuspecting stranger's bleak existence, and they basked gratefully in his glow—even as he tried to feel them up and take their phone numbers.

The world makes no sense, Tom thought as he watched the blonde chuckling and blushing at Dieter's jokes, *maybe that's why Dieter belongs in it and I don't.*

Handing Dieter the keys and describing the route to the rental car bay, the blonde glanced at Tom. Their eyes met for a fraction of a second and the young woman's expression suddenly soured, her eyes accusing him somehow. Of being a killjoy, he felt sure that was the message behind her accusatory glare. And in truth Tom felt like a death ray next to Dieter's warm glow. He'd managed to suck all the joy out of the blonde's first encounter with *The Laughing Guru* just by being there.

Tom turned away and pretended to look at a leaflet display on the counter, then yelped as Dieter's hand came crashing down on his shoulder. Dieter urged him to come along; the car was ready and waiting. Tom felt a strong urge to run, just run, the heck away but followed Dieter's quick—marching strides like a faithful dog. Thumbing the hard, smooth surface of the cell phone inside his pocket, Tom yearned for the familiar discomfort of home and the dependable awkward silence that dwelled there.

The rental car proved difficult to find. So difficult, in fact, that even the effervescent Dieter's mood had begun to sour by the time they had retraced their steps through the parking bays a third time. Tom remained silent as Dieter yammered on, flustered. Just as it looked likely that Dieter might head back to his blonde and tell her it was all over between them, they chanced upon the parking bay. It had eluded them by hiding under an overpass, the concrete pillars casting a deep shadow over the bays beneath. The serial number, painted onto the concrete was also partially obscured by an oil spill so dark it looked, from Tom's distance, like a hole in the ground. A gunmetal gray Ford Focus stood waiting for them in the shadows. Dieter's face filled with glee upon sight of the car; despite its budget status, it was still a symbol of America to him, of salesmanship. He punched the air and strode toward the vehicle in great lunging steps, overcompensating for his embarrassing failure to locate the car efficiently.

"Isn't she a beauty?" Dieter enthused.

Tom kept his mouth shut and watched as Dieter popped the trunk with all the excited exuberance of a child opening a gift on Christmas morning.

You'd think it was the fucking Batmobile or something, thought Tom.

As he stepped across the threshold from light into shadow Tom felt a shiver pass through him. Muscle memory conjured icy, talon—fingered hands clutching at his wrists, an aftershock from his vivid nightmare during the flight. He'd be eager to step into the car and warm up a bit, were it not for Dieter being there with him. Maybe, with a little luck, Dieter would stop chattering long enough for him to sleep during the journey. If not, he'd do his best to pretend he was sleeping—that might shut the big man up.

"Worth a try..." Tom thought out loud.

"What?"

"Oh, nothing."

"Jetlagged, huh? Didn't you sleep on the plane?" Dieter didn't wait for an answer. "We'll stop for strong coffee on the way. You'll be right as the rain."

Tom glanced up at the gray skies, rain clouds churning darkly over the concrete shapes of the parking lot. Gritting his teeth, he accepted his fate and climbed into the passenger seat next to Dieter.

Chapter Six

"We're not lost again? How can we be lost before we've gotten out of the airport?"

Tom was feeling as fractious as his voice suggested he was. He did nothing to hide it.

"We'll be fine," Dieter boomed. "Everything's back to front over here is all, because they drive on the left. Been driving in America so long I forgot how weird it feels. Aha!"

He'd spotted an exit ramp sign and accelerated towards it. The ramp was steep and gave way to a series of sharp bends that weaved through the concrete pillars of the parking complex like an obstacle course. Tom felt pressure on his knees and, looking down, saw that he was gripping them tightly with his hands. He did not like the way Dieter was driving. He was going much too fast, but Tom sensed that if he asked him to slow down, the fool would take it as a challenge to go even faster.

"Whoa!"

The shrill exclamation left Tom's throat before he could quell it. Up ahead, around the last of the sharp bends, he'd glimpsed a splash of vibrant yellow, the color as bright as the sun amidst the oppressive gray of their surroundings. Accompanying the yellow streak was a flash of ochre light. Tom mashed the floor beneath the dash with his right foot, applying ghost brakes that simply were not there and praying for Dieter to *slow the fuck down.*

As they cleared the bend, Tom realized the splash of color was the florescent jacket of a cop; the orange flash his bike's spinning warning light. The policeman stepped from away from his ride, which was parked up at the curbside, and held a black leather-gloved hand out to halt them. Tom felt the seat belt bite into his chest as Dieter overdid it on the brakes. Dieter opened his side window, electric motor whirring as the policeman stomped over to the car, a surly expression on his face. The juxtaposition of the electronic whirring sound over the image of the cop striding towards them made the officer look like something from a dystopian sci-fi movie.

Whirr, stomp, whirr, stomp.

Tom inadvertently grinned. The policeman leaned down and into Dieter's open window.

"Remain here until instructed to move off," he deadpanned, robotically.

"Something the matter, Officer?" Dieter asked.

"Crowd of protesters outside." Robocop's expression soured further upon noticing Tom's idiotic grin. "Something funny, sir?"

"Jetlag." It was all Tom could say without bursting into a fit of the giggles.

The cop threw him a look of contempt.

Great, thought Tom, *I'm about to get myself arrested in a foreign country for laughing at a police officer.*

To Tom's relief, the policeman withdrew and stomped back to his motorcycle. Dieter sighed, drumming his fingers on the steering wheel, only now glancing at Tom and noticing his mirth. The big man play punched Tom's arm and laughed along as though they were sharing some secret joke.

Great, now he thinks we're best friends. Way to go, thought Tom, wiping the smile from his face.

The cop waved them on and Dieter drove slowly and carefully through the remaining bollards to the outside world beyond the airport car park.

Crowds of people were gathered outside, lining the sidewalks as far as the eye could see in all directions. Many of the gathered throng waved placards daubed with slogans—*NO NEW RUNWAY* and *SPEND IT ON SCHOOLS* being among the favorites. Hundreds of voices chanted

41

in unison and Tom reached for the switch beneath his window to open it so he could hear what the protesters were saying. He clicked the switch but his window remained closed.

"Child lock," Tom muttered.

Dieter looked at him quizzically and Tom indicated the master window switch mounted on the driver's door.

"Oh." Dieter hit the switch, opening Tom's window.

As the glass descended, cool polluted air wafted in from outside. Tom inhaled it, enjoying its metallic artificiality as it chilled his nostrils and throat. Carried on the air, the unified voices of the crowd, shouting as one, "No way, no way, no new runway!"

"What are they chanting?" asked Dieter, his own window remaining resolutely shut.

"Environmental protest," Tom answered. "Airport wants to expand, looks like these guys don't want that to happen."

"Can't stop progress."

"No, but they're having a damn good go at it."

The rows of bodies nearest them were being held back by a single line of police officers who had formed a human chain, arms linked together at the roadside. Every now and then a ripple passed through the scores of protesters like a Mexican wave at a sports stadium. Each undulating swell of bodies tightened Tom's throat. He could see the police were finding it difficult to keep their chain from snapping, clinging to one another for dear life like passengers atop the deck of a ship on a stormy sea.

Dieter joined the line of traffic crawling through the tumult of human bodies and noise. The red braking lights of the hatchback upfront flashed in warning as the vehicle's driver slammed on the brakes. Dieter put the pedal down too and they halted with another whiplash-inducing lurch. Something was happening up ahead. The sound of the crowd had changed somehow, going from a unified chant to a colossal, defragmented roar in the space of milliseconds. Tom peered over the dash but all he could see was the red glow of the car lights in front, and a confusion of bodies beyond.

The roar grew and Tom glanced left to see the human chain of police officers buckle suddenly, their linked arms disentangling to let the tidal wave of protesters come crashing through. Within seconds they were upon the rental car, placards crashing against the windshield, feet slamming against the hood as people climbed up onto the roof to avoid being crushed in the stampede. The chanting continued amidst the animalistic roar and spread to the protesters standing atop the cars. They began to stamp their feet along with the chanting and Tom was alarmed to hear the metal canopy, under which he and Dieter sat, buckle with each tribal footfall.

"We have to get out of here," Tom said, his voice loaded with alarm.

Dieter glanced around and then his eyes met Tom's. Bodies were pressed up against and around the car. They had nowhere to go. Even if they could manage to force their doors open, climbing out now would place them in the crush of the crowd. Trapped inside the car, they watched as yet another mighty surge of bodies pushed more protesters into their path.

This surge was different though; whereas the previous movement had felt like it was driven by some kindred purpose, this one seemed to be the result of blind panic. The protest was changing shape, taking on the aspect of a struggle for survival rather than a righteous stand. The chanting turned to frightened screams and howls of aguish as protesters were knocked against each other. Some fell beneath the torrent of human limbs, crushed underfoot by their fellows. Others were wedged up against the line of vehicles, gasping for air and unable to free themselves as they were pinioned by the sheer dead weight of bodies behind them. The tidal wave hit Tom's side door and the car rocked and tipped in Dieter's direction. For a breathless moment, Tom thought the car might topple over, but as the protesters on the roof held on for dear life, the vehicle righted itself.

A cold stinging sensation exploded across Tom's left eye as a hand penetrated the inside of the car. In shock, it took Tom a few seconds to realize his window was still open. A protester had gotten wedged up against the car so tightly that he had tried to protect himself by putting a hand out to steady himself against the car, managing to strike Tom's face in the process. Tom looked up at the protester, who was struggling to free himself like a bear in a trap, snarling and cursing as yet more insufferable pressure was visited upon his limbs from the press of bodies behind him. Their eyes met, a strange meeting through the dark frame of the car window. Tom saw just how young the protester looked, he couldn't be more than twenty years old. The boy's hair was a tangled mess of dreadlocks barely restrained by a colorful knitted Alice band. Tom felt a tightening against his chest and saw that the protester's arm had become ensnared in his seat belt. The kid's eyes were almond shaped and a deep hazel color, giving his face the aspect of a frightened rabbit's as he struggled to free himself from the seat belt. The more the boy struggled, the tighter the belt pulled against Tom's chest, squeezing the very air from him. He glanced out the windscreen and saw a blur of bodies as his vision turned misty. Gasping for breath, he felt he might pass out any second. He clawed at the seat belt, trying to force a thumb under it to pry it away but it was squeezing him tighter than a boa constrictor and he couldn't get a purchase on it. Tom felt a warm, sticky trickle creeping down from his eye socket to his cheek. He touched the warm spot and studied his fingers. He was bleeding from the blow through the window. Tom turned to Dieter, who was sat absolutely still in the driver's seat, knuckles as white as snow as he gripped the wheel in abject terror.

"Drive," Tom gasped.

Dieter looked at him, mouth agape.

"Just drive." Tom's voice was no more than a pained whisper.

Dieter gunned the engine.

Chapter Seven

"What the fuck are you doing?! Stop, you crazy Yank bastard, stop!"

The protester was still entangled in Tom's seat belt and found himself being dragged along by the suddenly moving car. Inside, Tom had managed to twist his upper torso to face the door, and was gripping the seat belt and trying to wrench it free from the kid's forearm. The mad scene was underscored by the panicked wails of protesters as they struggled to escape the path of the oncoming rental car. Dieter's teeth were locked in a grim rictus as he accelerated through the morass of human bodies.

Now the crowd's shock at the car's movement turned to rage and they started lashing out at the vehicle as it crawled past them. Blows from placards and fists rained down on the metal skin of the car like hailstones. The sound was deafening and, as he struggled on with the seat belt, Tom imagined this was what a war zone must feel like to a soldier. He and Dieter had become idiot infantry, lumbering through some foreign land in the perceived safety of their vehicle while all and sundry took a pop at them. The protest had turned from peaceful banner waving to a free-for-all brawl within a matter of minutes. The ensuing atmosphere had begun to feel palpably nasty to Tom.

Fear gripped him like paralysis. If they had to stop, they surely would be dragged from their car by the people they had, in essence, tried to mow down. Violent images of him and Dieter being beaten to death by the angry placard-wielding mob flashed before his eyes and he put all of his fear into removing the seat belt from the young guy's arm. Using his right arm, he managed to locate the catch holding the buckle in place. It took several attempts to press the little red button down with his thumb, and then he got to work on the problem area of the belt with his left arm. Pleas and obscenities gushed from the kid's mouth as Tom wrenched and pulled at flesh and belt in equal measure. Tom used his right hand to twist the kid's arm as far back as it would go, and his left to pull at the belt with all his might. The protester howled with pain as pinpricks of blood blossomed across his forearm. The edge of the seat belt was flaying his skin, shearing off downy little hairs as it went. Tom continued pulling with one hand and pushing against the protester's chest with the other. Then the kid screamed and fell backwards into the braying crowd.

The crushing discomfort of the seat belt left Tom's chest instantly. He breathed deeply, but found little respite in the air that filled his lungs. It smelled of fear—of all the rank sweat and ripe breath coming from the crowds of protesters all around them. Their numbers closed around them, blocking out the already faint daylight. Dieter was forced to take his foot off the gas as the sheer weight of numbers made their current escape route and velocity impossible. The engine dipped as the crowd seemed to let out a collective sigh and, for a moment, Tom felt stillness. It was as though he had passed through into the world reflected in his wing mirror; the image distorted and slightly off-kilter—soundless, and out of time. Then a sound, like that of a colossal wave crashing onto the asphalt, shook the car windows.

Tom looked on, awestruck, as a torrent of water slammed into the crowd of protesters beyond the windscreen. The blast knocked them away from the car, scattering them like they were rag dolls, their screams swallowed up by an artificial ocean wave. It was like something from a disaster movie. Tom looked to the right, across Dieter, and saw the source of the rapids. A row of police vehicles was advancing on the protesters' flanks, a huge water cannon taking center stage. Riot police officers marched either side of the vehicles, each one decked out with protective helmet and clear reinforced plastic shield. The riot cops fanned out around the perimeter of the crowd to capture the stragglers as they ran to escape the Niagara jet of the water cannon. Tom watched as bodies skated past, unable to withstand the power of the blast. Road signs and advertising hoardings buckled. Young trees, some only saplings that were still encased in clear plastic tubing, were uprooted from the concrete sidewalk. A woman slipped and fell facedown on the tarmac. She lifted her head and Tom saw blood dribbling from her nose. Yet more riot police waded in and lifted her to her feet, dragging her away. Tom peered out the side window to see where they were taking her. A group of police vans had assembled at the edge of the car park entrance. Scores of protesters were being treated there for minor injuries sustained in the stampede. Some of their fellows were in mid-argument with the police, shouting at them in protest at the use of the water cannon. Others had already made the mistake of getting physical and Tom watched as a couple of the more irate offenders were dragged away to the police vans by a half-dozen or more riot cops.

Tom stroked the tender flesh above his solar plexus where the seat belt had done its worst and glanced back at the airport terminal. They had traveled approximately a half-mile toward their destination and, already, he felt like getting on the next available flight back home. A sudden violent rapping on Dieter's side window put Tom's heart into his mouth. They glanced at each other, then at the motorcycle cop out the window—it was the same guy who had pulled them over during Tom's unfortunate attack of the giggles. He gestured to Dieter to back up, then to kill the engine. The officer had placed them in a row of cars containing other travelers who had become caught in the waves of protesters. Dieter did exactly as instructed then he and Tom waited their turn to be processed and questioned by the police. It was going to be a long evening.

The impromptu Q&A session at the police force's pleasure kept Tom and Dieter sitting around for a total of four hours. They both repeated their stories a total of three times, to three different officers, in three different interview rooms, the last of which was a barely heated portacabin. The biting cold coupled with lack of sleep had made Tom irritable and he couldn't help but snap a couple of times during what had, by that point, begun to feel like an interrogation.

"Are you going to keep me here indefinitely?" he'd said, answering a question with another question rather than give the stock answer he'd already learned from the two previous interviews.

"Just as long as it takes," the rotund police officer had replied.

The officer, a fellow called Travis, had had an unlikable face and demeanor; all red cheeks and puffy eyes. He'd wheezed between sentences and had often coughed before finishing them, adding to the torturous delay. During one such coughing fit, Tom had fixated on the man's temple, where a thick vein protruded from his receding hairline. It looked like a huge earthworm had burrowed under his skin and was wriggling to get free. Tom had looked away from the rasping man's reddening features and wondered if the vein might burst.

Maybe if it does, he'd thought, *I can get out of here sooner rather than later.*

No such luck.

The cop had rasped a request for a plastic cup filled with water from a junior officer and, gulping it down noisily, had continued questioning Tom for another half hour. By that time, Tom had to admit defeat and dutifully reeled off his blow-by-blow recollection of events from the moment they left the terminal to the arrival of the cavalry and its water cannon. He'd left nothing out; hoping his attention to detail might curry favor with the pen-pushing jobsworth who sat opposite him. Nothing that was, except for the part about the motorcycle cop and Tom's embarrassing fit of the giggles. That minor detail had been on a "need to know basis" only—and he had decided the fat man certainly did not need to know. The chubby officer had scribbled notes in a little flip pad furiously as Tom recounted the moment where the young, dreadlocked protester had struck him through the window and gotten trapped in the seat belt. The officer had asked him if he wanted to press charges, but to Tom the incident had already become a thing of the past, an unfortunate accident. Officer Travis had looked a little disappointed with Tom's reply and remained silent as he circled something in his notepad with his well-chewed pencil.

Over at last, the interview was rounded off with a request for Tom to provide contact details in case the police needed any further information, so Tom dug out the address of the guest accommodation in Douglass from his hand luggage. The fat guy raised an eyebrow when Tom admitted he was unable to confirm exactly how long he'd be staying there, so he also gave him The Consortium H.Q. address in California.

"Enjoy your stay in the United Kingdom," Travis said without much enthusiasm; adding, "and try to stay out of police custody."

Tom bit his lip at the fat man's glib parting shot and chuckled inwardly.

Yeah, you'd crap yourself if you ever met one of San Francisco's finest, thought Tom as he recalled his one and only brush with the law on his home turf following a minor parking violation. He glanced at the cop and realized what was perhaps the starkest difference between the U.K. police and the ones back home—no guns. Even the riot police he and Dieter had seen earlier, charging into the crowds with Perspex shields raised, had not been equipped with a single sidearm between them. Instead of obvious firepower, this land was one of harsh words hidden behind seeming civility; the past four hours had been testament to that.

Tom popped the address of the guest accommodation back into his bag, closed the zipper and headed for the door. Glad his detention at *Her Majesty's pleasure* was over; he now had the joy of an airport hotel room to look forward to. He was keeping his fingers crossed there would be a bathtub. Only a long, hot soak could save him now.

Tom stepped out of the stifling chill of the prefabricated cabin into the tactile, freezing cold of night and found Dieter leaning up against the gunmetal hulk of the Ford Focus like the captain of a ship. There was no way on God's green earth he and Dieter would be driving through the night to get to Douglass, thought Tom, he was completely wiped and they'd be better off starting afresh in the morning. Dieter had been waiting twenty minutes for Tom and it turned out they were *on the same page*, as corporate speak would have it. Arriving at the same conclusion, Dieter had used the wait time to get on his smart phone and book rooms at the nearest available hotel to the airport. Both too tired to speak, they drove the short distance to the hotel parking lot in silence across the urban landscape that had become a battlefield just a few hours earlier. The only indication that there had even been a violent protest was the occasional crunch of a placard as it was crushed beneath the blackly indifferent tires of their rental car.

The hotel was a redbrick budget affair two lanes of tarmac away from the entrance to the airport parking lot. As they drove into a bay near to the main entrance, Tom glanced up and saw the hotel crouching over them on its concrete stilts, looking like some weird cubist nightmare against the evening sky. Purple floodlights helped exaggerate the building's sheer size and ugliness. Backlit advertising displays announced *All you can eat* breakfast deals and free wi-fi access (*for twenty minutes, hourly charge thereafter*).

Dieter caught Tom's look and his hand hesitated at the ignition, engine still running.

"Like me to try somewhere else? This was the nearest that still had rooms."

"No, no," Tom replied. "It's perfect."

"Want to check in then regroup? Grab a bite to eat?"

Dieter was eyeing the golden arches reflected in the rear-view mirror. Tom glanced at them too and bristled at the thought of gulping down a Big Mac and fries with a side order of uncomfortable silence. Besides, he found it vaguely distasteful to have flown halfway across the globe to Europe only to pay a visit to the monolithic giant of American fast food. He glanced, instead, at the illuminated advertising boards punctuating the dead concrete space between the rental car and the hotel. The image of a giant pepperoni pizza floated in the night, that staple of European foodstuffs. At least he would be sampling local cuisine, in however tenuous a form.

"I'll get room service," Tom mumbled quietly, marveling at the almost three-dimensional way the pepperoni slices had been rendered on the advertisement, making them look bigger than the average hotel pizza ever turned out to be. Tom had eaten lousy pizza in lousy hotels many times on his travels. The experience always provided him with a kind of reliable disappointment—a taste of home.

Dieter killed the engine and they heaved their luggage out of the trunk and headed inside to check in. As soon as his key card was in his hand and he'd confirmed the room had a bathtub, Tom made his excuses and left Dieter at reception, heading for the elevators. The big man looked almost grateful to have been given the chance to chat up the receptionist, a pretty brunette with *Lucy* emblazoned on her name badge. She was a big girl, positively curvaceous in fact; she could fend for herself. Tom had already forgotten which room number Lucy had told him was his. He glanced at the room number scribbled on the branded keycard holder. The glossy paper holder bore a reminder; *Don't forget to hand your key back at Reception on check out.* His room number was 507. *Fifth floor.* He swiped the card in the elevator keycard reader, hit the *UP* button and waited to ascend.

Tom's room was basic, air conditioned to a comfortable temperature, and clean. The carpet still had that new smell, like that of a showroom or his office when it had been given a refurb. Advertising standees, a huge card-backed menu and laminated instructions for the use of the TV, air-con and room service were dotted around the room in strategic places like clues to some obscure corporate treasure hunt. Tom gathered them up, one by one and deposited them in the slide-out drawer beneath the fitted wardrobe. The menu was the last to go. He gave it a cursory glance but decided he really was too tired to eat. He surveyed the room once more, now that he had made it feel even sparser. Truth was, Tom liked staying in hotel rooms like the one he was standing in. They were impersonal, unfussy and felt somehow anonymous. Though fewer and farther between than perhaps he might have liked, especially with his home life being so difficult, his business trips afforded him the opportunity to disappear for a while. Thankfully he could already feel himself slipping out of existence, somewhere on the horizon point between the mauve carpet and the beige skirting boards.

He wandered over to the window and pulled back the double-glazing panel, then the gossamer-thin net curtain covering the outer window. He located both handles, either side of the window frame, yanked them down and pushed. The door swung open about two inches then stopped with a dull clunk. He glanced up and saw a thick coil of cable, bolted into place to prevent the window fully opening, along with a window sticker proudly proclaiming that the window device was there, *For the safety and security of all our customers.*

Tom peered down at the parking lot six floors below and wondered how security might be an issue this far up. Safety perhaps, as one too many nights in a hotel like this could make even the most enthusiastic person lose the will to live. How would it feel, he mused, to drop suddenly from this anonymous room and hurtle anonymously to an insignificant death on the parking lot below?

Don't forget to hand your key back at Reception on check out.

With a sudden sensation not unlike vertigo, he remembered his nightmare on the plane and those talon-like hands pulling him up, up and away through the choking soot of the chimney and out into the icy black of night. He shivered and rubbed at his wrists, drinking in a deep breath of air from the two-inch gap between the window and its frame. The air smelled as metallic as blood and as poisonous as air fuel. It was strangely delicious, and probably more nutritious than any hotel microwave pizza would prove to be. He breathed his fill of the toxic concoction, then stripped off his clothes and sloped over to the bathroom where a sign above the faucets warned him: *Caution: Hot Water.*

Emerging bright pink from his bath a full forty minutes later, Tom wrapped a towel around himself, killed the lights and kicked back on the bed. The polyester curtains danced in the cool breeze from the window. A song of aircraft engines, traffic and distant sirens floated in on the back of the breeze. As he lay there listening to the machine cacophony, Tom fell suddenly and deeply asleep.

Chapter Eight

Jupiter Crash sat in the back of the camper van, smoking the joint down to the roach in brooding silence. Pinpricks of pain in his lips and fingertips shocked him back into the here and now as the last few millimeters of rolling paper burned away. He yanked the jay away from his lips and its hot-rock tip fell away and onto his lap. He hissed with pain as the ember, a little orange glowing demon, burned through the corduroy fabric of his trousers and into the tender flesh of his inner thigh. He scrambled to his feet; a maneuver made all the more difficult by the violent movement of the camper. The rickety old VW always rattled and groaned at speeds of above fifty miles an hour and at present it felt like it was doing fifty-five. Cursing, Jupiter tried to steady himself with his back to the blacked-out window of the van, brushing the vicious little hot rock from his leg.

"All right back there, Jupes? Want me to pull over?"

Kegger turned the steering wheel hard left and the camper veered onto the hard shoulder for a few seconds. In back, it felt like the vehicle had rolled off a cliff and Jupiter cursed louder and more descriptively than before as he fell on his ass—and his fellow travelers.

"Whoops," Kegger deadpanned. "Sorry, Jupes!"

Jupes. Jupiter hated it when Kegger called him that, which was of course why the bastard did it.

"Oh, I'm fine, Kevin, don't you worry about me."

It was the perfect riposte. Jupiter could feel Kegger smoldering at him from the driver's seat. He disliked his real name almost as much as Jupiter disliked the man himself. He'd only had Kegger come along because he had a clean driver's license and enough cash to cover some petrol, unlike most of the losers on his team. Jupiter rubbed at the tender spot on his inner thigh where the joint had burned him. It smarted, but not as much as his arm. The medic at the protest had told him he was lucky it wasn't dislocated when the car had dragged him along the asphalt.

"Want me to kiss that better for you?"

Denny was grinning beside him, relaxed in a heap of knitwear with Amber, who snickered at the joke.

"What, my arm or my leg?" Jupiter scowled at Denny, not waiting for him to answer. "How about you just kiss my arse?"

"The one you just fell on? Sure!" chuckled Denny, sharing the joke with Amber.

Jupiter scowled as he watched them do that annoying nuzzling thing with their noses. They started to make out through their giggles and the frown on Jupiter's face intensified, his pale features beginning to look like curdled milk.

"Get a fucking room. Oh sorry, I forgot, you're freeloaders who are living, eating, sleeping—and whatever fucking else—in *my* van."

Denny came up for air. "You invited us, bruv, I said we'd pay for some fuel when we get our cash..."

Jupiter smacked his teeth, loud and clear. He'd heard Denny's bullshit one too many times, especially the fantasy tale about how he and Amber were going to contribute to the group's expenses. The pair of them never spent a bean because they didn't *have* any beans. He glanced at their kitbags, filled to bursting with clothes and outdoor gear. Between them and their luggage they were adding a half-ton of dead weight to the camper's payload and expending even more fuel in the process. They were a total waste of space.

He turned away from them in disgust and his gaze fell on Charlotte's sleeping form. A sticker on the side window opposite her had peeled away a little, allowing a tiny beam of daylight through. The golden light danced across her face, bringing out the fiery red of her long, thick hair. Reflected fires danced in Jupiter's eyes as he gazed at her.

Amber caught Jupiter looking at Charlotte and leaned across to him.

"Relax, mate, she'll be awake soon and you can ask her to kiss it better for you," she teased.

"Fuck off."

Jupiter struggled to his feet once more and went to sit up front with Kegger. Even his company would be welcome after tolerating the freeloading bastards in the back for what felt like an age on the road from the airport. They were, even now, chuckling maniacally behind his back.

He clambered ungraciously into the passenger seat next to Kegger and sighed, looking out at the gray expanse of four-lane motorway stretching out ahead of them. Jupiter reached into the cluttered side pocket mounted on the passenger door. Navigating his fingers past layers of used napkins, tissues and junk food wrappers, he located a cassette tape and pulled it out, studying it. *Megamixtape* said the legend, scrawled in metallic gold Sharpie across the gray, smoked-plastic surface of the tape. He slid the tape into the cassette player and it lurched into life, midway through an old shoegaze track that sounded like it had been recorded through a wall—and a crumbling wall at that. The camper had come supplied with this anachronistic audio equipment and Jupiter hadn't the cash or the desire to replace it. One time, Charlotte had offered to buy a little plastic gizmo from the petrol garage that would turn the old cassette player into an iPod interface. Jupiter had then allowed himself a little momentary glimpse of him and his camper joining the twenty-first century, but when they'd realized none of them actually owned an iPod, iPhone, or anything *current*, it was back to the trusty tapes. Hearing more giggles from the lovebirds in the back, Jupiter cranked up the volume and the indie guitar track gave way to some machine-driven trance dance.

"Remind me to kick those bastards out when we get to the next services," Jupiter growled. "Bloody freeloaders."

"What's got you so riled anyhow? Usually pretty chipper after you've had a smoke."

Jupiter blinked incredulously and held up his bandaged arm.

"Were you actually *conscious* when I was dragged along the road by my arm by two fascist fucking American blokes?"

"Still hurts then, does it? Least you got it looked at and that. Bandaged it up nice."

Kegger could be a total moron at times. This was proving to be one of them. Jupiter bit his lip and remained silent, barely able to suppress the torrent of abuse that was building up in retaliation for Kegger's inane comments.

"What did they say to you then, the coppers?"

Jupiter narrowed his eyes and looked at Kegger. He was already beginning to regret his decision to sit up front. Glancing over his shoulder, he saw Denny and Amber making out under Denny's big army surplus overcoat. Amber giggled shrilly as Denny groped and tickled her.

"They asked a bunch of inane, pointless questions."

"Like what?"

"Name, age, address—all that kind of crap—asked me if I'd been to any protests before…"

"You tell 'em?"

"Of course not."

"What about your name?"

"What about it?"

"Well, you couldn't exactly tell them it was Jupiter Crash, could you?"

"Why not?"

"'Cos it's a made-up name and…"

"I *gave* them a made-up name, idiot."

"Really? Won't they check?"

"Check where? Gave them a false address too."

Kegger's monobrow descended, casting a shadow over his nose and making him look even more Neanderthal than he usually did, if such a thing was possible.

"What name did you give them, then?"

"Kevin Payne."

"But that's…"

"Your name, I know."

Jupiter fixed Kegger with a cold stare, then cracked up laughing at his own joke.

"I'm just pulling your leg! I made up a name on the spot, can't even remember what it was."

Kegger thought for a moment, if such a creature was capable of thought.

"What *is* your real name? You know mine. S'only fair I should know yours."

"Like I'm going to tell you that," Jupiter laughed.

Kegger looked crestfallen, so Jupiter decided to spin him a line.

"Think of it as damage control, yeah? If we get into real trouble with the fuzz, we give them our nicknames; tell them we don't know each others' real names. If I don't tell you mine in the first place, there's nothing to worry about, is there?"

"Did the pigs ask you for my name, then?"

"No, of course they didn't. Why should they? What did you do, wave a placard around then try not to fall over when they turned the water cannon on us, like everyone else? Don't sweat it, man. No, once the cops asked me all their questions—I had a few of my own for them."

"What like?"

"Well, where I could claim compensation for my injuries for a start. We live in a world of litigation now Kegger, every little incident has its price tag. Those bloody Yanks nearly ripped my arm out of its socket, that's what the paramedic on the scene said, and he should know thing or two about injuries, don't you think? Lucky I had the presence of mind to ask the medic for his details in case the police needed a statement. He was happy to oblige of course and told me if I wanted to press charges I should speak to the investigating officers on-site. Well, they were intent on questioning me anyhow, so I let them do their thing..."

"Then what?"

"I laid out the whole story. How the Americans deliberately drove into the crowd, how I got my arm caught when I tried to wave them down and stop them—and how the panic they'd caused started a riot."

"You told them all that?"

"Yeah. Takes the heat off the protesters, doesn't it? I mean, it was peaceful until those fuckers came along. The police seemed mightily interested in what I had to say about the driving into the crowd thing, especially. I mean, they hate it when protesters are clued-up like me, we've all seen how powerful it can be when we mobilize and consolidate our ideas. Whether they like it or not, they'll have to look into it. That's what they do; it's in their job description. A complaint has been filed in the bureaucratic hive machine and the worker ants within that system have to now check all the variables. *Compute/does not compute, Okay/Cancel*—you get me?"

Kegger clearly did not.

"All I have to do meanwhile is call one of those 'no win, no fee' places to make my claim," Jupiter concluded with relish.

This, Kegger could actually understand. "So you really think you might get compensation?"

"I know I will. Litigation my friend; an accident that was not my fault, blood spilled on England's green and pleasant land. The hive mind will not allow that—it *does not compute*."

"But...how will they send you the money if you gave a false name and address?"

Jupiter fell silent. He wished Kegger had done so too.

A soft voice piped up from the back of the camper van. Charlotte had woken up.

"His real name's Brian," she said.

Chapter Nine

He heard screams.

The sound a child's mind makes when it snaps, unable to endure the dreadful sights invading it. Pure unadulterated pain, torture and death unfolding like diseased flowers before him. Hatred and madness in full bloom. And those hideous eyes watching from the fireplace, glowing like hot coals. Taloned fingers reaching out and grabbing at the tender flesh of his wrists, holding him fast, just so. Making him look. Making him see. Then dragging him up, up into the trees.

"He's in the trees..." Monroe's dying words, each one a death rattle as brittle as the frozen pine needles scratching him on his ascent. *"He's..."*

"...waiting."

Tom jolted awake from his dream on the sweat-drenched hotel bed.

He gasped for air like a patient being resuscitated on a hospital gurney. Darkness enveloped him, save for two angry red eyes glaring down at him from the firmament. He blinked, his chest rising and falling with each frightened breath. The red glowing eyes were still there, glowering down at him, daring him to move. He had no choice. Reaching out to his side, he fumbled for the light switches built in to the night table next to the bed. He clicked the wrong switch and activated the main lights by mistake. The room was flooded with several hundred watts of cold wall and ceiling lighting, dazzling him. Tom squinted skyward and saw the angry eyes for what they were—two red LEDs blinking at him from the smoke alarm that was embedded in the smooth beige plaster of the ceiling. He breathed a sigh of embarrassed relief and flopped back down on the bed. His hair and skin were slicked with sweat. Pools of the stuff had drenched the polyester sheets and pillowcase beneath him. He felt clammy and unclean. Further cold wetness coated his crotch and thighs and he thought for a moment that he'd wet himself once again. Closer inspection revealed the source of the dampness to be the bath towel he'd fallen asleep in.

Still dazzled from the sudden room lights, Tom fumbled for his smart phone on the nightstand and tapped it awake. Sitting up to avoid the clammy pool of sweat beneath him, he slid his index finger across the smooth screen of the device and entered his PIN number to unlock it. A facsimile of a ticking clock was revealed, complete with twitching needle beating out the seconds as they passed.

Four a.m.

His jetlagged brain struggled with the math, but after a couple of tries he figured out it would be eight in the evening back home due to the time difference. He glanced around the bare room and thought of Julia sitting quietly on the sofa in the intense, ordered space they called home, just as she did night after night. Thumbing the shiny surface of his phone, Tom toyed with the idea of texting her again. Not calling, that would be pointless. After all, what on earth would they talk about, with him jetlagged beyond reason and her drugged up on meds? He wondered if Ellie was there, fussing over Julia and frustrating the hell out of herself in the process.

"The trick with Julia right now is to keep her on an even keel," her doctor had told him when she'd first been prescribed the tranquilizers. *"No stress, no surprises, just routine."*

He'd fought against the prognosis initially, disliking the zombie he found lying next to him each morning. But then, as with most of the disappointments in his life, he'd gotten used to it. Maybe he'd try texting her in the morning, when he'd thought of something to write. That way, if Ellie intercepted Julia's phone (as she was bound to do) even she couldn't deny he'd at least made an attempt to contact his self-medicated, fractured wife during his business trip.

He yawned, shivered, and scooted over to the dry side of the bed.

As soon as his head hit the pillow, he knew he wouldn't be able to fall asleep again. What he wouldn't have given for a couple of Julia's pills. His stomach gurgled at the thought of swallowing them down and giving himself over to a few hours of prescription-induced oblivion.

Staring up at the intermittent flickering of the smoke alarm lights, Tom left the bedside lamp switched on and waited for morning to come.

A hot shower, with the showerhead set to its most powerful setting, went some way to reinvigorating Tom's senses. He pressed the wall-mounted soap dispenser, treating himself to another palm full of pink ooze. The shower gel smelled like fruity herbal teabags that had been kept in a plastic container for just a little too long. As he massaged the soap into his skin, he inhaled the aroma of the lather, enjoying its artificiality.

The large wall mirror above the sink had steamed up by the time Tom finished showering. He realized he had turned the exhaust fan off at the isolator switch before hopping into the tub the previous night. He looked at his vague reflection in the foggy glass as he brushed his teeth, resisting the temptation to wipe a peephole in the condensation so he could see himself. Tom preferred the distorted pink blur of his reflection, not caring to see how tired he looked. He rinsed, spat and wiped his mouth with a hand towel, leaving the steamy mirror to censor the effects a day on a plane and a night in an air-conditioned room may have visited upon his skin.

Packing didn't take long, as Tom had removed so few personal effects from his luggage the night before. He unplugged his phone charger last of all and stowed it in his laptop bag along with all the other cables, mouse, and USB memory sticks that accompanied him on the ride whenever he was on business. Pulling on his jacket, he ran his fingers through his still-damp hair, glanced at the little pile of advertising and instruction leaflets he'd made atop the desk, and left the room.

Tom found Dieter tucking into a plate of scrambled eggs, toast, bacon and mushrooms when he arrived in the restaurant. Dieter eyed Tom's luggage as he brought it over to the table.

"Why didn't you leave that in your room?" he mumbled through a mouthful of breakfast.

"I'd rather get going."

Dieter swallowed his huge mouthful prematurely. Looking like he might choke, he reached for his glass of orange juice.

"But don't rush your breakfast," Tom added. "Is it edible?"

"Not bad." Dieter shrugged. "A little...lukewarm."

Tom wandered off in search of sustenance.

Heated metal trolleys were lined up at the far end of the restaurant, the stainless steel lids embossed with the names of their contents. He lifted the lid marked *Scrambled Eggs* and peered at the watery, rubbery contents inside. He replaced the lid, which looked like a gravestone in memoriam of the food that had died beneath it. Opting out of the lukewarm food option left only breakfast cereal, which was stacked up in tiny individual boxes next to jugs of fruit juice and milk. He selected a couple of vaguely healthy-looking cereals, tore open the cartons and inner bags, then poured the contents into a bowl with milk. Grabbing a spoon, he tried a mouthful of the sugary, lactose mess and found it to be surprisingly tasty. What he really needed was coffee, and a quick one-eighty of the room revealed a few filter jugs of the stuff lined up next to a caddy containing stacks of warm cups and saucers. Ignoring the saucers, Tom poured himself a cup and drank it down in just two gulps. Grabbing a tray from the caddy, he poured a couple more cups and carried them, along with his cereal back to the table where Dieter and his luggage awaited him.

When they were done eating, the two business travelers huddled together around the road maps that Dieter's blonde squeeze from the car rental company had given to them. Double-checking the route against the one suggested by Dieter's smart phone, they ascertained the drive to Douglass would take them at least four hours. Taking into consideration the rugged terrain beyond the motorway, plus a couple of rest stops, Tom suggested it might even take closer to five or six hours. He gazed at the printed map, marveling at the fact that there seemed to be no straight roads in Scotland. In fact, there didn't really seem to be many roads at all. The closer their route took them to Douglass, the more dense and expansive the areas of green that represented forests became. Tom had lived in the city so long that the landscape mapped out before him looked like some alien world. They could have been trekking into the Amazon there were so many trees. A little frisson of pleasured excitement passed over the surface of his skin as he gazed down at the printed forests, Godlike, from above. With several miles of motorway to get through first, Tom was itching to get on the road.

"Good to go?"

"Okay," Dieter said, gulping down the remnants of his fifth glass of OJ, "I'll go pack. Want to wait here, or I see you at the car?"

"At the car," Tom replied. "Have to make a phone call anyhow."

"Okey dokey."

Tom's phone already felt heavy as a brick in his pocket as he walked out of the hotel lobby and onto the parking lot. He was not looking forward to calling Julia, and was dreading the possibility that Ellie might pick up. Just as he was cycling through the list of possible excuses he could invent in order *not* to call, Tom felt his phone vibrate in his pocket. He pulled it out and looked at the screen, dreading what he might find.

The text message had been sent from Unknown Contact #0838 and read: *Welcome to Scotland and welcome to Scotnet, your network home from home. Check with your provider for roaming charges.*

He chuckled at the message, its bland robotic delivery offsetting the tension he'd felt before opening it. Feeling ridiculous, he thumbed the screen and brought up his list of contacts. Thumb hovering over the name *Julia*, he glanced up at the early morning sun.

Of course, he remembered, *it's eight thirty a.m. in Scotland, which means it will be after midnight back home.*

Score.

He popped his phone back into his pocket and promised himself he would text later when it was a more acceptable time for Julia.

Tom had forgotten all about his promise to himself by the time he reached the rented Ford Focus. He leaned back against the gunmetal gray bodywork, luggage at his feet, watching jet planes thunder overhead as he waited for his driver.

Chapter Ten

Self-styled eco-activist Jupiter Crash (a.k.a. Brian) had sulked for the entire journey to the rendezvous point.

The atmosphere in the camper was calm, as the lack of banter from their glorious leader had given each of the passengers some quiet time to doze, or simply to watch the endless blur of motorway turn to rural splendor, then back to motorway again, as the sun went down and the stars came out overhead. Jupiter had succumbed to sleep when Kegger slowed the camper down and pulled into the final services before the coast. A fleet of similarly beat-up old vehicles lined the parking bays at the services, along with lines of motorbikes and a couple of vintage buses that had been converted into bohemian motor homes. Sitting on and around the vehicles were droves of the same people who had been waving placards at the airport protest earlier that day.

Jupiter came to as Kegger found an empty bay, parked up and killed the engine. Brushing his dreadlocks from his eyes, Jupiter peered at his brethren through the condensation coating the window. The motorway services had become protester central, a nomadic army marching on the injustices of government. It was a sight that never failed to fill him with civic pride.

"Brothers and sisters," he said, his voice thick with nicotine and herb. "Time to stretch our legs and see what's what."

Kegger stretched and yawned. His huge frame wobbled as he extricated himself from the driving seat.

"Anyone else hungry? I could eat an ox," he said, rubbing his bloodshot eyes.

"Absofuckinglutely starving," Denny said.

"They have a KFC," Kegger said, sounding like he had found Nirvana.

"Christ's sake," Jupiter said. "Why not give your money to Life Sciences and be done with it?"

"What?" Kegger asked, "I'm not a *veggie-tarian* like you. Can eat chicken if I want."

"Whatever's in those boxes isn't chicken," Charlotte said, joining the fray, "Brian's right—you may as well give your cash to animal torturers, poor little things don't see an ounce of daylight."

Jupiter glanced over to Charlotte and nodded in solidarity.

She looked nothing short of gorgeous in the cobalt glow of the car park lighting.

"Jupiter. J-U-P-I-T-E-R. How many bloody times do I have to tell you?"

"All right, chill out, why do you have to be so confrontational all the time?"

An uncomfortable silence fell over the group.

Kegger lumbered off toward the Colonel's disembodied face, glowing atop a post like a head on a stick.

"Hey, wait up!"

Denny ambled after him, smelling the possibility of a free meal. Amber shrugged at Charlotte and followed her man.

Faced with the choice of joining the majority or being left alone with Jupiter, Charlotte muttered something about needing the bathroom and took off after them.

Great. He'd managed to turn a bonding opportunity into another reason for Charlotte to keep her distance. He loved the fact she was a vegetarian like him (he had neglected to mention that, unlike her, he ate fish), but he wished to high heaven she would stop using his given name. Taking the keys that Kegger had left in the ignition, Jupiter locked up the camper. If any of them returned looking to crash, they'd have to bloody well remember his proper name when they came looking for him to let them in. Stomping away from the van, Jupiter headed for the larger of the custom buses, in search of intel on the day's activities.

Mama Cath was right where he expected to find her, surrounded by her entourage on the lower deck of her vehicle, an old pillar-box red London Routemaster bus. The lower deck had been converted into a living room complete with sofas and a standard lamp that had been bolted to the floor. An ornate red velvet lampshade cast an exotic glow over the room, which was thick with smoke. Mama Cath's living room also served as a meeting house at times such as this, when she held court in a rickety old rocking chair with a Mac Book laptop atop her skirts. Assorted longhaired, shaved, tattooed, pierced and heavily bearded folk were gathered around her on the repurposed bus seats that lined the room.

"You're late," she said, as Jupiter skulked on board via the step at the rear of the bus.

"Pigs keep you long, did they?"

The whiny voice belonged to Bill, Mama Cath's beau. Jupiter had no idea why she would shack up with a sniveling bastard like Bill, but they were thick as thieves. For as long as Jupiter had been on the circuit, Bill had expressed an increasing dislike for him. The feeling was mutual, and Jupiter ignored the question.

"Good crowd tonight. Still buzzing from the airport gig. Did a good job, I thought. Ranks held, saw some telly cameras in the fray. If they hadn't turned the pumps on us, we'd have been solid..."

Mama Cath's eyes were eating him whole. He looked into them. They were wide, all-seeing orbs bright as fireworks. She knew their protest had been a failure as well as he did. Her ensuing sigh underlined the fact. Her eyes fell and she set about rolling a cigarette using her trademark jet-black liquorice papers.

"Glad to hear you're so upbeat about it, Mr. Crash."

Bill had decided to speak for his missus, as he often did. Mama's eyes twinkled, her gaze still fixed on Jupiter.

"How many did you bring, out of interest?"

Jupiter faltered.

He had promised at least a couple hundred, roughly one third of his Twitter following. It had seemed a reasonable estimate during the planning stages, but he hadn't taken into consideration the fact that many of his followers hailed from the south. Anything north of the Watford Gap was clearly too far out of their comfort zone. Consequently, only a handful of his chapter had turned up.

"Just out of interest?"

To Jupiter, Bill's nasal snarl sounded like a wasp buzzing in his head. He wished he could swat the voice, and its owner, away.

"Two dozen, I reckon."

No sooner had Jupiter uttered the words than a ripple of laughter passed through the gathering aboard the bus.

"But the weather's been foul and most of them are southern sissies."

"Takes one to know one!" Bill laughed.

The crowd laughed along with him.

Jupiter bit his lip, silently cursing the Home Counties accent that made him sound posh to pretty much anyone outside Surbiton.

"Does it, Bill? Really? Where were you when the cannon went off, then? Could've sworn I saw a pub near the terminal..."

Bill's eyes narrowed, his pointy features taking on a rodent-like aspect as he scowled openly at Jupiter.

"Now, now, boys," Mama Cath said, exhaling liquorice smoke. "Let's be friends, eh?"

She leveled her gaze at Bill, who looked daggers at Jupiter, then withdrew. Returning her attention to Jupiter, Mama Cath turned the laptop around in her lap so he could see the screen. She had his profile up, for all to see.

"You have hundreds of followers, no?" She did not wait for his answer. "We need the young'ins, Jupes, it's the only way we can beef up the numbers. And numbers are what we need right now more than anything. A couple of van loads of your mates ain't enough to make The Six O'clock News—you feel me?"

Jupiter nodded. He was the youngest person aboard the bus. Perhaps that's why he felt like a schoolboy being given a ticking off in the head teacher's office. He so wanted to be a part of this, perhaps it had been a mistake to promise such high attendance figures.

"What did you tell them? The cops?"

Bill again, lurking like a rodent in the shadows.

So that's what this Q&A session is all about, thought Jupiter.

He made sure not to pause for too long before answering.

"I got hurt," he said, lifting his bandaged arm slightly for dramatic effect. "Guy who did it drove headlong into a crowd of us. If you were in the thick of it, you'd know all about it of course."

Jupiter stared at Bill with relish as the pointy man felt the sharp end of his barb.

"Cops wanted to know all about the blokes who drove at us, that was all."

"That right?" Bill asked, his nostrils breathing suspicion like smoke.

"Yeah."

"And who were they, these fellers?"

"Couple of dorky Americans. Gave the cops their details, let the CCTV footage do the rest. Made sure to tell them I'm interested in pressing charges."

"You did good," Mama Cath interceded before Bill could speak. "Assault on a protester could be bad, very bad *ju-ju* for the police— especially after what happened in Parliament Square."

Jupiter remembered the protest as clearly as if it had happened yesterday. Hemmed in by the police tactic of "kettling" outside the Houses of Parliament, scores of protesters had been rushed to the hospital after collapsing in the crush of bodies. An elderly man had later died from internal injuries, and the Metro Police Chief had resigned soon after.

"You did good," Mama repeated. "Just get the numbers up next time. Keep the police cameras off the old faces. Give them a smokescreen to disappear into, yes?"

Jupiter nodded his agreement and thanks for the endorsement.

"Now fuck off," said Bill, taking the wind out of Jupiter's sails. "Us grownups got some proper business to discuss."

Jupiter jumped off the back of the bus and headed for the bright lights of the services. He glanced back over his shoulder to make sure Mama's boys hadn't followed him, then quickly doubled back toward the Routemaster. Ducking around the side, keeping low to remain out of sight of the gathering, he sidled up to an open window on the driver's side of the bus. He could hear Mama Cath's voice just as clearly as though he were still inside the bus with her.

Jupiter crouched down and listened intently—so intently that he did not hear the footfalls of Bill and cronies until they were upon him.

He tried to cry out in pain as they grabbed his damaged arm and wrenched it around behind his back, but a big, powerful hand was clamped over his mouth, keeping him from making a sound. His assailant held him fast as Bill and the others closed in around him, raining kicks and punches on him like an angry mob at a stoning. His body wanted to double up as a boot found his groin, the impact sending his testicles deep into his abdomen, but those powerful arms held him erect and vulnerable to more punishment. A fist split his lip and he felt warm blood spew over his chin, tasted its salt metal tang. Something blunt glanced across his forehead accompanied by a dull cracking sound and his eyes rolled back.

They were still punching and kicking him as he fell unconscious.

Chapter Eleven

As the rental car engine droned on, Tom watched a huge bird of prey wheel across the tousled highland landscape. He thought the bird could be a Red Kite, though he wasn't one hundred percent sure. He toyed with the idea of asking Dieter for his opinion, but thought better of distracting him while driving on such a tricky road, which weaved this way and that at the whim of the surrounding mountain range.

The drive had, as predicted, taken five hours and he and Dieter were still several miles off from their destination. Neither of them minded, not with views as spectacular as the one beyond their windscreen. They had shrugged off the airport, then the city and the blank corridors of motorway some hours back and Tom felt lighter the more distance they put between their rental car and civilization. Their rest stops had been brief, affording just enough time to grab a coffee and a snack before urinating, then getting back on the road again. Tom could see Dieter was tired from the flight and the hours of driving, but something like a compulsion had gripped the both of them to reach Douglass.

Tom craned his neck so he could see the bird of prey riding a slipstream of mountain air high above their car. It soared out of Tom's view for a moment before it reappeared on Dieter's side of the vehicle, then soared back toward his side once more. He gasped as the majestic bird hovered for a moment in midair, then tucked its wings either side of its body and took a nosedive toward the ground at frightening velocity. Again, Tom lost sight of the creature as the car rounded a sharp bend. Then, it rose up, powering itself aloft and clinging to its prey—perhaps a small rabbit—with talons as big as butcher's hooks. The bird's black eyes glinted and Tom felt for one penetrative moment like it was looking right at him, welcoming him into the wild. The rabbit twitched, barely able to move in the grip of those powerful claws.

In the dark of his nightmares the night before, Tom had known what it felt like to be that rabbit, dangling helpless beneath its abductor. But in the cold, autumnal light of day, Tom felt something else entirely. As the powerful bird flapped and glided off into the far distance behind them, accompanied by the ever-droning soundtrack of the engine, Tom smiled to himself. He felt privileged, like he had witnessed something secret, something primal and utterly pure. The feeling elevated him just as powerfully as those talons had carried him aloft in his nightmares. His senses soared.

This must be what it feels like to escape, he thought.

The mountains parted, like great curtains of green velvet, and the car began its descent into the lower slopes where, presumably, Douglass was hidden. Dieter slowed his driving pace a little with the new terrain, something for which Tom was thankful as they passed over a wooden bridge that offered a view of the landscape behind them. It took Tom's breath away to gaze at the mountains again, then at the foaming torrent of a waterfall spilling over a shelf of rocks just beyond the bridge. Turning a bend deeper into the valley, the road became nothing more than a track. The wheel arches of the rental car clicked and popped with the impact of loose stones and gravel kicked up by the wheels. It sounded as though the car, too, was excited about reaching its destination. Then, Dieter gasped and hit the brakes, causing the car to skid to a sudden halt.

Tom felt the seat belt bite into the tender spot in his chest, a stark reminder of the violent mayhem they had witnessed at the airport protest only the night before. Hearing bleating sounds, Tom looked up from the dashboard just inches from his nose and saw the source of Dieter's alarm. A flock of sheep was making its way slowly across the track from one grassy plain to the next. The animals bleated, cajoling each other as they made their crossing. A large ewe, bigger than her sisters, paused for a moment in front of the car. She fixed the occupants of the Ford Focus with stern black eyes and bleated as loud as an angry teacher berating her pupils.

"That told us," Tom laughed.

"Sure did!" Dieter replied, finding the ewe's protest equally amusing.

Dieter moved off when the last few stragglers had joined their fellows in the field to his side of the car. Looking out the windscreen, Tom spied something above the dense tree line in the distance.

"Is that...?"

"Yes it is."

Tom peered up the track ahead of them. At first, he'd mistaken the plume of smoke above the fir trees for yet more mist. But unlike the mist, the smoke had purpose.

"Where there's smoke, there's..."

"A public house!" Dieter said as they neared an elderly building with *The Rock in a Hard Place* emblazoned beneath its eaves.

But his joy quickly subsided as they passed the building. It had been boarded up long ago. The source of the smoke now looked to be from deep within the forest, not from the pub as Dieter had imagined, and the sky had darkened as the thick green of the firs became a huge verdant wall either side of them.

"Is this really the place? Could we have taken a wrong turn somewhere?" Tom asked.

He was already reaching for the map he'd tucked away in the glove box with his bottle of water. Their smart phone map apps were not an option out here in the wilderness. Dieter remained silent, eyes fixed on the road ahead, looking for anything resembling a landmark in the thick of the trees. Tom's consternation turned to relief as they drove past a weathered sign at the roadside and he left the map where it was.

The wooden sign was clinging onto its moss-covered post for dear life via a cluster of huge nails. Rust stains had formed around each nail—blood red, like gunshot wounds. The sign was framed with a green border of mold. Its painted letters were peeling from the surface of the wood after what looked like several human lifetimes of wet weather had been visited upon them. Tom blinked as they shot past the sign, the letters imprinted on his vision: *Douglass*.

They drove on for another mile or two and, just as Tom was planning how to break it to his boss that the village was no longer there, they arrived in Douglass proper—though the streets were deserted.

"Where is everybody?" Dieter muttered.

"Expecting a welcoming committee?" Tom said.

"Hardly," Dieter replied.

And he had a point. Tom felt a little uneasy all of a sudden at the thought of steaming into this remote little village on a mission to buy up all the land for biofuels development. He doubted they would be welcomed with open arms, or even an open hotel.

"Weird isn't it...not a soul out today? Oh wait, what have we here..."

The first sign of life came in the form of a cluster of little picture postcard cottages, set back from the road behind higgledy-piggledy walls constructed from irregular blocks of local stone. Tom glanced at the thatched roofs and saw smoke spiraling out from a couple of the chimneys, proof positive that their owners must be home.

"Guess it's not a ghost town after all."

"*Ja,*" Dieter muttered. "But there's not much life here either by the looks of things. What's the place called again?"

Tom took the slip of paper from his pocket.

"The Firs," he said. "How imaginative. Damn well hope it's in better shape than the place we saw back there."

Dieter nodded, as he drove on at a crawl through the village. Among the few other buildings they encountered was a little post office and general store, which looked to be shut. They followed the road as it swung a right through the impenetrable forest flanking it and clanked over a metal cattle grate. About five hundred meters farther on, they finally saw the sign for The Firs and its parking lot, which another sign declared was *For Patrons (and their animals) Only.* Dieter chuckled at the sign and Tom could tell the big man had already added the gag to his ongoing comedy routine for future use in a potential romantic situation.

They parked up alongside the only other vehicle in the car park, an elderly, mud-encrusted pickup. Dieter killed the engine, and they both removed their seat belts and clambered out of the rental car.

As he listened to Dieter groaning and stretching after hours in the driver's seat, Tom marveled at the freshness of the cool mountain air. It was damp, loaded with the scent of pine and the deeper he breathed the giddier he felt. There wasn't a single sound to be heard, save for his own breathing.

"Amazing," Tom whispered.

"You think?" Dieter looked unfazed.

"You're from the countryside?"

"Not from. But my family moved to the Alps when I was a boy. Lived there 'til they sent me to school in Cali."

"I envy you. I lived in the city my whole life. Places like this look like pop-up books to me."

"They lose their appeal in the bad weather, believe me," Dieter laughed. "Okay when the snow comes, at least you can go skiing then, but in the fall—damp can be a total bitch, gets right into your knee joints, you know?"

Now it was Tom's turn to laugh.

"You sound like an old man."

"And right now I feel like one," Dieter said, stretching his aching limbs, "Come on, let's find a fire to sit beside. And some food..."

Dieter popped the trunk and he and Tom retrieved their luggage. Locking the car, a city dweller to the last, Dieter led the charge to the side door of the pub.

The door, which had *Guest Reception & Lounge* hand painted on it in elegant golden letters, creaked as Dieter held it open to let Tom inside first. Tom made his way down the short corridor that led to the reception area, glancing at framed watercolors of rustic landscapes that lined the walls. The corridor opened up into a lobby where an unmanned reception desk stood at the foot of a carpeted stairwell. A log fire crackled in the hearth of the adjacent dining room. Tom peeked inside and saw half a dozen tables, each surrounded by high-backed wooden chairs that overlooked leaded windows and views of the fir trees beyond. The warmth from the fire had permeated the entire area, making a mockery of the cool mist outside, and Tom removed his coat. Folding his coat and placing it atop his luggage next to the reception desk, he tapped the brass bell with the flat of his hand. The bell rang out shrilly and the sound had all but faded when Tom and Dieter heard the creak of footsteps on the stairs above.

"Ah, you must be our American guests."

The voice wafting down the stairs was soft and lilting, like birdsong. It was a male voice, but one with a range a few octaves higher than the average. The Scottish intonation added an intoxicating bent to the delivery, making the most ordinary of words sound exotic, almost magical.

"That's us," Tom said.

He peered up the stairs to get a view of the extraordinary voice's owner.

A rake of a man appeared, navigating the last few stairs with great care and holding on to the banister so tightly that he could have been a passenger on the *Titanic*. In his early sixties, he had thinning white hair, combed back and left long at the back and sides so it crowned his slightly feminine features like wisps of cotton candy. His skin was flushed pink and beads of sweat glistened on his forehead, presumably due to the exertion of his rapid descent. As he maneuvered himself into a practiced position behind the reception desk, the old man took a handkerchief from his breast pocket and mopped his brow.

"You know, we we're expecting you yesterday," he said, leafing through the ledger on the desk before him. "Get lost along the way?"

"Trouble at the airport," Dieter said. "We called ahead this morning. You get our message?"

"Message? No, no message."

The old man stroked his chin for a moment, deep in thought.

"But the girl said..."

"Ah, that'll explain it. My Holly is adept at taking messages, but passing them on is a skill she's yet to master," he chuckled, then turned the ledger around on the desk. "If you could both sign here please."

Tom glanced over the names and signatures of previous visitors, with a column for their place of residency filled with obscure names: *Gravesend, Downton,* and *Grimsby* all sounded like fun places. Then, Tom saw a familiar name, and that of the most recent guest—*Monroe.* Tom wavered for a moment, remembering the man's final words to him as the blood had spiraled around his head after his fall.

"He's in the trees... He's waiting..."

Goose bumps erupted across Tom's forearms, a microscopic mountain range of chilled flesh. Tom's hand faltered above the ledger, pen hovering, poised above the dead man's name.

What the hell happened to Monroe that he was so damn frightened?

"How was Mr. Monroe during his stay?" Tom asked, hoping that by mentioning the dead man's name aloud he might will the gooseflesh away.

Their host towered over Tom, scrutinizing him in the way a teacher would scrutinize a student in an exam.

"Quiet man, kept himself to himself. Oh, he was nae bother. A good guest."

Nae bother. The turn of phrase amused Tom and he shared a surreptitious smile with Dieter. Then, hearing a rapping sound, Tom saw the old man was now tapping the pen against the ledger with a slight scowl on his face. Tom took a sharp intake of breath, then signed and dated the ledger on the next available empty line. He was struck by a welcome distraction; another curious place name.

"*Kintail* sounds interesting, where have I seen that name before?"

"On the map," Dieter said.

"Aye, the Kintail Mountains are north-northwest of here. Lovely place. But you'll have to wear your long johns if you're to visit this time of the year," their host quipped.

Dieter took his turn to sign the guest ledger, his eyes on the roaring fire and dining tables in the adjacent room the whole time. He pushed the ledger back across the desk to the old man, who lifted it up and studied it intently with those glassy eyes of his.

"McCrae?" he said, scanning Tom's entry in the book like it was forensic evidence.

Tom nodded. "Tom. Pleased to meet you, Mr....?"

"I'm a Tom too, funnily enough. Tom MacGregor, but most folks call me Tommy," the hotelier said in that musical voice. "You have family up here, I suppose?"

Tom shook his head.

The old man looked perturbed.

"*Have'nae* had anybody by the name of McCrae in Douglass for...well..."

His voice trailed off, and Tom and Dieter waited patiently while the old man finished his scrutinizing. Their remaining patience was sorely tested as he then took his sweet time locating their room keys.

"Upstairs, through the fire door and along the corridor," the old man instructed them as he handed over their keys. "Your rooms both have telly, en suite bathroom, and if you're hungry and thirsty there are tea and coffee facilities—and complementary biscuits."

His last statement was delivered with great relish, as though he'd just announced a free Michelin-starred banquet.

"I don't think tea and biscuits are going to sate this beast." Dieter's stomach growled, as if on cue. "I'd like to place a lunch order, say fifteen minutes—after I freshen up. How about you, Tom, hungry?"

Tom nodded. He'd forgotten how hungry he was until Dieter mentioned food. Breakfast was a distant, fading memory and the snack stops they'd made during the drive hadn't constituted a proper lunch. He was just about to articulate his hunger, when the old man frowned and interjected.

"Oh, I'm afraid lunch is finished for the day, gentlemen."

"Finished?" Dieter sounded bereft.

Tom felt Dieter's pain. His stomach growled too, as though in protest.

"How can lunch be finished?" he asked.

Their elderly host turned to a clock mounted on the wall opposite the stairs. It was a garish thing, its hands inlaid with mother of pearl, and a brass surround that could have done with a good polish. It was just after three in the afternoon.

"Lunch is served from twelve until two."

"That's insane," Dieter said. "Lunch is when guests want it, surely?"

"In the city, perhaps," the old man replied calmly, his eyes twinkling. "But this is not the city. Only the two of us to run the place; our cook defected to Edinburgh some time ago."

"But what are we supposed to do?"

"Dinner service starts at six..."

"I'll have died of starvation by then. Is there somewhere else to eat?"

"The Rock used to do good food, but it's..."

"Closed down, I know," Tom struggled not to sound annoyed, but the old man's manner was beginning to grate. "We saw it on the way here."

"Of course you did." The old man smiled.

"So is there anywhere else?" Dieter snapped.

"You'd have to go up to Plockton, they have a good restaurant there."

"Great." Tom tried to sound positive through his grimace. "Plockton sounds nice. Is it far from here?"

"About an hour and a half—with a prevailing wind."

"Ninety minutes?! Ninety damned minutes...for lunch?!" Dieter had clearly had enough.

"We are rather remote."

"You're not fucking kidding."

Dieter strode over to a cardboard rack filled with tourist attraction leaflets and started rifling through them, presumably to avoid a charge of assault and battery on an elderly man.

Tom leaned over the desk, lowering his voice to offset Dieter's rage.

"Could you make an exception this one time? Rustle something up for two hungry travelers? We'd be very grateful."

The old man looked at Tom like he'd just asked him for permission to screw his wife on the reception desk. Torturous silence passed, marked by the loud ticking of the ugly brass clock, before he spoke again.

"I suppose Holly could make you some sandwiches."

"Sandwiches would be great," Tom enthused, before Dieter could say something he might regret later.

The big man's face had reddened from the pain of keeping his mouth shut.

"You'll have to eat them in the bar, you understand," their host added.

"In the bar, in our rooms, wherever is just fine."

"I'll tell Holly. What do you gents like? Ham? Cheese?"

"What else do you have?" Dieter asked, his pent-up bile free at last.

The old man pondered for a moment. "Ham. And cheese," he replied.

"We'll take it," Tom said, ushering Dieter and their luggage up the stairs, intent on avoiding a diplomatic incident.

Chapter Twelve

Cosmo tended the fire because it was all he had, apart from the girl.

Throwing handfuls of dry bracken onto the fire, he knelt down and blew into the base of the flames, listening to the life-affirming crackle and pop of the newer wood igniting. Those branches that were more recently deceased still had sap and moisture locked inside them, causing them to spit and whistle like the cadavers he and his comrades had torched in the old days. His army days, Kosovo days. The mere thought of the place conjured the same fleshy stink that had clouded the very air he'd breathed. He shut his eyes and tried to blot out the phantom screams of the women and children, screams that had followed him throughout his war and across the sea to this place.

My forest, my home, my trees.

Cosmo opened his eyes again and looked skyward, to the place where the tips of the firs met the sky. The forest, his forest, was in a state of perpetual twilight due to the thickness and density of the foliage. Here on the forest floor, alone with his fire, his roasting rabbit, nothing could reach him. No one could see him, nobody could find him, and yet he felt altogether vulnerable. He turned the rabbit, a quarter turn on its spit, out of habit now rather than hunger. The smell of the flesh had become fused with the scent memory of those burning mothers, their screaming children. Burning alive, some of them. He heard a Red Kite's cry echo across the treetops and his flustered mind conjured screaming children, begging him to rescue them from the funeral pyre he and his brothers had built for them in the old storehouse that day. Muscle memory made his hand hot with shame, just the way it had felt when he'd pressed his fingers against the red bricks of the storehouse. Six inches of stone and mortar was all that had separated him from the dying on the other side of that wall. The more the smoke had billowed from the airbricks and cracks in the structure, the fewer the cries of anguish. The fewer the cries for help. The little lambs inside had lain down and gone to sleep. Even now the words of his little lullaby to them came back to haunt his lips. Each and every syllable the last breath of a pregnant mother; a defiled and weeping child.

He felt heat, white hot, at his fingertips and looked down at his right hand. He had inadvertently placed his fingers inside the fire. Careless. He watched the skin of his fingertips, transfixed, for a few moments as it blistered and blackened. Multiplying the sensation across the dark web of his memories, he imagined the hair of the women burning up like tapers in the inferno. The roasting rabbit's flesh sizzled and spat beside him as the layers of fat melted over its pinioned carcass. He blinked and saw a ghost image of a thousand chubby little child bodies roasting and spitting as they writhed in agony, hammering their little hands on the walls until, baked brittle, they broke and burned up.

Cosmo doubled over and dry heaved into the carpet of ruddy leaves beneath him. It had been a while since he'd last eaten, so the contents of his stomach were nothing more than hot spools of bile, which steamed horribly as they dribbled onto the forest floor. Cold tears streamed from his eyes and mucous oozed from his nose like snail trails. Sobbing, he glanced back at the rabbit, the fire. He had intended to eat some of the meat, and then wrap the rest for later, but he no longer felt like eating.

Elena would surely be hungry when she woke. He would take all of the meat back for her. An offering. Wiping the mucal detritus of his woe from his face and nose, he crawled back to the fire. He removed the cooked rabbit from its spit and wrapped it in the animal's own pelt. He placed the warm, furry bundle inside his backpack for the girl. Cosmo had already left the entrails for the denizens of the forest, and hoped they would appreciate his humble tribute. He was certainly undeserving of the forest's bounty today, but not them—not the wild things that graciously shared their forest home with him. And he was a wild thing too, but not yet one of his forest fellows. He was a man of muck and murder, forever stained by blood indelible.

Removing his paratrooper boots and partially rotted socks, he stood up and walked over the flames until the fire was extinguished. With each step, he said a silent prayer for the ones he had burned. The calloused flesh of his feet began to melt painfully as his body weight fused skin and burning branch together. He held his breath and continued walking on the spot, knowing a thousand such steps across all the fires in hell would never be penance enough for the things he had done. So, when the fire was out—extinguished by his guilt—he tied his boots together by their laces and strung them onto his backpack. He would walk the long walk back to his girl and his shelter barefoot. Perhaps then the admonishing screams of pain would cease and he could sleep awhile. Until those screams returned with the next cursed day, the forest, the trees, and the spirit protecting all of them, would know how sorry he was. He began his walk on red, raw feet, and prayed a silent prayer for peace.

Afternoon was losing its daily battle to twilight when Cosmo trudged back to the house; a derelict like him. He paused for breath a moment, taking in the sky's orange glow, haloed around the ramshackle roof of the place he called a temporary home. Soon, the light would be gone from the sky and omniscient day would give way to imperceptible night, the time Cosmo felt safest of all. Most people, in his old-life experience of war and cities, felt most vulnerable in the dark. Not so for Cosmo, who wore night's black velvet like a protective cloak. Underneath the stars, none could find him, no one could see him. And *woe betide* any who did, for night was when he finally gave way to sleep. If any man were foolish enough to disturb the shallow meditation of Cosmo's slumber, they would find themselves going under—no sooner than he'd opened his eyes and looked upon them. He dropped his pack beside the door and made a quick perimeter check, just be sure. His traps and alarms bore no sign of having been tampered with. Satisfied, he headed back to the door, hoisted his pack onto his shoulder and crept inside, fearful of disturbing Elena.

The door creaked as he opened it and he made a mental note to oil the hinges with some animal fat in the morning. The building was decades old, and in a state of neglect that bordered on abuse. It had been a fine cottage once, somewhere to rent out to walkers in the summer months. Relics of this tourist trade were still to be found on the shelves in Cosmo's adopted home; old compilation CDs given away free with Sunday newspapers, yellowing books and magazines with damp, curling pages. Several tiles were missing from the roof of the two storey building and leaves, dirt and dust had made themselves at home as a result. Each floorboard creaked in welcome, or warning, as Cosmo crept across the living room. The exposed wooden boards were part-carpeted with rotting leaves and soil, as though the shack was intent on becoming at one with the forest—living inside out. A fir tree had erupted through the floorboards in the far corner by the window, further laying the forest's claim to the house by a process of natural assimilation. He reached the spot where the soiled rug lay between a festering pile of leaves and a moldy old armchair. Cosmo stooped low and pulled back the rug, revealing the hatch that had become his front door. From over his shoulder, he heard a whisper of wind in the fireplace. He was eager to climb below into his hidden home. Cosmo did not care for the atmosphere in the airy living room. The journey from the front door to the hatch always had his nerves on edge. The house creaked and moaned like a ghost, encouraging his exit.

He picked up the broken chair leg, sharpened to a point, which had become his door key and used it to prize open the trapdoor. He descended the first few rungs of the ladder, cringing at the noise he was making. Even though he was barefoot, his footfalls would be more than enough to wake Elena. Listening intently, and hearing nothing, he turned and carefully lowered the hatch with one hand, while tugging the rug back into place above it. When his fingers were all but wedged between the floor and the hatch, he snapped them back and lowered the hatch into place. The escaping air would be enough to ensure the border of the rug concealed the lip of the hatch. His perimeter was secure, of that he was certain, but a good soldier left nothing to chance. Being proactive kept a soldier alive.

Get sloppy and you're as good as inviting Death to your party, his drill sergeant used to tell him, *the Devil is in the details, but you have to step back and see the bigger picture and your place in it—if you are to defeat your enemy.*

Right now though, Cosmo was home. With the perimeter checks complete and the hatch closed behind him, he could settle down for the night.

As he reached the foot of the ladder he saw the familiar shape of the girl on the cot bed in the corner, blankets bunched up around her so all that was visible of her was her beautiful fair hair.

Good, he thought, *still sleeping.*

He placed his pack in the coldest spot in the cellar, a brick-lined alcove that once held a wine rack until he ripped the thing out so he could make it his refrigerator. The rabbit would keep there nicely until morning. Elena would be pleased not to have to go outside before breakfast; the mornings were getting colder as autumn was drawing swiftly in. He untied his boots from his pack and stashed them in a high place where they would not draw damp from the cellar floor so easily. Removing his greatcoat, he hung it from a hook embedded into the largest of the ceiling beams. When he'd first explored the cellar, he'd found a net basket of garden toys hanging from the hook; a bright orange bucket, green spade and a sponge football all the colors of an oil slick in the sunshine. Deciding the garish plastic things had no place in his world he had buried them outside, drowning their rainbow hues forever beneath drab soil and dead leaves.

Yawning quietly, Cosmo stretched his arms up as high as he could reach them and felt his vertebrae crack and shift from long hours carrying his pack through the forest. His feet were both numb from cold and seared by the flames he'd stamped out earlier, and he craved the warmth beneath Elena's blankets. Carefully, quietly, Cosmo pulled back the woolen layers covering her and stole into bed. She lay with her back to him, and he curled his body into her tiny form until they were making spoons under the blankets. Breathing in the soft, sweet fragrance of Elena's hair, he pulled the blankets up and over his head.

Nobody could find him, no one could see him.

He closed his eyes and let sleep take him down.

Chapter Thirteen

Tom leaned against the bar and finished his sandwich. He and Dieter ate in silence, listening to the beauty serving them from the other side of the copper-topped bar. If their host's voice was music, then Holly's was a symphony performed by a full orchestra with a choir of angels. Her sweet Scottish accent had a lovely lilt to it, making a jewel of every vowel sound that passed her fulsome pink lips.

Tom watched Dieter watching her, and then sneaked a glance for himself as she reached for the coffee jug, turning her back to them. She was a rare beauty, mid-twenties at a push, with messy red hair, shoulder-length and eyes as green as a cat's. Her skirt was daringly short and her mohair sweater was flimsy thin, accentuating her curves. He and Dieter had remained quiet ever since they'd laid eyes on her. She hadn't stopped talking for a moment, keeping them entertained with small talk about the weather in Douglass and where the best local fishing was to be had.

Tom glanced at Dieter again. The big man looked absolutely smitten as he laughed at Holly's jokes on cue and drank his coffee down so he could get another refill, and another look at her rump, on the house. Any complaint about the lack of a hot lunch option had been forgotten the instant Holly had appeared, smiling, from behind the bar. In fact, Dieter looked to be genuinely enjoyed the simple fare, even complimenting Holly at one point on the fine taste of the mustard she'd slathered between the layers of cold meat and tangy cheese. All local, she'd told him with a smile, including the bread, which was as spectral white as Holly's skin and tasted a little stale to Tom. But their hostess transfixed him just as much as she did Dieter, so he remained quiet on the subject—opting to chew his way through the matter rather than spoil the convivial atmosphere.

He'd brought his laptop with him from his room and, finishing his sandwich and pushing the plate away to make it clear he required no more, he opened up the screen and powered up the laptop. The little start-up chime rang out in the empty lounge bar like a call to action, but Dieter didn't seem to notice, or care—his attention was fixed on Holly.

"Thought we might run through the itinerary," Tom ventured.

Dieter was still in the process of stuffing his face with a doorstep of a sandwich and mumbled something unintelligible through his mustard-flecked lips.

"Okay, join me when you're done," Tom said before asking Holly if she minded him plugging his laptop in somewhere.

She graciously directed him to a table near the window, below which was an electrical socket. Tom had been meaning to launch a ticket in The Consortium Inc.'s I.T. support system to request a new battery. He was lucky to get a half hour of juice out of the thing on a good day and, back home, had to rely on the coveted Caltrain power sockets to keep working during his commute. Usually only one carriage had them, and unless you were willing or able to pay premium fares, it was potluck to get one in Standard. Plugging the power cord into his travel adaptor, then into the wall, Tom glanced out the window at the curtain of fir trees; such a different landscape to the one outside of his windows back home.

Julia would love it here, he thought sadly, before correcting himself. *Scratch that, she would have loved it back in the days before she became a zombie.*

Logging into his machine, Tom got connected to the pub's free wi-fi connection. The connection was okay, three bars out of four, which was one more than he sometimes got back home. He grabbed the virtual network key from his bag—a gray plastic key fob with a tiny digital display that gave him a code to tap into his computer so he could access the company network on the road. The display refreshed with a new code every minute, so he opened the virtual network window and entered his login details first. When the key refreshed with a new code, he cracked his knuckles and then typed it in. Next, he opened his Outlook mail window and it was just like being at his desk in the office, save for the fact that he was sitting in the lounge bar of a Scottish pub, surrounded by beautiful forests of Douglass Firs.

You've got mail.

One hundred-forty-eight unread messages, to be precise.

The sight of his inbox, crammed with office memos and other time-consuming crap he could better do without filled him with dismay. He had only been gone a couple of days and he already had a half day of work cut out for him if he were to process all the junk.

Deciding he'd trawl through it later, he searched his mail for messages from the CEO and Division Head first, as those would be the most urgent. Sure enough, there were just five, each with a zipped file of attachments for him to peruse. He unzipped them and saved the contents to his desktop folder named *Douglass Deal*. The first was a series of maps and schematics, which would form the basis of the surveying work he and Dieter would undertake during their stay. The next was a PDF document, watermarked *Eyes Only*, which detailed the point-by-point requirements of The Consortium's purchase of Douglass and its surrounding forests. Tom looked over the paragraph he'd just read a second time, and the penny dropped. His masters had sent him out here not only to buy land, but also to purchase the actual village itself.

He glanced over at Holly, who was laughing dutifully at Dieter's jokes. Maybe it was Tom's inherent paranoia, but her eyes seemed to look straight through him and at the trees outside the window. He adjusted the laptop screen, a reflex action because there was no way Holly could see it from where she was standing, and turned his attention back to the document. A few moments later, Dieter came over and sat down opposite him, placing a welcome cup of coffee on the table for Tom.

"Thought you could use this," Dieter said.

"Thanks," Tom replied, his voice a little distant.

"What's up?"

"Just reading through the schedule," Tom said. "We've got our work cut out for us. This is one heck of a big deal."

"Nothing we can't handle," Dieter said, sipping his coffee.

"True. But I'm not sure the locals will find it so easy."

"Ah. Buyout?"

Tom nodded. "Monroe did some good preliminary work by the looks of things..."

His voice trailed off and he glanced over to the bar again. Holly had left.

"You okay?" Dieter asked.

"Fine. It's just, did you see Monroe's name in the guest book?"

"Didn't notice. Sorry."

"It was just a little weird after what happened at the office. The last time I saw him, he didn't look so great."

"Word on the wire was he was under a lot of stress."

"Evidently."

Tom sipped his coffee. It wasn't great, but infinitely better than what had been on offer at the chain hotel that morning.

"So, back to the business at hand. Our first port of call should be a guy called..."

He scrolled back through the onscreen document, scanning each line for the name.

"Lithgoe," Dieter said.

"That's it," Tom said, mystified.

"He's the local laird, as they call it 'round here. Pretty much owns the village and everything in it, including the lease on this place. Nothing gets done without his say-so. Dinner's at eight, he'll join us here. A table right next to the fire you might be pleased to know."

"But how did you..."

"While you were over here playing with your laptop I got the inside track from the landlord's daughter on all the great and the good in the village. Seems there isn't a whisper or a fart goes on here that she doesn't know about," Dieter chuckled. "Not just a *very* pretty face."

Tom marveled at the smug grin creeping across Dieter's face.

Maybe it wasn't so bad to have him along for the ride after all.

Chapter Fourteen

Dieter's smug grin had all but vanished when it became apparent that Lithgoe was a no-show. He and Tom had left voicemail with the laird's assistant, twice, and they were at a loss what to do next, other than order main courses. They had taken their time with the starter, a thick broth of beef and vegetables, and were both ravenously hungry after their late, but light, lunch. Tom waved Holly over and she brought their menus to the table once again.

"No need for those," Dieter said, grumpy with hunger, "I know what I want. The roast lamb."

"With gravy and all the trimmings?" Holly asked, her voice effervescent as always.

"All the trimmings you got—Tom?"

"Oh, same for me," Tom said, sounding as tired as he felt.

Holly nodded and smiled at them both before ducking back into the kitchen.

Dieter watched her go, his eyes devouring the tiny strip of exposed flesh between her apron strings and the waistband of her black miniskirt.

"Lovely girl, shame the food's not quite up to snuff," he said.

"You don't like the broth? I quite enjoyed mine."

"Too salty."

The fire crackled and Tom glanced across at the pub's only other diners; an elderly couple with a combined age of a couple of centuries if they were a day. Tom frowned as he watched the old man slurping soup through his thick moustache, a process that generated a sound not unlike a suction pump. The old woman opposite him pecked at her food like a bird. He watched her taking tiny morsels of bread from her plate, which she then rolled between her fingertips until they were little pellets.

"It's like feeding time at the zoo over there," Tom whispered, vaguely disturbed.

"What? Oh," Dieter said, noticing the old couple as if for the first time. "Date night."

"Jesus," Tom sighed, hoping he and Julia would divorce before they ever ended up like that.

He knew in his heart there was every possibility that would happen, a feeling that gave him little solace so he turned his eyes back to the glow of the fire.

"Think I should call again?" Dieter asked.

"No, when he gets our voicemail he can decide how to play it. Let him chase us now, but if we don't hear from him by lunchtime tomorrow..."

"Call again, got it."

Holly emerged from the kitchen carrying two large plates of food. She held them both with a napkin in each hand to protect her fingers from the heat.

"Careful the plates are a wee bit hot," she chirruped as she placed the plates in front of Tom and Dieter. "Can I get you gents anything else?"

Dieter smirked and winked at her and she turned and smiled at Tom.

"He's a cheeky one your friend," she said, polite as ever.

Oh, he's not my friend, was what Tom really wanted to say, but he chose instead to return Holly's smile.

She held his gaze for a few seconds and Tom felt his cheeks flush a little. It was like they were sharing an intimate joke, a feeling Tom had not experienced for some time. It felt nice.

"All good, thanks," he said.

Feeling suddenly bashful, he rearranged his napkin in his lap.

"You devil," Dieter chuckled as Holly walked away, "I think she likes you."

Tom filled his mouth with roast potato, avoiding a riposte. Then he winced as the unmistakable charcoal taste of burnt food assaulted his taste buds. He turned one of the other potatoes over on his plate and was shocked to discover it was jet black underneath.

"What's wrong? Not cold, is it?"

There was raw panic in Dieter's voice; the naked fear of a man who loved his food almost as much as his women.

"Burned, look," Tom said, tipping his plate up slightly so Dieter could see.

Dieter checked his own plate and found his to be the same. He sliced open one particularly char-grilled specimen and prodded its insides with his finger.

"Stone-fucking-cold inside," he said, looking around for Holly.

She was no longer behind the bar, so he got up and stomped over to the doorway leading to the kitchen, calling her name. A few moments later, she reappeared. Tom noticed how she straightened her apron and hair as she stepped out from the kitchen doorway. Dieter led her to their table, pointing at his plate like he was a cop unveiling fresh evidence at a crime scene.

"What is this?" he said. "It's cold, and burned."

"Oh, I can't imagine how that happened, let me take them away and get you something else. How about fish and chips?"

"I don't want fish and chips, lady. I want the roast, preferably cooked today, not resurrected from the dead tomorrow."

"It was freshly prepared, I assure you..."

"Don't try that crap with me."

Dieter picked up a black-bottomed potato and held it aloft.

"These aren't fresh, they're leftovers from yesterday or God only knows when. They've been reheated, but all that's done is burn them on the outside and leave them cold on the inside."

Holly's mask fell for a moment and she looked at Dieter as though he had just described himself. She looked down at Tom.

"Is yours okay, sir?" she asked.

Tom just shrugged, placed his knife and fork on his plate and wiped his clammy hands with his napkin.

Dieter glowered at him, waiting for backup. Holly looked back at him with an air of disappointment. Tom had a sudden and overwhelming urge to go upstairs to bed.

"I'm sorry for the inconvenience, gentlemen," she said. "How about the fish and chips, they won't take long and they're cooked from fresh, I assure you."

"I ordered the roast."

Dieter was like a bull with a red rag in its sights.

"I'm afraid the roast is finished, it would take too long to make another and I don't want to keep you waiting..."

"You're out of leftovers you mean," Dieter snapped. "Let me talk to the manager."

"Please, just let me get you something..."

"The manager."

Holly looked flustered. She forced a smile at the elderly diners, who had taken an interest in the impromptu cabaret unfolding before their rheumy eyes.

"I'm afraid, he's not—he's not here," she stammered.

"Not here?!"

"So it's?" Tom said.

"Just me, yes."

Holly looked crestfallen.

An uncomfortable silence ensued as Dieter realized he had few options to claw this one back. Holly's eyes widened and Tom thought she might burst into tears any moment. Then, she steeled herself and cleared their plates from the table.

"I'll just have some dessert," Tom said, in as diplomatic a tone as possible.

Holly nodded at him, looking almost thankful. Hearing Dieter groan, she scurried away as quick as her legs would carry her.

Dieter flopped back down in his seat.

"What kind of operation are they running here? Sandwiches for lunch, burnt offerings for dinner, only one member of staff in the whole building, no wonder the place is up for sale."

Tom gestured for him to hush, eyeballing the elderly couple.

"Oh don't worry about them, they're probably deaf as posts," Dieter said.

He sat back, and he and Tom watched Holly as she returned from the kitchen wheeling a huge trolley laden with cakes and desserts. Each confection was housed beneath its own glass dome, like a laboratory specimen. A bizarre, drawn-out ritual ensued, as the girl placed each and every dish atop the table beneath the picture window. Then she stood back behind the line of cakes and puddings, tiny hands clasped together, awaiting further instructions. Agonizing moments passed, before the elderly man cleared his throat and spoke up.

"The bill, please."

His voice had that same musical lilt as the landlord's. Holly hurried away and came back with the couple's bill, which the man promptly paid, in cash. He stood and helped the woman into her coat, before thanking Holly for their meal.

"Keep the change," he said, looking directly at Tom and Dieter.

The man whispered something into the old woman's ear then left the dining room.

Then, to Tom's surprise, the elderly woman approached their table. She cleared her throat and addressed them in clearly enunciated repetition of, presumably, what her companion had just whispered to her.

"Mr. Lithgoe thanks you for a most enlightening evening and requests that you see him at his office nine a.m. sharp tomorrow morning. Holly has the address..."

Holly stood quietly beside her display of cakes and puddings, a slight smile at play on her lips.

Tom stood up, bolt upright, on reflex.

"Wait a minute, you're telling me that was..."

"Mr. Lithgoe, yes."

The old woman stared at Tom like he was plankton in a petri dish before she turned and walked to the exit.

"And you are?" Dieter ventured—brash as ever.

Pausing at the door, the woman fixed Dieter with that same hard stare.

"Mr. Lithgoe does not wish to see you tomorrow, just Mr. McCrae here. Do I make myself quite clear?"

Dieter did not respond to her rebuke.

The old lady looked at Tom once more, her eyes shark-like. He nodded in swift agreement; looking and feeling for all the world like a scolded schoolchild. Apparently satisfied for the moment, she swept from the room with a swish of her overcoat and left them to consider the desserts in silence.

Chapter Fifteen

Tom lay awake in his room, listening to Holly's sobs through the paper-thin walls. The argument, something about the burnt food and the lack of takings in the restaurant, hadn't lasted long before Tom had heard the unmistakable sound of the landlord's hand striking her. At that point he'd struggled to stop himself from marching next door to confront the old man. He had refrained of course, knowing any argument between father and fully grown daughter was their affair entirely and nothing to do with him. Tom winced as he heard the old man slam the door and stomp past his on his way to the stairs, and the bar below.

Hell, Tom would have only made it worse if he'd tried to intervene; at least that was what he was telling himself. Lithgoe's ruse to conceal himself while Dieter stomped about like a G.I. on steroids was a savage enough indictment of their current form on the Scottish business stage. Still, something good had come of it at least—Tom would take the meeting in the morning alone. He felt sure he could handle things better without Dieter's swagger getting in the way. The CEO had instructed him to cosy up to the locals; a tall order, taking into consideration their shaky start, so Tom had his work cut out for him. As Holly's sobs showed no sign of subsiding, Tom abandoned his plan to get an early night and turned the bedside lamp on again.

He cast his eyes around the drab room, which looked like an expressionist re-imagining of a hunting lodge. He rather missed the airport hotel with its air-con and neutral, almost nonexistent decor. His new digs were decked out like a set from a 1970s British sitcom, with the predominant color being dark brown, right down to the flecks in the well-trodden carpet.

Feeling the urge to empty his bladder, Tom climbed out of bed, rooted through his luggage and fished out a sweater, which he pulled on over his pajamas top. He crossed to the en suite bathroom and clicked the light on. The cord pull had been knotted in several places along its length, where it had clearly snapped and been patched up by the frugal landlord.

Under the harsh light of a single bare lamp the en suite bathroom was an eyesore, decorated with what Tom could only think of as pea soup green. The bath, sink and toilet fittings were the exact same sickly green hue as the walls and tiling. Adding to the grim effect the same layer of dust that coated every surface Tom had encountered after checking in had even taken hold in the bathroom. As he relieved himself, he had noticed an elderly toilet brush lurking behind the crapper. He frowned at the yellowing plastic of the brush holder, trying not to think of the bacteria making a home there and vowing not to touch the thing for the duration of his stay.

The bedroom itself was small, and had looked cosy upon first inspection, but now night had fallen so too had the temperature. Compared with the precise microclimate of his Mountain View apartment back home in the States, his room at The Firs was testicle-shrinkingly cold. Folding his arms and rubbing his hands across his body, Tom saw the curtains rise and fall slowly, as though a specter had moved right through them. He reached out and pulled back one of the curtains. It was cheap fabric, dark brown velour, and felt flimsy in the palm of his hand. No wonder it was having a tough time keeping the draft from the aged leaded windows at bay. He could feel icy air blowing through the gaps between the window and its frame—no double-glazing here like there had been at the airport hotel. But the view was infinitely superior to the street lit parking lot the chain hotel had offered.

Tom pulled aside the yellowing lace curtain to reveal the moonlit treetops beyond the glass. His breath fogged the windowpane as he moved his face closer to it, peering out into the night. Beneath the wash of moonlight, the trees appeared fused together like an impenetrable dark wall of interlocking branches and spiky needles.

Clouds drifted across the moon and, as the light dipped across the lower branches, Tom saw something lurking at the foot of one of the trees. He squinted closer to the window, feeling the cold glass kiss his forehead. It looked like a person—a male from the figure's stature, though he could not be sure at that distance—was standing there very still, gazing out from the edge of the forest. But gazing at what?

Tom quickly crossed to the bedside table and killed the lamp, hoping that by extinguishing the glow he would be afforded a better view of the unexpected stranger. He returned to his lofty vantage point and peered out once again, cursing as the cloud layer thickened and cancelled out the moonlight completely. By the time the clouds had cleared and the trees were once again painted silvery white beneath the moon glow, the figure had disappeared. Tom glanced up and down the ranks of trees, checking to see if the stranger had simply moved off, but he was nowhere to be seen.

If I saw him at all, Tom thought, yawning.

Tiredness could play tricks on a mind already fatigued by an overseas flight, not to mention an interminable drive with Dieter. Holly's sobs had subsided next door and Tom was contemplating climbing back under the sheets to give sleep another try when his cell phone vibrated on the desk, scaring the very breath out of him. The phone's screen flashed, illuminating the room with its electronic glow. He picked up the smart phone and looked at the screen to see who could be messaging him so late in the evening; *Number Withheld* was displayed there. He unlocked the device and navigated to the incoming messages window. A little green speech bubble filled with gibberish popped up on his screen; *xmKYsFighjkzx.*

Must be a glitched attempt at a spam message, he thought. But he still had that nagging voice at the back of his head. *If it is just a spam text, then why is it making you feel so damn uncomfortable,* the voice asked, *is someone fucking with you, maybe?*

But where had "they" gotten his number from, and why the garbled message—why not get straight to the point? He thumbed the touch screen and deleted the message. The little speech bubble diminished from the screen like a deflating balloon being popped by a pinprick.

His thoughts returned to the figure he had seen—or had *thought* he had seen—on the tree line moments earlier and he crossed to the window again to take another look. The clouds were moving faster across the moon's reflected brightness, casting dizzying shadows on the ground at the foot of the tree trunks. The shadows undulated like a weird black tide, an impenetrable swirl cast by the shapes of the branches that were silhouetted by the flickering moonlight. That was explanation enough for Tom; he must have imagined a figure amidst the dark dance of the shadows. Even now, the trees were swaying slightly in the wind, which had picked up so much that the net curtain flapped slightly from the imperfections in the elderly windows. Tom felt instantly cold, as though a ghostly breath had enveloped him. He drew the flimsy brown curtains and, shivering, climbed back into bed, taking his phone with him as a makeshift flashlight.

Huddled under the covers, he activated *Silent Mode* on his phone so he could still receive messages but not suffer a coronary in the event that he got one—especially if it was another gobbledygook waste of time glitch of a message. Reeling through lines of random text characters in the way that some might count sheep, Tom's eyes finally rolled back into his skull and he fell asleep.

As he began to snore, the wind blew a chink in the curtains, allowing a sliver of moonlight in. The curtains fluttered in a whisper of wind, the moon's light making new shadow shapes that spread across his bedclothes like tendrils.

Tom's eyelids flickered as he entered dream sleep and his subconscious mind conjured an old familiar melody.

"Jack Frost nipping at your nose..."

Chapter Sixteen

When Jupiter awoke, he felt like he'd been on the business end of a ten-ton truck. He opened his eyes and winced at the sharp pain that flashed behind his eyelids like a lightning strike to his nervous system. Instinctively, he touched his right temple and felt a jolt of pain so severe he thought he might pass out, or vomit, or both.

He heaved himself up into a partially seated position, letting his body weight rest on the hard, lumpy object just above his rib cage. As he moved, he felt a tightening in his sternum, like someone was pressing a booted foot against it, and the details of the assault started to come back to him. His addled brain pieced together the vicious sequence of punches, kicks and taunts he had suffered at the behest of Bill, that two-faced bastard. Pulling his legs up around him so he was kneeling on his side, his groin burned where they had kicked him repeatedly in the nuts. Sensation returning to his body with the flow of his blood, he could feel his left ear—sopping wet with blood after they had kicked him in the head. A sudden polarizing thought gripped him and he panicked.

What if I'm brain damaged, what if I can't walk, or talk anymore?

He clutched his head, the contents of which now felt like a stockpot boiling over, and tried to speak. Nothing came out but a pitiful moan. His voice sounded like the slurred dumb show of a boxer who had gone a few too many bouts in the ring. They had made mincemeat of him. He felt like crying, and would have done so if he didn't suspect it would hurt too much.

He placed his hand on the ground next to him. It felt rough and unyielding beneath his palm. Trying to focus, he peered down at his hand and squinted. His surroundings sharpened a little with his concentration and he realized the hard object that he was leaning on was the barrier at the edge of the car park. He looked up, expecting to see Mama Cath's bus, but only the painful glare of the floodlights greeted him. He quickly shut his eyes to cancel it out and, dizzy, he slid sideways across the curbstone until he was almost horizontal. His ribs screamed as he rolled over onto his front. Gasping for air, he crawled onto what felt like dirt and gripped a rough, springy plant. He was on an intersection planted with shrubs. The smell of manure repulsed him, but he lacked the energy necessary to push himself any farther. Collapsing facedown in the stench, Jupiter moaned and kicked his feet out with the last of his strength.

Then his world tilted and spun. He felt hands gripping his wrists and his ankles as a familiar voice murmured something beyond the fog of his consciousness. He blacked out again as the hands held him aloft and carried him away.

Jupiter was still clutching a fragment of the shrub in his hand, like a totem, when he awoke. His eyes opened less painfully this time and the vibration all around him told him he was safe and sound inside the camper.

Stretching his arms and legs out as much as he dared in light of his injuries, Jupiter glanced around the van, getting his bearings. Dim, gray morning light seeped through the side windows, which were covered in a film of dancing sleet. Beneath the frosty display sat Charlotte, nursing a steaming mug of tea, her tousled red hair going off like a firework atop her head.

"He's awake."

Jupiter looked toward the front of the vehicle and saw Kegger glance over his shoulder from the driver's seat. He looked vaguely glad that Jupiter was still alive, if such empathy was possible in the empty void between the large man's ears.

Denny and Amber peeked out at him from the confines of their sleeping bag. They couldn't have looked less interested in Jupiter's wellbeing if they had tried, he noticed with bitterness. He made a mental note to drop the fuckers at the next service station—for real this time.

Charlotte took a sip of her drink and then crawled over to Jupiter, taking care not to spill a drop as the van rocked her slightly. She offered him the cup and he took it, grateful for its warmth in the palms of his hands. He lifted it to his broken lips gingerly and as he did so his damaged arms, the first still hurting from the protest and the other from the attack, twinged with pain. He gritted his teeth, not wishing to appear weak in front of Charlotte, and inhaled the deep aroma of fennel—Charlotte's favorite brew.

"Drink some, you'll feel better."

Her voice was as soothing as the scent of the herbal tea.

Jupiter took a sip and winced at the sudden sting of warm cup against the tender flesh of his mouth but drank on, feeling as brave as a wounded soldier on his way home for leave.

"Thanks," he whispered.

He returned the cup to Charlotte as she sat down close beside him.

"Bill's lot did this, I suppose? Couldn't get much sense out of you when we picked you up—other than that you didn't want an ambulance."

"They did."

"Why?"

"Why does Bill do anything?" Jupiter fixed her with a pained look. "Is it bad? My face?"

"You look as pretty as a picture," she replied as she fished in her little shoulder bag for something, "A picture by Francis Bacon," she added.

Charlotte located the thing she'd been looking for; a compact makeup mirror. She pressed it into his hand.

"Careful, it's an 18-certificate, your face," she warned, apparently only half-joking.

"Christ. Oh, Jesus Christ," Jupiter said under his breath.

The face looking back at him from the little circle of glass in the compact was barely recognizable as his own. His bottom lip was three times its natural size, the skin broken in three places where the flesh had been slammed against his teeth. His right eyebrow was swollen and bruised, crowned with a glistening red semi-circle of a cut. The hair above his ear was matted with dried blood where they had kicked him. Worst of all, his right eye was bloodshot, giving it the appearance of a crimson pool ball where the blood vessels had burst around the iris.

He reached for the tea again and Charlotte handed it over, gesturing for him to finish the cup. A shiver passed through his body as he clung to the cup for dear life. Seeing his injuries had reactivated his nerve centers and he was beginning to feel their pain anew. He pressed his back against the vibrating metal body of the camper van. A wave of nausea hit him and it was all he could do to keep the contents of his stomach down. He must have turned deathly pale, because he became aware that Charlotte was inching away from him. She looked at him with the concerned disdain of a child minder tasked with looking after a projectile-vomiting toddler.

The nausea subsided and Jupiter, cold sweat clammy on his forehead, sipped more tea in the hope it would settle his churning stomach. He forced a smile, which from the look on Charlotte's face had only made him look more dreadful than ever.

"What time is it?"

"Coming on for ten o'clock. You've been under all night. We thought you'd gone with them at first, but then Kegger spotted you when he went back for Hot Wings."

"So I owe my life to Kegger's insatiable need for junk food? I'd kiss him if he didn't stink so bad," Jupiter snarled. "Where the hell are we?"

"On the road to Islay."

"Islay? What the fuck's in Islay?"

Coughing emanated from the sleeping bag at the front of the

vehicle. A cloud of reefer smoke surrounded the bag's occupants like a cloud.

"Distillery tour, bruv," Denny said, mid-toke. "Bit of culture on our travels."

"Distillery? What the hell are you on about?"

Jupiter winced again as the fresh scab on his lip started to separate, causing the wound beneath to bleed afresh.

"He's joking," Charlotte said, putting Jupiter out of his misery. "Islay's the next meeting place. We got word at the services that there's going to be a protest against the Forestry Bill."

"That bill didn't make it through Parliament," Jupiter said.

"A lot can happen while you are unconscious. Story broke while you were...incapacitated. Some bloke from the Forestry Commission was on the radio earlier. He sounded gutted, saying they'd all lose their jobs and the forests will go to the highest bidder, to be privately run..."

"You're shitting me. It went through while I was *sleeping*? But the House of Lords blocked the bill. How on earth could it have gone through?"

"The Lords voted against the previous bill, true. But the fuckers tweaked it on the back of some private sector kick-start scheme and got a marginal in the House of Commons. God knows who they bought and sold this time."

"Bloody hell, it's like the Land Bill all over again."

Jupiter stroked his jaw.

"You feel up to it? The protest I mean?" Charlotte asked. "We didn't know whether to go for it or not with you in such a state. I thought you'd probably want us to. So, anyway, we put it to a vote."

"You did good. We made our feelings clear about that new runway; we'll do the same with the forests. Fuckers can't just pass a law in Whitehall and expect us to stand by while they chop all the trees down in Scotland. Fuck's sake..."

He paused for breath, lowered his voice, leaning in close so only Charlotte could hear him.

"Mama Cath's lot know about this?"

"Don't know. They left the services in that bus of theirs before the news broke."

"They must know about it. If it's been on the radio, it must have hit the freak network by now."

"Why'd they give you such a kicking anyway? What did you say to them?"

"Not so much what I said, more what I heard."

Charlotte looked puzzled. "Go on."

"Let's just say I learned a couple of things last night."

"What things?"

"Stuff Bill would rather nobody knew about, or Mama Cath for that matter. Let's just say there's a hierarchy to our little protest movement, a hitherto unknown fiscal dimension to proceedings…"

"What are you going on about?"

"Bill and his gang are on some kind of payroll. I heard Mama Cath talking about it on the bus before I got whacked. Couldn't hear all the details, but I got the message all right. Someone is paying Bill and his boys to whip things up at protests."

"That can't be true. It would go against everything Mama Cath stands for."

"That's what I thought too."

He locked eyes with Charlotte.

"But if it isn't true, then why did Bill and his boys see fit to knock seven shades of shit out of me?"

Charlotte bit her lip.

"It was a warning," Jupiter continued. "They know I'm on to something."

"So what do we do?"

"We get to the protest site, lay low, find out what Bill is up to…"

"And then?"

"Then we fuck the bastard over good and proper."

They were so close now that Jupiter could feel Charlotte's breath on his face. He chanced a hand on Charlotte's thigh. She didn't ask him to remove it. He kissed her as hard and as deeply as his injuries would allow him to, then sat back and swigged the last of the fennel tea. He felt a little better now he had some fire in his belly and the fennel taste of Charlotte on his lips.

Chapter Seventeen

The drive to Lithgoe's place was tense to say the least. Dieter coughed and turned the in-car heating up a notch. He had not looked his best at breakfast, complaining of interrupted sleep caused by a lumpy mattress and rattling windows. The landlord's offer of a different room had apparently sated Dieter—that was, until he discovered the replacement's bathroom had not been cleaned and went on the rampage again. Tom knew the source of Dieter's angst was Lithgoe's dinnertime ruse; pretending to be a regular customer so he could get a look-see at the fish-out-of-water Yanks. Dieter was a sore loser and had let Lithgoe get to him, but Tom found the whole charade mildly amusing. What better way to get to know a potential client than by spying on him? The entire business was, in Tom's book, no different than Googling someone before a meeting to get the skinny on their personality and activities.

Dieter yawned, blinked his eyes and rubbed a hand across his face. The car's heating was making him drowsy.

Tom watched as the big man turned the heat down a notch, then opened the driver window a crack to let some fresh Highland air in. Tom did the same, glad of the fresh air in the stifling closeness of the car. Like Dieter's, his eyelids were heavy. He could count the number of good nights' sleep he'd had in the past year on his right hand and still have a couple of digits left. Yet he could not blame the dilapidated hotel room at The Firs for his poor sleep. After his sighting of the mystery man in the trees—an event Tom had tried to dismiss as hallucination caused by jet lag, and long hours on the road—he had fallen prey to the same screaming nightmare that woke him most nights. He had dreamed himself back into that room filled with crimson atrocities.

Again, like his nightmare during the flight, those cold hands had pulled him up and out through the chimney into the freezing shock of night before depositing him onto the forest floor in a mess of blood and leaves. He had then dreamed that his body was sinking into the roots of the trees that were closing in all around him, trying to scream as damp earth filled his airways. He had woken up several times during the night, each time clutching on to his chest with fright, and each time blinking away his night terrors and wishing it was morning.

Now that blessed morning had come, Tom gazed out of the passenger window at the awesome landscape. Every twist and turn in the road revealed new, weather-beaten wonders. When they had set off, thick frost still covered the mountainsides and fields like a silver blanket. Now that the sun was rising, an autumnal yellow, Tom could see the frost cover receding in places, gradually giving dominion to daylight. But the days were short and even in the comfortable microclimate of the air-conditioned rental car Tom could feel the cold in the air just by looking at the landscape.

Following Holly's directions, which she had kindly jotted down on a sheet of paper for them, Dieter took a sharp bend at the end of the high mountain road. The turn took them down a steep, winding road and deep into the lush, green wilderness of a valley. The land was so wild that Tom had difficulty imagining anyone living out there. But as they descended the winding track to the valley floor, the vista outside the windscreen opened up and Tom could see why an elderly gentleman like Lithgoe might make his home there.

The view was breathtaking, rolling fields either side peppered with foaming brooks; tributaries fed by melting ice atop the tallest peaks. Here the road became more of a narrow track that slalomed along the valley floor, twisting this way and that with the natural undulation of the landscape and its little rivers and tributaries. Rickety wooden bridges, silver green with age, created passing points at the widest sections of river. Tom marveled at how much the banks had eroded in places, presumably when the brook waters had swelled during heavy rainfall and burst them. Craggy rocks became a more regular feature of the landscape as they pushed on, some as big as demolition balls. The narrow track led them upwards again, as a high as a hill, and as they cleared its brow Tom saw the waters of a loch, as smooth and still as glass.

Overlooking it was a stone house, gray and impressive amidst the green. They drew nearer and Tom could see the vast slated roof, beneath which rows of leaded windows looked out across the flood land. There were enough windows for the place to have at least a dozen bedrooms, and the huge chimneystacks at either end of the structure spouted white plumes of smoke that drifted across the loch like mist. Dieter steered the rental car through the high gates, hewn from the same rock that had been used to construct the house.

Both gateposts were crowned with an elegantly sculpted bronze of a stag, complete with proud antlers. Dieter drove between them and brought the car close to impressive stone steps that led to the huge black-painted doors of the main entrance. Tom peered out of his passenger window at the broody sky reflected in those many dark windows, each one a weather eye, gazing out across the craggy landscape to the loch. This close, the house was a behemoth, looming over their little car and casting its shadow far and wide. If it wasn't so damned beautiful, Tom would have thought it haunted.

He and Dieter stepped out of the car, both stretching out their limbs and muscles after another long drive. The air was chill, with a biting crosswind that rose up off the surface of the loch and made light work of the businessmen's overcoats. It seemed to Tom that wherever he and his driver might go on their business trip, thick woolens might make be a more appropriate dress code than suits.

They climbed the steps and Tom knocked at the door using the huge brass knocker that had been cast in the shape of a lion's head, complete with mane rendered like a fiery sun. The sound of his knocks boomed like cannon fire on the other side of the door. Whatever room lay beyond the threshold must be vast to create an echo of that magnitude. The door soon opened with a click and a creak, and Tom and Dieter were face-to-face once again with Lithgoe's elderly female chaperone from the restaurant at The Firs the night before. She peered out at them through the gap in the door, looking them up and down before addressing Tom.

"You may come in," she said in that peculiar brogue of hers.

Tom and Dieter both took a step forward, eager to be out of the chill wind.

"But you must stay out here," she finished, looking directly at Dieter.

His face fell, and he struggled to find a retort.

Before he could find one, the old lady spoke again.

"Mr. Lithgoe was clear that he would only grant audience for Mr. McCrae here. You may wait in your automobile. I'll send out a cup of tea."

"And something to eat?"

Dieter sounded hopeful, like a Dickensian schoolboy asking for *more*.

The woman made no attempt to disguise the frown etching itself across her wrinkly forehead. She had evidently frowned a lot during her long lifetime.

"I'll see what I can do."

With that, she ushered Tom inside and slammed the door shut behind him, leaving Dieter to walk the long walk back to the car on his lonesome.

The entrance hall was as vast as the echo from the door knocker had suggested, and then some. Each wall was festooned with flags from all over the British Isles and beyond; dusty treasures from a bygone age and a forgotten empire. The Lithgoe family had traveled, that much was certain, and had no shame about announcing the fact with trinkets and baubles collected or conquered during their tenure as lairds of the land.

Tom walked the hall with his mouth wide open in wonder at the stuffed animal heads lining the walls, some of which included beasts it was no longer legal to hunt, let alone kill, then stuff and mount for decoration. He could barely take in the number of paintings the walls boasted, framed beautifully amidst ornate tapestries and yet more flags. Several times, he felt the urge to take a closer look, but the old woman marched so quickly through the hall he had to quicken his pace to keep up. Whatever was in the fresh air in this part of Scotland, it had put a spring in the old dear's stride. Tom hoped he would be left to see himself out, giving him time to marvel at more of the treasures on display in the entrance-cum-gallery.

He turned a corner, following his guide's quickstep through a side doorway and into a smaller room, paneled with oak. The room was deathly quiet, and lit only by the scant light from a single window and a table lamp with thick tortoiseshell lampshade. It was a dark room—masculine, claustrophobic and clearly intended to put a visitor in his place before being granted an audience with the laird of the manor.

"Wait here, Mr. McCrae. And make yourself comfortable, our Mr. Lithgoe winds his own clock."

Tom waited in the antechamber and waited for Lithgoe to arrive, as the old lady had instructed. He was still chuckling to himself about Dieter, marooned in the car outside while he trod the hallowed halls of Scottish gentry. He found it difficult to make himself comfortable though; both armchairs in the antechamber were as hard as the rough boulders outside, and low enough to accommodate a child. He chose to stand instead, pacing the last of the car travel-induced stiffness from his legs.

Several minutes passed with no sign of his host. Tom was tempted to leave the antechamber to go explore the hallway and its wonders when he heard the slow tread of footsteps approaching from down the hall. Tom froze, for reasons unknown to him, and positioned himself by the window with his back to the door, to make it look like he was taking an interest in the gathering gloom outside.

Seconds later, he heard Lithgoe enter with a creak of the floorboards, put on his corporate smile and turned to greet the old man. To his surprise, the old man passed him by without even looking at him. Lithgoe reached out and opened a hitherto unseen door that was set into the paneled wall of the antechamber. The door mechanism made a hollow clicking sound and Lithgoe stepped through the opening, leaving Tom grinning like a fool by the picture window.

Allowing the smile to fall from his face, Tom gave chase and stepped into a huge room filled wall to ceiling with framed maps. There was more window than wall in the room, giving it the aspect of a conservatory. The natural light levels explained why it was in now use as a map room, assuming it had not been designed for that purpose from the outset.

Lithgoe plodded over to a high-backed chair at the head of a long mahogany table and sat down to face Tom. He looked at him now, the old man, with an open gaze that suggested he had taken hundreds, maybe thousands of such meetings over the years.

"Do you like maps, Mr. McCrae?" he asked.

"Sure I do. This is quite something," Tom replied.

Lithgoe gestured for Tom to sit down at one of the chairs to the side of the table.

"Then you'll feel right at home here. Would you like some tea? Or coffee? I'm afraid it will be tea from a bag and coffee from granules. Us old folk do everything instantly you see, we're running out of time to brew leaves or grind beans."

"I'm...fine," Tom said, unsure how to reply.

"To business then. I see you are man on a mission. My assistant filled me in on the gist of the proposals your corporate masters FedExed to us."

"Hard copies, as you requested."

"Not me, Mr. McCrae. I do all my business via email, and keep tabs on my grandchildren over Skype. It's Lottie who won't abide such devilish technological advances, you see. She'll read stuff for me, but it has to be printed. And don't tell her I said this, but she gets quite excited when the courier comes. Makes her feel important; email cannae do that. We make our own entertainments out here in the hills."

Tom smiled politely, fighting the urge to laugh out loud.

Lithgoe was a quaint old sort, and the revelation that the surly old bird out front was named Lottie was adding to his mirth. He had imagined her name to be something more forceful; less cute.

"So, just to get you up to speed, Mr. Lithgoe, I'm here a week. During that time, I'd like to capitalize on the excellent groundwork my predecessor, Mr. Monroe, laid down with you guys. Access to the local power plant substation, assessment of the lay of the land *vis-a-vis* any private businesses that could cause delays or other interference with The Consortium's plans..."

"Of course, that won't be a problem."

"Great. I would also like to take a meeting with the Forestry representative who will be handling things on their end. I understand the paperwork is due to be signed off between the charitable trust gatekeepers and the government in Whitehall within the week?"

"Aye, you understand right. Forestry organization can't delay anymore than they have. They're as cash-strapped as the rest of us."

Tom let the comment slide.

The idea that the owner of the ancestral pile he was sitting in could be cash-strapped struck him as preposterous. He felt Lithgoe's eyes studying him, probing him. It was an uncomfortable feeling, like being a specimen under a microscope.

"How is Mr. Monroe?"

The question threw Tom, coming completely out of the blue.

"He's..."

Tom blinked away an afterimage of the man's skull, leaking blood on the polished surface of The Consortium Inc. H.Q. floor.

"He passed away. Unfortunately. An accident at work."

He winced at his words no sooner than they had escaped from his mouth.

An accident at work? Poor bastard had a desk job like everyone else.

"Unfortunate indeed," Lithgoe replied, without emotion.

The old man stood up and crossed to the window, clasping his hands behind his back as though tethering himself to the musty air in the room.

"And how do you like Douglass, Mr. McCrae?"

"Sure, I guess, I mean...it's very different to what I'm used to."

"Is it now? And what are you used to that's so very different?"

"Well, hardly any trees for a start. I haven't seen this many since my last business trip, up in Seattle."

"Are your masters going to cut them all down?"

Tom did not know quite how to respond. He remained silent.

"The trees. Is your company going to chop them down? Raze them to the ground?"

"No, sir."

Tom took a breath, hoping his hesitation would not sound like subterfuge.

"Some of the trees will have to be removed, that's all in the plans we mailed to you, but that's just so the plant machinery can get in, build the ops base for the biofuels division."

"And then?"

"Development of the village will happen concurrently. Modernization of the existing houses—owned by residents who don't want to stay, of course. Construction of new homes and facilities for the workers."

"And?"

"Well, the teams will start their research. It really is all in the documents..."

"No matter about the documents, Mr. McCrae. You and I both know they barely skim the surface of your employers' plans. It is what lies between the lines that I am interested in."

Lithgoe still had his back to McCrae. The effect was disconcerting, but Tom did his best to keep his voice measured, calm, businesslike.

"Okay, Mr. Lithgoe. What do you need to know?"

"The business model is built on research into solid biofuels, correct?"

"Yes. The Consortium has other operations researching advanced alternatives including recycled sources in South America, Scandinavia. But the European model is wood-based biofuels. Pellets, briquettes...we are keen to tap into that, see where it can take us, and the industry."

"So there would be some manufacture alongside the research, to make it pay?"

"Just to make it pay, yes."

"And wood pellets and suchlike come from forestry work, am I right?"

"Sawdust is damn near impossible to dispose of, the beauty of such a solution is that something green comes out of, well—something green."

"How green is it to cut down trees though, Mr. McCrae? Whatever you're turning them into, the man on the street will simply see a global corporation taking advantage of a loophole law dreamed up by greedy politicians in the south."

"You're opposed to The Consortium's plans, personally?"

Tom wondered if the meeting might be over already. There was more to discuss and he and Dieter had driven over an hour—it would be a shame not to make better progress than he had done. Above all else, Tom needed to know if the laird was going to be a problem. The Consortium's legal eagles had done their due diligence. Lithgoe knew that Tom knew he owned over fifty percent of Douglass and everything in it. He needed the old man on side or negotiations would take longer, and the bill would get higher.

Lithgoe fell silent, and sighed. His shoulders rose and fell and his back arched a little. He looked like a hot air balloon shrinking after a long, soaring flight.

"I'm not opposed to anything that makes me money," Lithgoe said after a pause. "The bell rings and the Maypole spins, Mr. McCrae; that's how the world turns. Seasons change with or without us, just as we change our environment with or without permission from a higher authority. Walk for long enough from a city and you'll find some trees, but when you pass through them, you'll find yourself in another city, soon enough."

Tom pondered the old man's words.

Lithgoe unclasped his hands and turned to face him.

"The good people of Douglass will not stand in your way if you want to 'develop' their little village into something your people can use. But they might take issue with you felling those trees. Many of those firs have been standing far longer than you and I."

"I'm confident we can offset that with our renewables pledges, incentive schemes for local people wanting a stake in the future," Tom offered.

"Everyone has a price, you mean?"

Tom nodded.

Finally, they were on the same page.

"Well, the people 'round here like to have beef on their table, bread in the larder and single malt on tap. You'll have to offer them something *real*."

"I'll take that under advisement, thank you."

Lithgoe snorted, then chuckled a little.

"You can visit the substation this afternoon. If you get moving, you'll have enough daylight left for a recce. Follow the road out of Douglass, but instead of taking the main track up to the bridge that leads out of the district, turn left onto the narrower track through the trees. Park up at the gates before the footpath, then it's on your boots from there."

"Thank you," Tom replied.

"Listen. The locals, such as they are, won't cause your masters any problems. I own a big enough stake in most of them to prevent any delays anyhow. The only folk to watch out for are the Greysons."

"The Greysons?"

"Aye. They own the farmland and pick-your-own produce

plantation up beyond the forest nearest the village. No one could get them to sell out. Not even season afore last, when things were really *bloody bollocksed.* No one. Not even me, Mr. McCrae, and I'm used to getting what I want."

Tom did not doubt it. He stared at the furrows in Lithgoe's brow, sensing some kind of disappointment was circulating the rapier mind housed inside that noble head.

"Then I'd better meet them. If they're going to cause problems, it could cost my employers thousands in legal fees and even more in wasted time."

"Everyone has a price. I'm sure you'll do a good job. Good day, Jack."

Lithgoe turned back to face the window. Trouble was brewing in the skies overhead.

"Lottie will see you out, there's a good fellow."

I'm sure you'll do a good job.

On his way back to the car, Tom wondered where he had heard those words before. As he climbed back into the passenger seat, he remembered Mathers had said the exact same thing to him before sending him on his assignment. And he and Dieter were halfway back to Douglass before he realized Lithgoe had called him Jack when they departed.

Must be going senile, loony old bird, Tom thought.

Feeling his forearms prickle with goose bumps, Tom turned the heat up a notch in the car. He looked out at the landscape. It was a drab blur, now that rain clouds had extinguished the sun.

Chapter Eighteen

The lengthy journey back to the forest bordering Douglass meant that it was mid-afternoon by the time Tom and Dieter hit the footpath leading to Electricity Substation D-5.

Old Lithgoe's directions were sound, and it was only a half hour before Tom and Dieter found the building. An electric company representative awaited them there, dressed in his fluorescent tabard. The garment was emblazoned with his company logo—a tree being struck by a jagged lightning bolt. Standing between a wall of trees and the substation's high railings, Tom felt suddenly uneasy. He realized he could feel the hum of electricity from the power station in the earth all around him. It permeated the ground on which he stood, vibrating through the soles of his shoes and into the soft tissue above his ankles. He reached out and leaned one hand against the trunk of a tall tree. Standing first on one foot then the other, he twisted his feet in their sockets to rid himself of the tingly feeling caused by the power hum.

Taking his hand away from the tree trunk, Tom stood erect and looked at the metallic fence separating the substation grounds from the rest of the forest. The railings were painted green and were as sharp as spears at their tips. A row of trees lined the other side of the fence like silent sentries. Looking up at them, Tom saw their evergreen branches had turned a sickly yellow color, as though all the life had been drained from them. The throbbing power of the substation seemed to be making the trees sick on the other side of the fence, where they were separated from their healthier cousins. Tom glanced at the dense wall of healthy trees lining the path behind him. They looked like mourners at their own funeral, forced to spend an eternity watching the slow deaths of their fellows on the other side of that high and mighty fence.

Breathing deep, Tom could almost taste the scent of pine. It seemed odd to him that the energy from the power station could be killing the trees—organisms which were like batteries, their chemical make-up designed to soak up and recycle man's poisons before turning it into breathable air.

Tom heard a metallic clanking from up ahead and saw their guide unlocking the thick chain that was padlocked around the security gates leading into the compound. Catching up to Dieter and the company man, Tom joined them at a second high gate. It was topped with coils of razor wire and adorned with a huge, vivid yellow triangular sign marked *Warning: Danger of Death.* A cartoon like illustration accompanied the macabre words, showing a stick figure being electrocuted by vast black lightning bolts. Tom felt discomfited by the image, and thought it strange how it mirrored the power company's logo.

He watched as their guide lifted a little plastic rain cover on the gatepost. There was an electronic keypad beneath the cover, with a little red LED light to show the gate was armed. Four beeping sounds emanated from the keypad as the company man entered a code and, with a click and a buzz, they were in. Tom followed Dieter and their guide into the substation grounds, feeling that omnipresent hum in his chest as he passed beneath the power coils feeding the cables overhead. Four low, redbrick buildings were huddled together, forming a courtyard into which the three men stepped. The guide, silent until now, gave them a potted history of the facility, and a quick breakdown of its output and service record. He left Tom and Dieter to talk shop, retreating to a patch of dying grass at the fence where he sparked up a Marlboro Red and tinkered with his smart phone.

The location was ideal as a base of operations for The Consortium's biofuels division. The only thing troubling both Tom and Dieter was access. It had taken a good half hour to walk to the facility via the track, which was so narrow in places they had to travel single file. Dieter assured Tom the forestry sign-off would prevent any problems with clearing the forest from the turn off in the road right up to the gate. Calling the power company man over, Tom asked a few questions about companies in the area which might undertake the tree-felling work and road building necessary to make the site viable. The man, who looked a little perturbed to have his cigarette break interrupted with such questions, answered them in the clipped fashion of someone who was used to working alone for long periods. When Tom's plan became clear to him, the man made clear his uncertainty that the electric company would allow such an extensive remodeling of the substation and grounds. He told them the necessary planning applications alone would take months to process, and asked if Tom might be better off considering a different site nearer the village. It was then that Tom revealed the nugget of information he had held back from Lithgoe during his meeting that morning. The Consortium had completed an aggressive takeover of the power company itself while Tom was en route to Scotland. As major stakeholders in the company, Tom's masters owned the very power station and grounds in which they were standing. Work would commence just as soon as the contracts were drawn up. Lithgoe knew as much of course, his comments about tree felling had given that much away. The old bird had probably gotten Lottie on the case just as soon as the visit to the substation had been mentioned in the The Consortium's mail-out brief. Lithgoe had made it clear to Tom that he had no problem with the plans, just so long as he got his cut.

"Everyone has his price, Mr. McCrae."

There was just one fly in the ointment left for Tom to consider; the plantation farmers that Lithgoe had warned him about. Calculating risks was Tom's *raison d'etre*, and the Greyson family name reeked of risk to him. Cutting a deal with the family epitomized the "excellent job" that Mathers had sent him to Douglass to perform. Without such a deal, he might as well fly back to California empty handed.

Thanking the company man for his time, Tom strode past the dying trees inside the compound and returned to the path that led back to the Douglass road. On their way back to the car, he instructed Dieter to set up a meeting with the Greysons for the following day. Dieter's mood seemed more buoyant, now that the day's work was done. Even the prospect of more culinary punishment in The Firs restaurant hadn't dampened his spirits. As they broke the tree line and walked down the steep section of track to their car, Dieter opened the driver door and held it open, like a chauffeur.

"What are you doing?" Tom asked, puzzled at the idiot grin bisecting Dieter's face.

"You drive."

"Very funny."

Tom headed for the passenger door, tugged at the handle. It was child locked.

"Seriously, guy of your age needs to drive."

"Why's that?"

"Long-term relationship. You'll have kids someday. Kids need a taxi service. And that is the sole domain of the daddy driver."

"Like I said, very funny."

Tom tried the passenger door again.

"Just down the hill, 'til we hit the main drag into the village, then I'll take over. My free gift to you. She drives like a dream, trust me, you'll enjoy it."

"Quit fooling, Dieter, I'm not even insured."

"Now, now, let's not get all risk-averse. The working day is done, dude. Unwind a little. C'mon, take her for a spin..."

Dieter rounded the vehicle and gently led Tom to the driver's side.

"All you gotta do is steer. Brake pedal is the one in the middle. Piece of cake."

Tom peered into the driver's side of the car—the undiscovered country.

"Try it for size. If you don't like, fine."

Dieter smiled, that same winning smile that made the hearts of blue-collar females flutter wherever he went.

"Just as far as the main road..."

"Right."

Tom climbed in.

Dieter's long legs meant the seat was set too far back for Tom to reach the pedals properly. He felt under the seat, expecting to find the lever for seat adjustment.

"It's on the other side when you're in the captain's chair," Dieter said.

He sounded like he was enjoying Tom's uncertainty a little too much.

Tom found the lever, overcompensated and shot forward until he was all but impaled upon the steering wheel.

"Easy, tiger," Dieter laughed. "You'll deploy the airbag, then we'll have to get you cut out of there."

Dieter's joke conjured a series of road-death scenarios too frightening for Tom to consider. He adjusted the seat more carefully a second time and then set to work on positioning the mirrors, as Dieter coached him along.

"Okay, you're all set, turn the key and start the engine...no not that way...that's it, and don't forget your seat belt."

The seat belt was the first thing Tom would normally reach for upon entering a car, especially with Dieter driving—he could be a little trigger-happy with the accelerator at times. Strange that Tom had forgotten it, and as he pulled it across his chest it felt weird pressing against his other shoulder. He'd been a passenger for so long. All his life.

Tom gripped the wheel until his knuckles were bone white as the car lurched into life and crept down the hill. He pressed his foot against the brake pedal to slow their progress, overdoing it as he had done with the lever under the seat. Trying to listen to Dieter's continuous instructions whilst getting used to the sensitivity of the brake pedal was proving difficult for Tom. The car kangarooed down the hill in fits and starts, sliding this way and that on loose earth as Tom tried to straighten up.

All too quickly, Tom could see the junction where the dirt track met the road proper. He glanced at Dieter, who now had beads of sweat on his forehead and a look of consternation plastered unconvincingly across his still-grinning face. Tom hit the brakes again as they veered into the road, but nothing happened. There was a dull snap from somewhere beneath their feet, and the car slid out onto the road, picking up speed. With the road's gradient providing yet more forward momentum, Tom panicked and steered hard left to try and slow the car down. His maneuver put them into a spin and Dieter cried out as the Focus hit a ditch at the roadside, then hurtled along it towards the trees. Tom shrieked, a feral sound, and put his hands over his face—

Like that's going to do anything!

—still pumping his foot into the unresponsive brake pedal as the car crashed through dense foliage and fallen bracken until *slam*, it hit a tree and came to a rest some forty yards from the track entrance to the road they had just exited.

Tom pried himself off of the steering wheel that had all but fused with his rib cage. No air bags had been deployed. Steam hissed from beneath the crumpled hood, fogging the cracked windscreen. Beside him, Dieter groaned. With a yawning grind of metal, Tom opened the driver's door and tumbled out onto the ground beneath the tree. Positioning himself on all fours, he crawled to the other side of the tree trunk and sat back.

One of his shoes was missing. The sock of his shoeless foot dangled like a clown's shoe from his toes. The tree supported him, but the world was still spinning. He heard a crash as Dieter's door opened then fell off its hinges, followed by an extended bout of cursing from the big man who was now visible through the cracked glass of the windscreen. Tom felt a burning in his lungs, a reminder to breathe. As he did so, he realized the car was a write-off, and they would have to walk back to the village.

He set about locating his errant shoe.

"And so ended Tom McCrae's first, and last driving lesson."

The entire pub, it seemed, erupted into raucous laughter. Tom lifted his pint to his lips, wishing he could fall, body and soul, into the glass rather than face the crowd.

Dieter had held the drinkers in rapt attention since he had started his tale, embellishing it with a few carefully plotted additional details along the way. These details were, of course, designed to maximize the comic effect of his story, at Tom's expense. Dieter went on to describe how he and Tom had struggled out the wreckage and staggered back down to the hill to the village before placing orders for stiff drinks at the bar. They had been there for almost two hours now, Dieter getting progressively drunk and regaling any new arrivals with a newly exaggerated version of his and Tom's car crash tale. Holly had stood patiently by, looking pleased to see so many villagers patronizing the bar. She looked even more pleased when Dieter ordered another round of chasers—doubles.

The place must be taking in more than they have done all season, thought Tom, as Holly pulled him a fresh pint of ale. *No wonder she's pleased.*

He recalled the night before, when her plaintive sobs had echoed through the thin walls of his room. The increased bar take would go some way to placating the surly landlord over her handling of the restaurant fiasco. Dieter seemed to have gotten over his disappointment at the facilities, anyhow. Tom peered at him from the bar, marveling at the way the man seemed able to blend in with any crowd. In any social hierarchy or situation, the big man was who you wanted as your wing guy. He was the affable jock, the epitome of the most popular and charismatic headshot in the high school yearbook. Tom had not yet quit disliking Dieter, and that wasn't about to change anytime soon, but he was finding it hard to actually hate him. If anything, Tom was developing a growing admiration for him and his happy-go-lucky style. It rather took the heat off Tom, even if the price he was paying was to become the butt of Dieter's current humorous tract about "off-road vehicles".

As his jovial wingman solicited yet more swathes of guttural laughter from the gathered locals, Tom turned back to Holly and took his pint. Their fingers brushed together for a fraction of a second and Tom felt a surge of electricity pass between them. She smiled at him, a lovely genuine smile of warmth and *there-there, dear, he's only having a laugh* before she turned her attention to the customers waiting at the other end of the bar. He watched her go, eyes lingering on her slender form and the way she moved her hips. Casting a furtive glance around the room, he knew he was safe from being caught eyeing up the landlord's daughter—all eyes were on Dieter, the court jester, after all.

Tom waited until the laughter had subsided before joining Dieter at his table. He padded over in his sneakers. His search for his missing shoe had been fruitless and he was thankful he'd thought to pack the sneakers. Taking an empty stool at the table, he heard that the conversation had moved on to what the American visitors' plans were for the duration of their stay in Douglass. It wasn't long before the Greyson name came up, and an uncomfortable quiet descended over the room. Before Tom could interject, Dieter, bold with alcohol, let slip their plans to go up to the farm and meet the Greysons the following day. Tom could have wrung the big man's neck—such information about an important meeting wasn't something he wanted broadcast around the village before it had actually taken place. As it was, he didn't have to worry. Within seconds, a burly man in his fifties, wearing a scruffy woolen sweater and battered weather cheater, stood up and announced himself.

"I'm Joe Greyson."

He looked daggers at Dieter and Tom.

Many of the locals averted their gaze from the man's eyes, peering into the bottoms of their glasses. They were evidently wary of him—afraid, even.

"There, so you've met me already," he continued. "So there's no need. No need."

Tom put his pint down, cleared his throat.

"We'd still like to discuss a couple of matters with you if that's agreeable, Mr. Greyson. As my friend here has outlined, our ride is out of commission, is your land within walking distance?"

Your land.

He had inadvertently let slip what the meeting was to be about.

The ale was strong, 6.8 proof, and had clearly loosened his tongue even though he was a couple of drinks behind Dieter. He hoped Greyson hadn't read between the lines.

"You'll need your car checking over, I suppose?" Greyson said.

"That would be great, do you know where we could..."

"I'll have my boys tow it up to the farm," the gruff man replied before Tom could even finish his sentence. "First thing. We'll give her the once-over, see what can be done. Although from what laughing boy here tells me, it's a write-off."

"Thank you. We'll be happy to cover any, um, costs of course."

Joe Greyson seemed satisfied with that. He finished his drink and wiped the foam from his graying whiskers. He pulled a wide-brimmed, waxed, brown canvas hat from his pocket and strode over to the exit.

"Tomorrow, then," he said, his voice heavy as a thunderstorm.

"Tomorrow."

Tom watched the farmer leave, and felt the oppressive atmosphere of tension leave the room with him. Within minutes, the bar was once again filled with the happy hum of inebriated conversation. It was like someone had opened the window to let a bad smell out, and the fresh air in. Refusing the offer of a refill from Holly, Tom bade farewell to Dieter and his new fan club, and retired to his room.

He felt tipsy, and suddenly sick with fatigue. For some reason, he remembered the dying trees at the electricity substation, their trunks oscillating nauseously at the throbbing edge of the dense forest where their cousins stood in dark droves. Perhaps he felt like them; on the wrong side of the fence, an outsider looking in on an alien world, shaken by the power of his masters to do their bidding.

He went upstairs, lurched into his room and kicked off his sneakers before lying down on his bed, very quiet and very still. Downstairs, the low murmurs of pub patron conversation continued with a soft, altogether human power all their own.

Chapter Nineteen

Tom was running, lost in the forest and all alone. He careered into a tangle of low-hanging fir branches, almost losing his footing as he scrambled through to the other side. The branches clung to his clothing and tore at his flesh as he wrenched himself free of their grasp. Gasping for breath, he stopped and turned, attempting to find his bearings in the cloying gloom of the forest. Looking down, he realized he was no longer standing on bare earth, but had strayed onto a gravel path. As he walked along the path he began to recognize his surroundings. When he reached the high green fence his suspicions were confirmed; his panic had led him back to the electricity substation. He walked alongside the high fence, feeling that low hum throbbing against the soles of his bare feet. *Warning: Danger of Death* proclaimed the yellow sign, mounted on the fence like a grim portent. The hum at his feet certainly felt dangerous. Its powerful resonance was at its greatest when he passed the high gate, behind which stood the leprous forms of the dying trees.

The surging throb of power in the earth rooted him to the ground, and he looked up at the trees. To his surprise he saw a gigantic fir standing proud right in front of the gate. He couldn't remember seeing it before; if he had, then him, Dieter and the company man would have had to walk around it to access the power plant.

Strange, he thought, pulling his pajamas tighter around his neck.

A cold wind was blowing through the forest, making the branches sigh and sway. Tom heard a distant rumble and looked up at the evening sky. Great rolling clouds were moving in overhead, spreading their dark shapes across the sky like oil in water. The throb of electricity at his feet was now vibrating up his legs. His legs began to tremble and his knees buckled from the effects of the power emanating from the ground. He fell to his knees, sharp gravel penetrating the tender flesh there. Every hair on his body was standing on end as the clouds thundered overhead. He was sandwiched between the electrical power from the ground and the static electricity above him.

A deafening peal of thunder exploded above and around him like a huge gunshot. He clamped his hands over his ears to blot out the terrifying sound, which echoed through the forest. Then, just a few feet away from him, a massive bolt of lightning lit up the night sky like a white-hot flame. The lightning shot down through the twisted branches of the tree that stood in front of the gate, its electricity seizing hold of the trunk. Tom felt the raw power of the lightning meet that of the ground. The tree's branches had begun to smolder and he wanted to back away from it but was rooted to the spot, still on his knees.

With a horrid wrenching of torn wood and flayed bark, the tree split down the middle. Flames erupted from its center, filling Tom's vision with black smoke. He gagged on the stuff as it billowed from the rotten core of the tree, which seemed to be oozing shadows that had been trapped inside for an age.

Scrambling to his feet now, Tom backed away in fear of the dreadful shape forming at the crux of those shadows. The black shape was that of a man, his eyes burning red like hot coals. The man's fingers clawed at the destroyed trunk of the tree as he stepped from his prison, pausing for a moment to take in the fragrant night air, heady with the scent of electricity, fire and dead, burning leaves.

Then, those awful red eyes locked on to Tom's gaze and the great, black shape closed in on him like a charnel shroud.

Tom woke with a scream dying in his throat, and the stench of burning in his nostrils. He looked around, fearful he might see that great shadow standing at the foot of his bed.

But instead of shadows and stench, he found morning had come—and with it the smell of fresh roast coffee and a song of angels.

"Morning, Mr. McCrae..."

The soft musical voice was unmistakably Holly's. He rubbed his eyes, bringing the world into focus, and was relieved to see the red-haired beauty standing at his bedside.

"Time to shake a tail feather," she said.

Tom sat up against his pillows and gathered his bedclothes around him; a reflex action.

"What time is it?"

"Eight thirty," she said, setting down a small tray bearing a cafetiere filled with steaming black coffee on his nightstand.

"Eight thirty?" He grabbed his smart phone from the bedside and tapped the screen, which confirmed the prognosis. "I must have forgotten to set the alarm. Strange, thought it was on repeat..."

"Enjoy yourself last night, Mr. McCrae?" Holly chuckled. "More than a few sore heads in Douglass this morning I'll bet."

She crossed to the window and opened the curtains, letting the morning light in. Diffused by clouds and the net curtains the light cast a halo around her feline form. Tom studied her curves. She turned sharply and caught him in the act.

"Tom. Please call me Tom."

He turned his attention to the coffee, feeling his cheeks flush a little as he fumbled with the plunger.

"I'd let that brew a couple minutes more. I'm afraid the old skinflint buys the cheap stuff. It's fine enough, but needs a few minutes more than regular coffee to get...convincing."

She beamed at him, a twinkle in her eye.

Tom breathed a sigh of relief as she crossed to the door.

"Is Dieter awake?" Tom asked, desperate to sound businesslike.

"Who do you think sent me up here with coffee? He's on his second breakfast already. Don't know where he puts it all. Anyway now, I'll be getting the car ready. See you in a bit, Mr. McCrae—when you're decent."

"Please—Tom."

"Okay. Tom."

With another smile the lovely creature left Tom alone in the tangle of his bed sheets. The sound of her speaking his name jangled in his ears like wind chimes. He took a few moments to compose himself then pressed the plunger down on the cafetiere. Pouring himself a cup, he lifted it to his nose and inhaled. It smelled good, like the earth in the forest beyond his window, and dispelled the last wisp of noxious fumes from his nightmare.

He drank deep.

Feeling *compos mentis* again after a breakfast of more coffee and several slices of buttered toast topped with a mountain of scrambled eggs, Tom followed Holly and Dieter to her car. It was a Mazda hatchback, with lime-green paintwork and rust above the wheel arches. The car looked tiny after their rental car, and Dieter had great difficulty clambering into the rear seat. He positioned himself sideways on the seat so his legs would fit as Holly pushed her seat back into place. He looked like a daddy long legs that had been trapped in a child's matchbox, ready for a bout of show-and-tell. Tom smirked, glad to be riding shotgun.

They passed the spot where Tom had totaled the rental car, and he saw a smattering of debris by the tree where they had come to an abrupt stop. Muddy tire marks had been left behind on the road, presumably by Joe Greyson's boys when they'd towed the vehicle away. Farther up the road Tom saw an old VW camper, parked in a lay-by on the edge of the forest. Its windows were curtained off on the inside.

"Odd place to stop for a vacation," he thought aloud. "Aren't there any campsites up here?"

Holly glanced into the rear-view mirror.

"On the other side of the forest, but some folk like to be in the thick of it. Get a lot of walkers up here, even off-season. Shame they didn't check into the pub last night instead of bedding down in that old thing. We could do with a few more guests at this time of year. Or any time of year for that matter."

Tom nodded, keeping quiet and letting her navigate the twisting country road. If his meeting with Joe Greyson went according to plan, Holly could expect a lot more visitors to Douglass very soon. A few minutes later, Holly swung a right onto a dirt track that led them through the trees and out onto open farmland. Gravel crunched beneath the tires as Holly slowed the Mazda to a crawl, parking up near a row of sheds with curved, corrugated metal roofs.

They got out, and Holly pulled the driver's seat forward so Dieter could escape his confinement on the backseats. He clambered out and leaned against the car, stretching his legs behind him, groaning all the while like a runner after an arduous marathon. Tom rubbed his upper arms to keep out the chill that was biting through his coat.

"Sure there's someone home? Place looks deserted."

"They'll be in the work sheds no doubt," Holly said, pulling on a knee-length cardigan that was knitted in the same bottle-green color of her eyes. "Come on, a walk will keep us warm."

She strode off in the direction of the metal-roofed sheds and Tom and Dieter followed close behind. The farm was eerily quiet, save for the distant cawing of crows nesting in the trees that overhung the sheds. Ancient farm machinery, caked with rust, stood at intervals along the path. Some pieces were merely fragments—a piece of hoe here, a section of timber saw there—leaning up against the walls of the sheds like forgotten relics.

Tom studied the corkscrew blade of something that looked like a medieval torture device, its tarnished metal surface turned rust red from age and neglect. If the items had been grouped together under a gallery roof, they would make one hell of an art installation. But lining the path to the work sheds they had a look of foreboding about them; like sharp-toothed warnings. As they neared the last of the sheds, Tom heard a faint metallic clanking coming from within the structure.

"There they are," Holly said, quickening her pace.

Tom and Dieter followed her to the shed, where they found a sweaty, thick-set lad in his early twenties hard at work beneath the crumpled hood of the rental car. He appeared to be attempting to reposition the dented radiator using a monkey wrench, without much success.

"Hello, Rory, Joe around?" Holly asked.

The young man started at the sound of her voice. Banging his head on the underside of the hood, he uttered a torrent of curse words before turning to see who had interrupted his labors. Rory had the unmistakable look of his father about him. The same shock of hair atop his angry red face though his hair, unlike his father's, was thick and black. Tom watched as the young man wiped the oily fingers of one hand across the chest of his overalls. His hands were as big as Tom's feet. He was still clutching the monkey wrench, with an attitude that made him seem threatening. Tom felt himself shuffle a step backwards, into Dieter's protective shadow.

"He's out," the lad finally said to Holly, before turning to Tom. "Your car is pretty fucked up."

"Can you get it going again?"

"Aye," said the lad. "She'll go, but stopping? Stopping is another matter entirely."

Tom and Dieter exchanged glances. Rory walked from the open hood to the side of the car. Crouching next to the wheel arch, he beckoned them over. The wheel itself had been removed and was leaning up against the side door like a discarded limb. Its absence afforded them a view of the axle and buckled metal surrounding it. Tom and Dieter bent down with hands on their knees, peering into the wheel arch. The lad unclipped a small Maglite flashlight, no bigger than a pencil, into the hole.

"There. See?"

Tom could not fathom what Rory was getting at. The young mechanic sighed, reached into the crumpled cavity and pulled out what looked like a child's novelty drinking straw. He straightened the clear rubber tubing and squeezed the end. Oily fluid dripped out, lit by the beam of his little flashlight.

"Is that...?"

"Brake fluid, aye."

"Explains why I couldn't stop," Tom turned to Dieter, whose face had turned ashen.

"You should sue the rental company," Holly said from behind them.

She, too, was peering into the wheel arch, mesmerized.

"Aye, we should," Dieter said.

He was picking up the lingo, blending in, the smooth bastard.

"They got a beef with you? The rental company?" Rory asked.

"Not that I...know of," Tom said.

"Then I would'nae bother," he replied. "See this cable here? It's been cut deliberately."

Tom's eyes widened.

The little droplets of brake fluid continued drip, drip, dripping from the severed cable.

"Someone didn't want you fellers to stop," Rory said.

"Fuck me," Dieter whispered.

The kid looked blankly at them both.

"Will I down tools, or what then?"

"Don't touch anything," Tom said to Rory. He turned to Dieter. "Cops might need to take a look."

"I hear you," Dieter said.

The boy shrugged and turned off his flashlight. Tom led Dieter to the open doorway of the work shed with Holly in tow.

"Holly, would you mind giving Dieter a ride back to The Firs?"

She shook her head, then realized Tom wanted to speak with Dieter in private.

"I'll wait for you in the car," she said on her way out.

Tom lowered his voice.

"I want you to call the cops, tell them about the brakes. Then call it in to Head Office. Might be an ill-advised prank on the part of the locals, to scare us ahead of the deal sign-off. But if it's not..."

Dieter glanced over at Joe's boy, lowered his voice to a barely audible whisper.

"If it's not?"

"It could be a game-changer. Logistics-based risk assessment, that's one thing, but if the variables include someone trying to have us killed...well, it's another thing entirely."

"Gotcha."

"After Holly drops you off, get her to come back and pick me up."

"You're going to try to find Greyson?"

"Shame if it's a wasted journey."

"Okay."

Dieter gave Joe's son one last cursory glance, then ducked out of the workshop.

Tom called after him.

"And before you guys hit the main road—get her to check the goddamn brakes."

Dieter paused, and nodded. He looked almost as perturbed as Tom felt.

Tom returned his attention to Joe's boy, who was now working on the giant engine of a partially dissected tractor in the back of the shed. He felt a little apprehensive about sneaking up on the kid, especially as he was once again wielding that hefty wrench of his.

Tom coughed as loud as he could to announce his presence. Rory startled again, swearing like a sailor under his breath.

"Might you tell me where I can find Mr. Greyson?" Tom asked.

"He's out."

"Out, yes. You did say that. Out where?"

"Checking on the Chrimbo trees probably."

"Chrimbo trees?"

"Aye, that's what we sell in the winter, mister. Pretty much all we sell when the fruit season is over. Rest of the time is pick-your-own."

"What the heck are Chrimbo trees?"

The boy looked at Tom like he was something he'd found caked onto the tractor's tires.

"Trees for Christmas of course."

"Of course. And your father is checking on them, you say?"

"Aye."

The boy then got back to his work while muttering something about apple trees, an avenue and a right turn.

"Apple trees, huh?"

The boy's accent was so thick, Tom wasn't sure if he'd followed what he had said. He turned to Holly for help, forgetting for a moment that she was gone with Dieter.

Rory just grunted back at him, his entire being now focused on hammering the wrench against a damaged section of the tractor's radiator grille. Tom was about to ask him to repeat his directions but his own voice was drowned out by the clanking.

He turned and strolled outside in search of apple trees.

Chapter Twenty

It didn't take long for Tom to find the apple trees. After a right turn out of the work shed, he'd followed the indentation of tractor tires along a dirt track past some polytunnels and storage sheds housing nursery plants and farm equipment. These gave way to avenues of apple trees, which stretched off into the distance for a few hundred meters.

A cold breeze snaked through the open avenues, causing red and brown leaves to flutter and fall from the branches of the trees either side of him. Now and then, the wind picked up and the leaves swirled up and around him; a benign whirlwind of autumnal colors. With the cool wind, a rich aroma of earth and rotting fruit rose up. Tom paused for a moment and looked down between the roots of the apple trees. Windfall apples lay discarded on the moist earth, decomposing. Fall offspring giving new life to their future spring siblings. With the tree branches swaying all around him, he closed his eyes and listened to the rustle of the drying leaves as they parachuted from their branches. He opened his eyes again and watched the leaves tumble and fall, borne gently to the ground by the wind where they joined the red-brown mulch of apple skins and earth. He breathed deeply, savoring the bittersweet smell, so unlike anything he'd experienced for years back home on the West Coast. Out here, on Greyson's farm, he could feel the turn of the seasons. In fact, he could smell them, almost taste the world changing.

A sound shattered his reverie; just the sharp snap of a twig breaking, but out there in the apple groves it was as loud as a warning klaxon. He whirled around to find the source of the sound, eyes darting this way and that between the rows of trees. Then he saw it, a figure standing no more than twenty meters away. Perhaps Rory had followed him up there.

"Hello?" he called out, but he already knew it wasn't Joe's boy standing there in the shadows cast by the taller, older trees.

"Mr. Greyson?"

But he knew in his heart that it wasn't Joe either, even before the words had dried up in his mouth. This was the same man he'd seen from his hotel window, standing at the edge of the trees, watching; Tom felt sure of it. He could not see the man's face as it was hidden in the shadowy folds of a hooded greatcoat the texture and charcoal black color of oilskin. In the partial shadow of the apple trees, the figure had taken on something of the aspect of the red-eyed demon that stalked him in his nightmares. Tom's eyes widened in fear as the man raised his right hand, revealing what he held there.

An axe.

Without a further thought, Tom took a deep breath and ran toward the end of the apple tree avenue. He could see the sharp green turrets of fir trees up ahead. Tom's heart pounded like a jackhammer in his chest as he reached the end of the avenue. Younger saplings were growing down this end, opening up the avenue into a junction. Tom skidded to a halt, almost slipping and falling on the uneven ground. He dared not turn around. Which way to go? Left, or right?

Straight on, Tom's senses screamed, *into the trees. Lose him in the forest.*

He ran on, straight ahead, his stomach doing somersaults as he went. His mouth was dry with fear and his throat began to burn from running in the cold air. Tom chanced a quick glance over his shoulder, but saw only a blur of green and gray. He pushed on, farther into the dense forest. Glancing again, he almost collided with a tree trunk. Instead becoming tangled in one of its lower branches, he was forced to stop and take stock.

Panting for breath, he peered into the distance, expecting his pursuer to come crashing through the foliage any moment. He put his right hand to his chest, willing his heart palpitations to stop. But just thinking about how panicked he was had the reverse effect. The act of becoming aware of how fast his heart rate was actually triggered it to beat faster. Tom grabbed the branch beside him for support, gripping it for dear life as he took great gulps of air. He began to wonder if he had imagined the man in the trees, to wonder if maybe his eyes were making a mockery of him. He blinked, and saw the shape of that axe head again; silhouetted razor sharp against his vision.

He's a phantom, he thought, though his blind panic was telling him otherwise. *He's a figment. He can't be real, can he?*

Then—*snap.*

Another twig, somewhere among the trees he'd careered through just a few moments ago. Cursing his pounding heart, Tom pushed himself off the branch and ran again.

This time, Tom did not pause to look back over his shoulder until he felt like he'd put some distance between him and his pursuer. Only when he neared a dip in the ground that opened up into a narrow path through the trees did he slow his pace enough for a backwards glance.

No one there.

He turned; now walking backwards slowly as he surveyed the shadows between the rows of tall firs. Still no one there. He had either outrun the axe-wielding stranger—or imagined him entirely. Tom felt unsure about which outcome was worse, but was glad of the opportunity to pause for breath. He was about to turn and stop walking backwards when he stumbled and fell down a sudden, steep slope.

Tom tumbled painfully down the slope, jarring his shoulders and neck as he came to a crashing halt at the bottom. He heard his clothing rip and felt the burning sting of sharp needles penetrating the flesh of his arms and back as he rolled to a stop. Rising to a kneeling position, he spat little needles from his mouth and raised his head to see where on earth he'd fallen to.

All around him were the sharp, spiky branches of Christmas trees. He had managed to fall directly into the plantation Rory had mentioned back at the work shed. Tom got to his feet gingerly, wincing at the sharp sting of yet more needles tearing at his flesh as he stood up. The plantation was vast, with festive trees of all shapes and sizes stretching as far as he could see to the very periphery of his vision. Some were fat-bodied Norwegian spruces, their limbs like the bristly blue legs of huge tarantulas. Others were the deeper green firs native to Douglass, many of which stood a full adult human in height above their Nordic cousins. All were pregnant with needles, each tiny pinpoint seemingly designed by nature to wound his tender flesh should he be fool enough to go any farther through their ranks.

He looked back the way he had come. The slope down which he had fallen was sheer, and he doubted the journey back up it would be as easy as his descent. Still, he had to try—the alternative would be to put his body through the mess of pine needles jutting out all around him. Treading carefully so he could squeeze between the branches of the trees lining the foot of the slope, he made his way painfully slowly to the edge of the tree line. Once there, he surveyed the slope. It offered little in the way of foot- or handholds. He located a single, jutting root and grabbed a hold of it with both hands, pulling himself up onto the slope. His feet slid on the muddy surface and the root pulled away from the ground, snapping off in his hands. He fell again, not as hard as before but again felt the unwelcome sting of pine needles as he came to a rest among the tree trunks. Tom lay there for a few moments, uncertain of how to overcome his predicament, when his pursuer decided the outcome for him.

He came out of nowhere, the axe-wielding shape, descending from above as though he had glided down the slope on a carpet of mist. He smelled the man's breath, rotten to the core, bearing down on his face like poison rain. He felt the cold kiss of the axe blade, biting into his throat as the man held him down with his free hand.

Tom thrashed wildly, kicking his feet and smashing his fists against his assailant's bulky form. He had no doubt now that the man was real. Kicking harder, he managed to slide from under the axe blade and get himself into a seated position. His eyes met those of his attacker. They burned red like hot coals from the dark of his cowl, just as they had from the fireplace of all his childhood nightmares. Tom kicked his legs up and under his body and bolted into the thick of the trees, careless of the death trap of needles all around him. The stiletto fronds slashed at his cheeks and a hot flush of blood blossomed there, warm trickles streaking his face. He ignored their sting, intent on outrunning the assailant at his heels, to be rid of his dark swinging axe for once and for all.

Driven by panic, Tom ran into a nest of pine branches thick as a nest of knitting needles. This time he did cry out; they tore through his sleeves and trouser legs, making mincemeat of his skin beneath. He thrashed and twisted, kicked and turned, but succeeded only in driving himself deeper into the lethal nest of needles. His mind raced, and he imagined the families that would come to this place in December, picking out their trees with babes in arms. The tree plantation was meant to be a haven for festive family activities. But now he was trapped inside it, it had become an arena of pain.

Desperate to escape he dropped to his knees and crawled like a child beneath the branches. Loose needles scraped his chin, hands and knees as he crawled—as low as a snake—to pass through the smaller, younger specimens. He kept crawling, blood from his wounds trickling into his eyes, turning his vision to a crimson wash. Remembering his recurring nightmare, he felt the dreaded touch of those hideous baubles, raining blood from the branches of that hellish Christmas tree.

And they were all around him now, those branches, brimming with pain, spiked with death. But Tom could now see there was light beyond them; an escape tunnel of light between the trunks of the saplings, some two hundred feet away. Tom gritted his teeth and crawled for it. When he finally emerged from the plantation, still crawling, sobbing with pain and fear, Tom crashed into something soft; something that enveloped him and held him fast.

A soft voice worried over him, told him to *be still*, asking what on earth had happened, where on earth he had been.

It was Holly. As Tom lay there, bleeding in her arms, he could not speak for lack of breath. His eyes were still fixed on the blanket of Christmas trees, through which he had made his escape, and the dark beyond them where the axman lurked. As the sensation returned to his fingertips, then his hands and wrists, Tom recalled the touch of that cold blade on his throat—and he shivered.

Chapter Twenty-One

Tom pushed away from the cloying warmth of Holly's arms and marched off into the trees.

"Where are you going? Car's this way, back at the farm," she called after him.

Her words fell on deaf ears. Tom was already several meters away, striding purposefully to God only knew where.

She followed.

"What's wrong, Tom? When you came out of the trees I thought you'd been attacked." A thought struck her. "*Were* you attacked? Did Joe's boys rough you up in there?"

At this, Tom stopped and turned to face her.

"It wasn't Greyson. It was... I was followed. A man, I've seen him before—he..."

Tom faltered. Fragments of his nightmares were spilling over into his waking life. After his ordeal among the Christmas trees he was beginning to feel he could no longer discern dream from waking reality. He was finding it difficult to think straight.

"A man? What did he look like?"

"Tall, with a long, dark coat..."

"Did you see his face at all?"

"He wore a hood...he..."

Tom was beginning to feel sheepish. Perhaps he had imagined the whole thing after all. Maybe the tall, dark, axman was a conjuration triggered by his recurring nightmare. It had alarmed him to find himself trapped in the needle pit of Christmas trees. The ordeal may have unlocked latent memories. Why then could he still feel the kiss of the axe blade on his neck? He absentmindedly pressed his fingers to his neck, finding swelling there. A weal had blossomed across his throat—but whether it was from his attacker's blade, or from the sharp branches, he could not tell for sure.

"And you say you've seen him before—where?"

Holly was talking to him like a counselor might talk to a suicidal caller over the phone.

Snap out of it, he thought, *what must she think of you?*

He pictured the figure standing at the tree line, only this time the man was looking straight up at his hotel window; seeking him out.

"Through my window, at The Firs."

She smiled; a beaming smile that flushed her face.

That's it, that's it; she thinks I'm nutty as a fruitcake.

"Cosmo," she said.

"What?"

"Not what—*who*. You just crossed paths with Cosmo. He's our resident local vagrant, spends most of his time out here in the woods. He's ventured into the village a couple of times, on Feast Days. Followed his nose, people say. Few starving men could resist the smell of a MacGregor spit roast; those with their bellies filled already have trouble enough. Oh but he's harmless enough, if you keep your distance."

"And if you don't?"

"You found that out first hand." Holly chuckled. "Ah, he's like a house spider that one. Folks are afraid of him up close, but really he's more scared than they are. And like a house spider, once he's made his presence known he soon slinks off back to the shadows."

Into the shadows, where he belongs, thought Tom.

"If he's so harmless, why did he attack me like that?"

"Maybe he saw you as a threat, I don't know."

"I'm not the threat here... I was only looking for Joe."

"Tell him that, did you?"

Tom fell quiet.

He hadn't really attempted to face the stranger and he knew it. He had bolted like a startled horse no sooner than he'd laid eyes on him. Tom could hardly blame the vagrant for being suspicious of him, given the circumstances.

"You said he spends most of his time in the woods?"

"That's right."

"What on earth does he do in here?"

"Come on, let's walk back. You need to get those cuts seen to. I'll clean you up." Holly smiled, her face beaming like the sun as she led Tom deeper into the trees.

Tom followed Holly as she led the way along a narrow path through the woods. In places, the path was no more than a shallow furrow in the ground and Tom had to keep his eyes fixed on where he was treading to avoid falling over.

The trees were crowded together in this part of the forest bordering the farmland and that, coupled with the already cloud-clogged sky, meant they had been traveling in near darkness for much of their walk. If it were not for the occasional caw of a crow in the distance, it could have been eight in the evening rather than the middle of the afternoon. Tom reached for his smart phone to check the time. It was gone from his pocket. He stopped and searched all his pockets, though he knew in his heart that he'd lost the damn thing, probably in his tumble down the slope into Christmas Land.

Up ahead, Holly became aware on instinct that Tom was no longer walking with her. She stopped and turned, looking at him with a bemused expression on her face.

"Okay?"

"Lost my damn phone is all. Shit."

"Want to go back and look for it?"

For a moment, he was tempted. He'd been putting off calling Julia again, but now his phone was gone he felt more than ever that he should do. And there was no way on God's green earth he would be heading back into the slice and dice of the Christmas trees anytime soon; not anytime ever.

"In those trees? Forget it. Doubt we'd find it in there, anyhow."

There was something strangely liberating about leaving the device behind in the depths of the plantation. Perhaps fate had dealt him a helping hand.

"Suit yourself." Holly seemed to catch the anxiety in his expression. "Feels like losing a limb though, doesn't it?"

She didn't miss a trick that one. Tom just nodded, and they walked on.

After a few twists and turns in the path, signs of human intervention began to appear. Branches and bracken, woven together to form makeshift fencing, cropped up here and there, keeping saplings a healthy growing distance from their towering forbears. The Greysons must have spent more than a few seasons performing the methodical, hard work of coppicing out there in the thick of the forest. By systematically cutting back and reorganizing the landscape, they had inadvertently created a hollow in the forest; a circular clearing through which he and Holly now passed. As they broke the trees, so too did the cloud cover, revealing the sun's rays for just a few seconds. And for those brief moments, Tom felt the warmth of the sky beaming down on him like a smile from above. The wind whispered through the trees, kicking up that delicious earthy scent of pine and damp soil. It was like a tonic, and he breathed his fill of it, the air spurring him on with a spring in his step that belayed his physical injuries.

They left the clearing and reentered the forest on the other side. Here, the path all but disappeared and even Holly, so sure of foot thus far, had to slow her pace to navigate the tangle of roots and tree trunks before them. Tom watched her footfalls, emulating her progress as well as his city-dweller's feet would allow. He slowly drew nearer to her, risking guilty glances at her feline form as they walked on. Then, they neared two colossal trees, their trunks five times thicker in diameter than any of those they had seen so far. Holly slowed to a crawling pace, rolling her shoulders back as she looked up reverently at the trees' branches above. She had a look of serene beauty, of peace, on her face. It was as though she were gazing up at the painted dome of some fabulous cathedral, not merely the canopy of some trees. As they passed between the trees, Tom saw there was something truly special about them. Holly stepped over the giant roots of one and as she did so, Tom noticed the largest root was joined to that of the neighboring tree.

"They're joined at the root," he said. "I've never seen that before."

"Aye, it's a rare thing."

Holly stopped, standing still on the other side of the root system and facing Tom.

"Local folk call them the Jack Tree and the Jill Tree." She reached out and touched—or rather *stroked*—one tree then the other, like they were sacred objects.

"*Jack and Jill went up the hill...*" Tom recited.

She giggled; a warm, infectious sound. Her red hair was a fire burning beneath the shadows of the tall trees.

"Aye, that's the kids' version. But us grownups also call them the Cunt Tree and the Cock Tree..."

Her eyes twinkled with mischief, her mouth making a meal of the words as she said them.

Tom felt shocked by her candor, and utterly aroused by the sound of her voice speaking the words. He cleared his throat, painfully aware of how his awkwardness was amplified out there in the woods.

Holly didn't seem to notice. She had both hands on the trunk of the female tree, caressing its lithe body, looking up into its branches as she spoke.

"It's *Sow-when* this weekend. Every year, local people have come here to worship and give thanks to these trees."

Sow-when. The word was alien to Tom, exotic, and yet at the same time strangely familiar.

Holly caught his bemused expression. "You might know it as Samhain. What you Americans call Halloween? Same thing. In the Celtic tongue it is *Sow-when*, the end of one year and the beginning of another; the cycle of the seasons, of life itself. A feast day, a night for celebration—and a time to give worship."

"To worship...trees?"

"That's right. Does it seem so strange to you, Tom?"

"Well yeah...it does, to be honest."

"Are you a religious man?"

"No, no I'm not."

"But you've been to church during your lifetime?"

"Sure, when I was a kid...they took me to..."

His voice trailed off. He didn't feel comfortable talking about the orphanage, never had; never would.

Thankfully, Holly continued on her train of thought.

"And what was the cross made of? And the altar?"

Tom didn't need to say anything, she had read his expression. He was beginning to get the impression she could read any man like a textbook.

"Why wood of course," Holly said smiling. "So you see, it really isn't that strange at all."

"Well, now you put it like that..." Tom cracked a smile too.

"Seems to me, people worship what they need in order to survive. Ages ago, folk out here would rely on the forests to give them their food, their shelter, their firewood to live through the harshest of winters. What do they worship where you come from, Tom?"

"Cell phones and money," Tom said. "The wrong things, I guess."

He felt that he meant it. At that moment he was glad to be rid of the dead weight of the smart phone in his pocket, burning a hole in his pants with the heat of its battery, desperate for him to take it out and thumb its screen into life—into usefulness. Without his devotion it was a purposeless thing. To hell with it now, he'd abandoned it in the forest. And the forest would still be there long after the thing had

149

rusted and rotted away to nothing.

He gazed at Holly, the delight on her face as she looked up at the Jill Tree, the freedom in her eyes and the youth in her curves. She was a fresh thing, a flower in her fullest bloom. She reached out her hands to him and he took a sharp breath and stepped across the threshold of joined roots. Holding on to her hands, their fingers interlocked. Her eyes met his as he drew near and they kissed, deeply and fully.

"I've loved these trees since I was a little girl," she whispered, nibbling his neck as he explored her body with his hands. "All little girls in Douglass are brought up here when they come of age. When I bled for the first time and became a woman, my mother led me up here and we buried my first drops in the burrow there."

She took Tom's hand in hers and pressed his fingers against the opening of a hollow in the tree trunk. He gripped the edge of the hollow and pushed her back against the tree, dry bark in the palm of one hand, her soft skin in the other. They gasped together and kissed some more, their clothes falling to the dirt of the forest floor. Naked now, their daily selves cast off all around them; they made love against the trunk of the tree. Slicked with sweat, Tom felt the razor-thin wounds from the plantation reopening on the surface of his skin. As he bled anew, Holly wrapped her legs around his waist and he rocked against her, into her. He threw his head back in joy and pain as his seed left him. The light between the leaves and branches gleamed down on him like white pinpricks of starlight.

Spent, he fell into Holly's wet, wild embrace and, for what felt like the first time in a year, he laughed. Holly laughed with him and, for a few precious minutes, she held him there with her against the tree. Then, slowly, she uncoupled from him and reached down between her legs. She raised her hand so they could both see their combined wetness there. She opened her fingers and their ejaculate glistened between them like the strands of a sticky ectoplasmic web. Then she reached her hand into the Jill Tree's hollow and smeared their twin fluids there.

"What are you doing?"

"An offering," she said; her voice slightly hoarse after their coupling.

Hearing it, Tom wanted her all over again.

"An offering? Like your...blood, when you were a teenager, you mean?"

"Aye, that's right. You learn fast for a city laddie."

Still naked, she danced between the trees, tracing a line from the Jill Tree's hollow, down and across the root system, then up the trunk of the Jack Tree to the first of its branches.

"They're joined, see, so one feeds the other—like you and I just did."

Tom could no longer hide the fire in his groin. Holly did not seem to mind.

She went on. "If a woman miscarried, she would make an offering to the Jill Tree too. It's long been believed that by doing so, the fruit of her despair would feed the Jack Tree and make her fertile again."

"You don't mean..."

Tom looked at the hollow in the Jill Tree, slicked with the mark of their lovemaking. What she had just described conjured images too dark to contemplate. The fire in his groin subsided, replaced by a queasy sensation, like acid indigestion bubbling away in the pit of his stomach.

"Come now, don't be so squeamish, Tom. Life, death, rebirth. We're all one and the same out here in nature, you know. We're like the roots of the trees, joined together, life and death cycles, with one feeding the other through all eternity..."

She grabbed his hand, pulled her back to him, and for a moment Tom thought she meant to make love to him again. Instead, she thrust his hand into the tree's dark hole.

"What do you feel in there, Tom?"

For Tom, her question was twofold. In his heart, he felt afraid; fearful of what he might find lurking inside the tree trunk. The axman, waiting to slice him open and pull him in. Instead, he felt something wet, something brittle, beneath his fingertips.

"Embrace her mysteries, Tom, grab a hold of something primal and take a look at it."

He closed his fingers around the wet, brittle thing and pulled it from the tree.

"Open your eyes. Be free."

Tom didn't even realize he had closed them. He opened his eyes and looked down at his hand. There in his palm was a little corn dolly, gone dry from age. Its little body was slicked with something dark red, and still wet.

"What is that stuff?"

"Strawberries."

Tom thought the word might be a euphemism. He lifted the corn dolly to his nose, both disgusted and intrigued, expecting to smell the copper taint of menstrual blood. Instead, he smelled the rich plasma of rotting fruit.

"I thought..."

"What, Tom? What did you think it was?"

A playful grin danced across Holly's face as she dipped her finger in the red and sucked at it hungrily.

"May my offering be made of flesh and blood, of hearth and home," she quoted, from some childhood ritual. "Or straw and berries," she added, laughing.

Her laughter turned to song as she hummed the familiar tune of a nursery song.

Tom felt on edge and queasy. He thrust the corn dolly back into the hole and pulled away from Holly. He looked down at his red-streaked hand and heard the ghost of a cry. Blinking away cold sweat, an image of Julia screaming, entangled in bloodstained sheets flashed before his eyes. He shuddered and sloped away from Holly, from the trees.

"Hey, where you off to?"

Tom didn't want to hear any more. The heat of the moment had passed, the stain of his passion drying on the pubic hair around his now-flaccid cock. He felt a shot of guilt, remembering Julia's stricken expression the day they had lost their baby. She had needed him and he had gone back to work. The moment had been too raw, too primal; and he hadn't been able to look her in the eye. He had done what he had always done; he'd retreated and lost himself in the surface logic of his working day. Holly's beliefs had led him down a dark path, and he did not want to go where it was leading him. She believed pain and loss were part of everyday life, that much was certain. Tom could not acknowledge those things as every day, he knew that now. To let them in would shatter his ordered little world, and it was that selfsame world he needed to get back to now, after his moment of madness.

Tom needed to be out of the woods, and away from Holly's words; her arcane superstitions and tree-hugging mumbo jumbo. He gathered up his clothes and pulled them on as he walked away, wishing for all the world that he hadn't dropped his damn smart phone.

As he stomped away, Tom recognized the lilting melody of Holly's song.

"Jack fell down and broke his crown...and Jill came tumbling after."

Chapter Twenty-Two

Cosmo watched the American man leave the spot beneath the sacred trees. He turned his attention back to the alabaster skin of the flame-haired girl who had lain with him, just fifty feet from his dugout. Cosmo was finding it difficult to lie still, watching the girl. Her breasts rose and fell as she stooped down to retrieve her underclothes, tugging them on over her smooth, white skin. He ached to touch her, to bolt from his hidey-hole like an animal and take her right there under the canopy of trees; to show her how a *real* man was. Not the simpering mess of a man she'd chosen to give her most secret gift to. A surge of guilt cooled his blood; his heart belonged to Elena, and the rest of him with it. The cooling effect continued, transforming his lust into anger and hatred.

Ever since he'd first laid eyes on the American up at the power substation, Cosmo knew they were enemies. Their paths were crossed forever; they could never be on the same trajectory. His military training told him a sworn enemy was an enemy for life; something to be feared and never trusted. And the only way to overcome an enemy was to understand it, to track it and study it and, ultimately, to know it.

Become your enemy so you might plot and predict his very next move—and the move after that. Wear your prey's skins and you may move freely among him, lull him into a false sense of security and then strike.

That was what his Base Commander had told him once, long ago, and the words still rang true for him—truer, even. Cosmo had watched from the sidelines as the American had fallen through the plantation of Christmas trees like a child; had bitten his knuckles almost to the bone to stop himself from roaring with loud laughter as the fool had almost eviscerated himself in the process. He'd watched as the scarlet witch had seduced him so easily it had been as though she were luring a bear cub into a honey trap. Cosmo had felt the blood rush of violence within him as he'd watched them coupling on the most sacred of spots in the forest—*his* forest.

Satisfied the pale girl was gone and not coming back, Cosmo risked breaking his cover and stealth-crawled his way through the bracken and nettles to the base of the Jack and Jill Trees. Kneeling at the roots of the twin deities, he held his head in supplication to them and vowed to do whatever was required to protect them and their brethren. It was time to give back, for something had been taken.

He pressed his fingers to the opening on the female tree and sniffed; scenting his prey. Cosmo knew his enemies, and it was only a matter of time before he could wear their guises, walk among them and make his move—in for the kill. The American was another stag, rutting on his territory.

It was a time to lock horns; and demonstrate his dominion.

Chapter Twenty-Three

Jupiter's stomach was gnawing with hunger by the time he and the others reached the outskirts of the village. Kegger had tried everything within his limited mechanical powers to get the camper going again, but nothing would work. After a couple of failed attempts at jump-starting the rusty old beast, Jupiter and Denny, pushing for all their might at the back with Charlotte and Amber cheering doing their bit at either side, they had put it to a group vote; the outcome of which was to ditch the vehicle and go in search of sustenance. They hadn't eaten a proper hot meal since the last town several miles, and hours, back along the road.

Jupiter remembered seeing a small post office-cum-convenience store on their way through the village, and a pub. They decided to pool their resources at the latter, and then stock up on a few supplies at the former if they had enough cash left. Jupiter was praying to the Fiscal Gods of Void Checks that the pub, and hopefully the store, would accept Charlotte's bank card for payment. The amount of real cash they had between them was pitiful and, as usual, the smallest contribution came from Denny and Amber. Jupiter had bitten his tongue when they'd laughingly placed their pitiful collection of pound coins and shrapnel on the floor of the camper. Charlotte had been in a great mood all morning, greeting him with deepest and most arousing of kisses, and he didn't want to waste the opportunity to build on that. He had aspirations to make it to home base with her by the end of the night. Recalling how she seemed to hate him being churlish with the others, he'd simply shrugged and added Denny and Amber's craptastic payload to the communal pot rather than unleashing a torrent of verbal abuse upon them as he was so inclined.

He watched Charlotte, bouncing along the track road a little way ahead of him, the cool, damp air making a hot fog of her breath. Imagining the smell of her on him, he smiled. She'd be more than worth the price of his admirable restraint. He just had to get her alone in the camper while the others were fooling around. Sending Kegger off for some firewood, with Denny and Amber in tow, ought to do it. He only needed a half hour at most; it had been a long time—too long— since he'd gotten his end away, and Charlotte was fine. So *very* fine. Maybe he only needed fifteen minutes after all.

They approached a turn in the road and Jupiter saw the sign outside the pub, swinging atop its post in the breeze—The Firs. Perhaps sensing his eyes on her, Charlotte turned and smiled at him. His smile grew into a fox-like grin.

They filed into the pub, noses twitching at the scent of fish and chips coming from the restaurant. Jupiter led the charge past the unmanned reception desk and into the cosy, carpeted enclave of the restaurant. An open fire blazed in the grate, warming them up no sooner than they'd stepped inside. A few locals and tourists sat at the far end, their backs to Jupiter and the others. Jupiter marched up to the little bar situated a little way back from the restaurant area. Like the reception, it was not staffed. A man in a sharp suit was perched on a barstool at the bar. His blonde fringe had fallen over his face and he was gazing into the depths of a whiskey tumbler, clearly on the main course of a liquid lunch. Jupiter cleared his dry throat and called out for service. He was ready to commit murder--of a pint of whatever ale they were selling the cheapest.

"Landlord will be back in a minute—he's just gone to change the barrels."

Jupiter looked around to see which of the patrons had spoken. It was not the man in the suit; he was still gazing inebriated into his glass. The voice had sounded familiar, with the rough edges of a heavy smoker's. As he glanced around the restaurant, Jupiter caught sight of a vehicle in the car park outside the window, almost as tall as some of the fir trees beyond. It was Mama Cath's bus. And even before the fellow crossed to the bar and slapped a faux-friendly hand on his shoulder, Jupiter knew with dread realization that the voice belonged to Bill.

"What took you so long?" Bill said, sneering. "Denny here told us you were on your way yesterday. Felt sure you'd have hit the pub by now."

Jupiter glared at Denny, who avoided his gaze by looking out of the window. His flushed face betrayed the fact that he'd rather Bill hadn't revealed his treachery. Jupiter would deal with Denny later; right now he had to find out what Bill was playing at.

Looking over at the corner table, Jupiter saw Mama Cath and a few of Bill's cronies eating and drinking. Some of the faces were all too painfully familiar—the same grinning bastards who had given him such a harsh beating in the service station car park.

"When did you get here?" Jupiter asked.

"This morning," Bill replied. "Landlord's cool about us parking up here so long as we put some cash behind his bar. Surprised you didn't think of stopping here—actually, scratch that, I'm not surprised at all. No tactician, are you, Brian, my lad?"

Jupiter winced at the sound of his real name and sighed. There was no talking to Bill; he was as single-minded as a rodent on a sinking ship, inseparable from his agenda—which usually involved bringing him down.

The landlord emerged behind the bar, and Jupiter ordered drinks. To his growing annoyance, Bill leaned in close by him, breathing down his neck.

"Funny you didn't mention this little protest plan of yours on the Freak Network," Bill breathed. "I'm beginning to think maybe you didn't want us to know. You can't imagine how hurt Mama Cath was to hear you were striking out on your own like this. Little silver-spoon scrapper like you? You need the support of your peers."

"I came up here because I care about the fucking forests, yeah?" The words escaped Jupiter's mouth before he could think twice about uttering them. "Word is some politicians are going to sell them off, and I'm dead against that. So are my friends—present company excepted..."

Jupiter looked daggers at Denny and Amber. They backed away, behind Bill.

"And we're willing to make a stand," Jupiter concluded.

Bill chuckled. "What are you going to do, Brian? Strangle them with your arm sling?"

The rodent's cronies laughed along with the barb, adding to Jupiter's ire.

Charlotte shook her head in warning to Jupiter, but it had been said now. Jupiter's vitriol was in full flow, and he was clearly intent on giving as good as he got.

"I don't know what the fuck it is you care about, if you care about anything," Jupiter went on. "But either buy me a bloody drink or piss right off. I've had enough of your rat face and your rat whispers. You're a fucking wind-up merchant. Get out of my face."

A thick silence fell over the dining room, the atmosphere crackling like the firewood that snapped and popped in the grate.

Bill reached into the folds of his leather jacket, achingly slow. The battered old sleeves of the garment creaked like the timbers of some ancient seafaring vessel. Bill never took his eyes off Jupiter as he did so. At length, he pulled out a crumpled note, which he passed to Denny in one fluid movement.

"Oh, I'll buy you a drink," he said to Jupiter, and then to Denny, "Get a round in, lad. You know what I'm having."

Denny did as he was told. Bill waited for the landlord to pull the foaming pints, grabbing them before the contents barely had time to settle. He turned to Jupiter and held one of the drinks out to him—a peace offering. Jupiter licked his dry lips, uncertain of Bill's smile, then reached out to take the glass. As he did so, Bill threw the drink into Jupiter's face, blinding him with beer. Before he could react, Bill smashed the other pint glass on the side of the bar, showering Charlotte, Kegger and the drunkard in the suit with its contents. Lightning fast, Bill grabbed Jupiter's damaged arm, twisting it painfully behind his back. He put the broken glass to Jupiter's neck, directly above his jugular. Kegger tried to intervene, but Bill jabbed the glass deeper into Jupiter's neck, a red lace of blood appearing there like a stark warning. Kegger backed off.

Jupiter gasped at the touch of the broken glass, eyes still stinging from the ale Bill had flung at him. Somewhere in the periphery of his hearing, Charlotte cried out in horror. A warm feeling snaked across his neck and he knew that Bill had cut him. He felt his legs go limp, feeling suddenly cold despite the fire crackling in its hearth. Then, he heard a voice, muffled somehow by the panic overpowering his senses.

"I said I know you—I've seen you before."

The voice was European, with a weird American twang. It reminded Jupiter of a sports presenter he'd watched presenting the Super Bowl on telly late one night when he was very, very stoned. Jupiter looked up and saw the tall, blond man who had been sat drinking at the bar when they'd first come in. He looked a little unsteady on his feet and his eyes were slightly red from the effects of three or four ill-advised chasers. For a moment, Jupiter thought the guy had been talking to Bill, but then he realized he was heading straight for him. Great, now he had two assholes to deal with, one psychotic and the other drunk—and *also* possibly psychotic.

"You were the one at the airport, the one who attacked my buddy in our car. No-one attacks my *buddyinourcarrr...*"

The drink was making it hard for the man to speak clearly, his words blending into one long sound as he tripped over the speaking of them. But Jupiter remembered the man's face now, as the events at the runway protest came crashing back. This was the driver of the rental car he'd tousled with; when the water cannons and the cavalry had come marching in.

"You were there too—*you're protesterrrrrs,*" the big man slurred, rocking on his heels.

He was addressing the entire restaurant now, pointing at the diners with an unsteady hand.

"You did it, didn't you? Fuckers. You cut the brakes on our car. No-one *cutssssthebrakesonmybuddy'ssscarrr...*"

His accusation trailed off into a roar. He sounded like a bear that had been baited to its limit, and then let off of its leash. As he took on the physical aspect of such a beast, the big man launched himself across the carpet at the nearest thing he could hit.

Bill.

Chapter Twenty-Four

The drive back to Douglass was proving an uncomfortable one. Tom could still smell Holly on his tattered skin, could still feel the memory of her hair and skin beneath his fingertips. They had driven along the bumpy track from Greyson's farm and turned onto the main road into Douglass before Holly spoke, breaking the ice.

"Did I offend you in some way, Tom? I hope I didn't. I get a bit carried away when I've... Well, you know...I'm sorry."

The smile that played on her lips was almost childlike, and irresistible. Tom had calmed down a bit after his march through the woods. Whatever guilt was gnawing at him was nothing to do with Holly; it was unfair of him to berate her because of it.

"No, I'm the one who should be saying sorry. I just... Some of the things you said back there affected me, I guess. Reminded me of stuff that's happened in the past, things I tried to bury."

"It's never good to bottle things up, Tom."

"Yeah, I know, but we all do it, don't we?" He looked her in the eyes and she could see he'd heard her sobbing in her bedroom at The Firs. For the first time since they'd met, he caught a glimmer of vulnerability in the backs of her eyes. Perhaps she was playing a part too; wishing stuff away just like he did.

She sidestepped his inference, the assertiveness returning to her expression. "If it helps to talk?"

"There's not so much to talk about," Tom sighed, looking at the banks of green firs whizzing by as they drove down the hill. "I'm married—or what passes for married where I come from—my wife and I, we had a bit of a drawback a few months ago. She had a miscarriage.

We've had difficulties coming back from it, truth be told."

"That must be hard to deal with," Holly said. "But in time I'm sure you'll get pregnant again—and again."

"You think so, huh?"

"I know so. Couples who miscarry are fertile at least. Maybe it just wasn't the right time for you both."

"I don't know if there will ever be a right time now."

Holly slowed the car's pace a little so she could swerve around some fallen branches at the roadside.

"Well, that's up to you both, surely? These things are sent to test us; they are all part of the cycle of life and death and rebirth. Those couples who live through them together come out stronger for the journey."

"You believe that?"

"I do. In a way I have to."

"Why?"

"Because then there's some hope in this world. For all of us. Even the damaged ones."

She looked at Tom, and again he felt she could read him. He wished he could read himself half as well. Ever since he'd boarded the plane, he'd felt a tangle of emotions regarding Julia. But since he'd met Holly he'd felt more at home than he ever had in his life before. He gazed into Holly's eyes, trying to find a way to articulate all that he was feeling.

She let him off the hook.

"I'm sorry your meeting didn't go as planned."

He looked down at his cut and bloodied hands, his ripped shirt and pants.

"A tad more exciting than the boardroom. My boss is gonna be pissed I didn't get to speak with Joe Greyson. If there's one thing they hate, it's delays like this one."

"If you'll take some advice, the best way to get Joe on your side is to...get to know him. Make friends."

"How do you mean?"

"There are two Joe Greysons. One you managed to avoid today—for one reason or another," she said, with a wicked look. "The other Joe only comes out after a few pints. I've watched him in the bar enough times to know that's when a laddie like you would do best to chat him up a bit."

"He's approachable when drunk?"

"He can be. It's a better bet than trying to negotiate with him when he's sober. Look, why not speak to him at the Samhain festival, buy him and his boys a drink. Show him you're one of *us*, not one of *them*. Blend in a bit..."

"And how do I do that, exactly?"

"Oh, I'm sure we'll think of something," Holly said with a twinkle in her eye as she drove the car into the village.

They both looked with surprise at the double-decker bus parked outside The Firs as they pulled up.

"Coach party? Your old man will be pleased."

"That he will," said Holly, looking anxious all of a sudden. "Jesus, I've been gone for a long time, leaving him to fend for himself with a bar full of customers. On second thought he won't be best pleased at all..."

She fumbled with her seat belt, hurrying to get out of the car. Tom unclipped his own seat belt and reached across to Holly, grabbing her shoulder gently before she could exit.

"Thank you," he said.

"For what?"

"Just, thank you."

Her face cracked a smile, then she was up and out of the car.

Feeling lighter somehow, Tom followed her to the side door leading into the reception.

"I'll go and freshen up," he said.

"You feel okay now?"

"Sure. It's going to be a little odd with your father, if I'm honest. I hope he won't be able to tell I've been getting fresh with his daughter."

Holly frowned. "My father? He's in Glasgow."

"I thought you said he was in the bar?"

"Hope not. Unless he's dug his way out of the cemetery and hitched all the way here on that bus..."

Tom was mystified. "But I thought Mr. MacGregor was your..."

"My Tommy?"

Holly chuckled. She reached out to open the door with her left hand.

Tom could not believe he hadn't noticed the tiny gold band on her wedding finger before. Maybe he had willed it away. Speechless, Tom followed after her like a lost pup.

Then he heard the sounds of raised voices—and breaking glass— from within the bar.

They ran inside.

Tom could scarce believe the scene unfolding before his eyes as he and Holly ran into the heart of the cacophony. The pub restaurant was in total disarray, tables and chairs had been upturned, a baying group of travelers were goading a small group that was embroiled in a bar brawl. It was like something straight out of a Western and in the thick of it stood Dieter.

He was holding one ruffian by the scruff of the neck, a dreadlocked young man who looked vaguely familiar to Tom. With his free hand, Dieter grabbed another combatant by his long, curly hair and slammed their heads together. The two men recoiled from the impact and fell back, clutching at their sore heads as Dieter let them go.

Another man was on the floor, cupping his nose with both hands as it gushed with blood. Behind them all, old Tommy MacGregor was frantically removing broken glasses and beer bottles from the surface of the bar, lest they become makeshift weapons.

Fearless, Holly marched into the fray. She positioned herself between Dieter and the others, shoving the big man back until he was square with the bar. Holly had Dieter by the lapels as she ordered him, in no uncertain terms, to calm down.

Tom watched as a couple of the roughnecks seized the moment and rounded on Dieter, intent on inflicting some punishment now that Holly had cleared the floor.

"Dieter? What the hell?"

Tom rushed over and waded in, brushing the dreadlocked guy aside. The young man turned and their eyes met. Tom recognized him as the protester who'd gotten his arm trapped in the window of the rental car back at the airport. The kid clearly recognized Tom, too.

"You," the kid said. "Should've known; corporate suit-job like you. On vacation, are we? Come to chop a few trees down?"

Tom blanked the kid and turned his attention back to Dieter, but he soon realized he need not worry. Holly stood between Dieter and the two men, daring them to make a move. The look of defiance on her face was enough to disarm the men. They cancelled their assault, throwing Dieter, then Tom, a vindictive look. Bolstered by Holly's support, the landlord stepped out to face the men.

"I want all of you out, right now. Police are on their way. If you're good little boys and girls, you'll have a head start. If not, you'll have the Inspector to answer to, and he's not the kind to discriminate. It'll be the highlight of his week to lock the whole bloody lot of you up in his cells."

"Bill, pay the man, we're leaving."

A wild-eyed woman, dressed in flowing skirts and until now a silent observer at the rear of the chaos, had entered the arena. She looked just as displeased with her foot soldiers as old MacGregor did. Tom noticed a skinny girl standing next to her as she tapped at the screen of her mobile phone then secreted it in her clothing. God help them if she'd been filming the whole sorry scene.

The bleeding man struggled to his feet and dug a few crumpled twenty pound notes out of his pocket.

"That should cover the food and drinks. This arsehole can pay for the damage," he snarled, eyes blazing at Dieter. With that, Bill tossed the cash at MacGregor before he and his cronies filed out of the restaurant.

Tom strode up to Dieter.

"What in the name of all that's holy do you think you're doing, Dieter?"

The big man swayed on his feet, still drunk.

"Just sampling some of the local delicacies, my man. One thing led to another."

"Holly, get him some coffee, will you? Strong—very strong."

The girl nodded and ducked behind the bar, MacGregor watching her like a hawk. The old man glanced at Tom with those rheumy eyes of his. Tom tried not to give anything away. The last thing he needed was to become part of a marital soap opera. He had one of his own to deal with, after all, on top of Dieter behaving like a maniac.

"How much did he drink?" Tom asked the landlord.

MacGregor just shrugged and waved his hand along the row of inverted liquor bottles behind him, indicating at least six different brands of Scotch had been sampled during Dieter's alcoholic odyssey.

Tom grabbed Dieter's arms, steadying him and led him over to an upturned barstool. God and Jesus, he weighed a half ton. Propping his coworker up against the bar, Tom knelt to pick up the stool then sat Dieter down, wincing at the distillery odor on the big man's breath. Dieter's upper body curled into the surface of the bar like a Slinky on a stairwell. Tom was mystified that Dieter had seen fit to get so wrecked in the middle of the afternoon.

"What in hot hell were you thinking, man? I told you to come back here and file a report with the cops, not to go on a drunken rampage."

Dieter looked at Tom, bleary eyed, as though he'd just met him at a party—then noticed his torn clothes and scratched face and arms.

"Hey, Tommy. What happened to you? Look like you went fifteen rounds with Mike Tyson."

"You should take a look in the damn mirror." Tom sighed.

He realized he wouldn't get any sense out of Dieter until he'd sobered up. Holly returned with a steaming pot of black coffee and, Tom was thankful, two mugs. She poured them both a drink before starting to tidy up the restaurant. A couple of chairs had been broken in the fray, and Tom watched as she stacked them in the corner. He then became aware that Dieter was watching him, watching Holly.

"Sly dog, McCrae," Dieter cackled. "So that's what took you so long, eh? Always knew you had some Scottish in you, with your name and all. She got some in her too, huh?"

Tom looked up and saw old man MacGregor, Holly's husband, back in his regular spot behind the bar not four feet away from them both. Caught off guard, the raw look on Tom's face must have told the old man everything he needed to know.

Great. First Dieter goes Frankenstein's monster on everybody's ass, now I'm a cuckold too. Old bastard will probably smother me with my pillow while I sleep tonight...if I can sleep tonight...

"Come on, Dieter, let's get some fresh air, yeah?"

Tom looked apologetically at the landlord, who glared back at him with open contempt. Pulling Dieter's arm around his neck, Tom heaved the hulking fool out of the restaurant. He avoided all eye contact with Holly as he passed her on the way out. He got as far as the Reception when Dieter heaved and vomited all over the carpet. Holly emerged from the restaurant, carrying broken furniture, and looked at the steaming mess Dieter had left on the rug with dismay. Legs buckling under Dieter's dead weight, Tom struggled outside, cursing under his breath and wondering if his day could possibly get any worse.

Dropping Dieter onto the edge of a large planter containing a weather-beaten spruce, Tom paced the parking lot in an attempt to contain his growing anger. It did not work.

"Listen up, Dieter. You cost us today, big time. Picking a fight with a bunch of protesters? Idiot."

"They started it," Dieter slurred. "Right after I accused them of cutting our brakes."

"After you what? As far as I know they only arrived here today, which would rule them out. We'd sure as hell remember seeing their bus, wouldn't you agree?"

"I'm sorry, Tommy, really I am. I had to say something about the brakes; I mean it must have been them. They followed us up here, you saw the guy with the braids..."

Dieter's voice was loaded with the kind of paranoia that came with putting away a half bottle of single malt. Tom had reached boiling point. Time to tell it like it was.

"First, my name is not 'Tommy'. Second, go sleep it off. Third, pack your things. I want you out of Douglass first thing tomorrow. I'll do what I can to pick up the pieces here, but if you have fucked our deal, I will make sure Mathers knows every last gory detail about what you achieved here today, you hear me, you drunken asshole?"

Without waiting for Dieter's answer, Tom marched back inside the pub. He could do with a stiff drink himself.

Chapter Twenty-Five

Jupiter stumbled on through the trees, his anger and bile overriding the fatigue in his calf muscles, which were crying out for stasis. Denny rushed on ahead of him, apparently intent on ignoring him for the entire walk back to the broken-down camper. Amber scurried along at her boyfriend's side, the two of them as thick as thieves.

How apt, thought Jupiter, *that's what they are, after all—bloody thieves.*

Jupiter could not let go of the fact that Denny had sold them out to Bill and his head frothed with indignation.

"After everything I've done for you, Denny, all the free rides, all the free meals; a crash pad for you and your girl. Hey, arsehole! Answer me, man! What did I do to you?"

Charlotte, struggling along with Kegger as they both tried to keep up with Jupiter, shouted at him to stop as he bolted through the trees and rugby tackled Denny to the ground. Winded, Denny coughed and spluttered on a mouthful of dead leaves. Amber tried to pull Jupiter away from her boyfriend, but Jupiter shoved her off of him. She careered back into Charlotte and they both took a tumble onto the forest floor.

"Answer me, bitch," Jupiter growled.

He had Denny pinioned, his knees digging into the wriggling man's arms, preventing him from defending himself.

Amber got to her feet again, intent on retaliating, but Kegger held her back.

"This is between them," he said, holding her by the collar of her jacket.

"You sold me out, bastard," Jupiter demanded. "You've been nothing but a user these past few weeks. Well, this is the last time, Denny."

"No!" Charlotte cried, as Jupiter rained blows down on Denny's face.

Careless of his wounded arm, Jupiter kept slapping and punching, turning Denny's skin the color of chopped liver. Unable to protect himself, Denny kicked and struggled, but he was rooted to the spot by Jupiter's knees.

And then Denny stopped struggling, and began laughing. It was a crazed sound, like someone had opened the stopper on a two-liter bottle of madness.

"What the fuck are you laughing at, Denny? I'm not laughing."

This only made Denny laugh even harder. Tears were rolling down his cheeks, his face red with mirth, and from the sting of Jupiter's blows.

"You sap, Brian," Denny chuckled through his tears. "I've been using you for longer than that."

Jupiter was mystified by Denny's statement. How could the guy have this much front? He'd kill him, so help him, he'd kill him right there on the spot.

"My name isn't Denny as much as yours is Jupiter."

Denny glanced over at Amber.

"Sorry, babe."

"What the actual fuck?" Amber stopped straining against the leash of Kegger's hand.

"We were real, if it's any consolation," Denny went on.

Amber renewed her attempts to reach Jupiter and Denny, but now appeared intent on wounding the latter. Kegger almost toppled over, holding her back this time; such was the ferocity of her anger.

"You're a copper?" Jupiter asked.

He glanced over his shoulder at the others, incredulous.

"He's a fucking undercover policeman!"

Denny's eyes narrowed.

"Much worse than that I'm afraid. Undercover? Yes. Police? No."

"He's a frigging journalist," Charlotte sighed.

"Bingo," Denny said. "Smart girl."

Jupiter snarled. "So you've been spying on me the whole time?"

Denny had been hiding his secret for months. It was a clear relief to be getting it off his chest.

"It's not about you, you dick. It's about Bill," he laughed. "My brief was to profile him and find out how he works. Whenever there's violence at a protest, he's there. Ask yourself why it kicked off at the airport. It was a peaceful protest until the big red bus turned up..."

Jupiter's mind raced. Denny, or whatever he was really called, was right. Whenever violence kicked off at a protest, Bill was there at the epicenter. He'd given Jupiter a beating when he was listening in at the motorway services car park. And Denny was driving Jupiter's train of thought.

"Why did he give you a good kicking that night? Ever asked yourself that? Maybe because he didn't want you hearing what he was really up to? What him and Mama Cath have been up to for months now?"

Denny grinned at Jupiter's ignorance. The journalist was enjoying this.

"My investigation took on a new aspect when I dug a bit deeper into the Freak Network Bill has so carefully constructed. I followed my lines of inquiry all the way back to the constabulary. And guess what I discovered?"

Jupiter tried to process what he was being told.

"Bill and his cronies are taking backhanders from corrupt policemen, who in turn take backhanders from corrupt politicians."

"What are you telling me, man? That Bill works for the pigs?"

"If you must put it that way, yes. The government wants to build a runway, the government wants to bulldoze the forests. Peaceful protests garner public support. They can't have that. But if the protests turn violent? Public and political favor can so easily swing the other way. Bills have been passed in the Houses of Parliament on the back of righteous indignation about riots, looting and carnage. And at the center of it all, corrupt cops..."

"And Bill," Jupiter said.

The penny had finally dropped. He felt as hollow as a jack-o'-lantern, and sick to his stomach, like his insides had been scooped out.

"Exactly," Denny said. "Now do you mind letting me up, I think the circulation is stopping in my arms."

Jupiter stood up, his mind a daze. He looked at Amber, crying now in Kegger's arms, then at Charlotte, who looked horrified.

"So why are you telling me this now?" Jupiter asked.

"Simple," Denny replied. "We can help each other. We have a common goal, you and I. Out of all the protestors I've met on this shitty detail, you are the only one who really believes in what he's doing. We can put that to good use, do an expose on Bill and promote your cause as viable peaceful protest. You'll be the hero of your movement. I get my front page by-line and an appearance on *Newsnight*. Trust me. What do you say, Brian, do we have a deal?"

"Trust you?"

Now it was Jupiter's turn to laugh, albeit bitterly.

"After deceiving us all like you did?"

Jupiter walked over to the others and stood with them, putting on a united front.

"You're a gutter hack, working for The Man. Do you really think the likes of us would work with the likes of you? Newspapers are just as corrupt as Bill, the police or any of them. The name's not Brian, it's Jupiter Crash, and no we do not have a deal. Fuck off, you're on your own, mate."

Denny glanced at the others. Seeing the same fury and disappointment in their eyes, he shrugged and sloped off into the trees.

"You're letting him go? That's it?" Amber protested through a mask of snot and tears. She stormed off in the direction of the camper, followed by Kegger.

"Guys? Where are you going? Guys?"

To Jupiter's dismay, Charlotte was leaving too. He grabbed her arm as she passed by.

"What?" she demanded. "You don't expect me to stand with you after what you just did, do you?"

Jupiter was perplexed. "What did I do?"

"Beating on Denny, how can you claim to be any different than Bill and his lot?"

"He's an undercover fucking journo! What would you suggest I do? Tell him my life story?!"

"I doubt your life story is that interesting."

She pulled away from his grabbing hand and jolt of pain shot up his arm.

"It's over for us before it's started, I'm afraid. You're just a thug like the rest of them, despite what you'd have everybody else believe."

He tried to reach out to her, to stop her from leaving him like the others. She held her hands up as a barrier and backed away.

"Leave me alone," she said, and ran away.

Jupiter ran after her, calling her name, but she had a head start on him and reached the road before he did. Seeing the familiar shape of Mama Cath's bus parked up at the roadside, he stopped short within the cover of the trees.

Peering out from behind the trunk of a fir tree, he watched as Bill and his crew helped get the camper started again via two jump leads connecting the engines of both vehicles. A few minutes later, Bill and Kegger exchanged quiet words. Kegger pointed in the direction of the trees where they had abandoned Jupiter. Bill would be looking for him, for sure. Amber and Charlotte joined Kegger on board the camper and drove away under the watchful eyes of Bill and his mates. Jupiter was desperate to make a run for it and try to hop aboard the camper before

Bill and the others knew what was happening. But to do so would be folly and Jupiter knew it.

His following had abandoned him to his fate, the turncoats.

Jupiter stood, alone, beneath the canopy of trees. He clenched his eyes shut in fury and dismay. Everything was falling to pieces, all because of Denny, that bastard, and Bill, and Mama Cath and the whole sorry lot of them. Gritting his teeth, he sloped off back through the undergrowth in the direction Denny had slithered. He didn't know what he would do when he found him, but he suspected it would confirm the accusations Charlotte had made against him. If she thought him a thug, then fine, he could live with that. Maybe Denny wouldn't, by the time he was done with him. Hell, he could even offer him up to Bill; tell him all about what the hack had been up to. A peace stone for Bill and Mama Cath, they'd have to show him some respect then.

Spurred on by this new plan, Jupiter careered between the tall, thick trunks of ancient firs, crushing twigs and branches beneath his feet as he ran. Violent fantasies of what he might do to Denny when he found him drove him on, into a gully and up a steep bank that did little to slow his pace.

Ascending the slope, he leaped over its lip and smashed into a tree. Catching his breath, he looked around, hoping for a glimpse of his quarry. Instead of Denny, he saw a dark shape between the trees, which were so crowded together they forced him to slow to a jogging pace, then to a stroll.

The shape was a structure, embedded deep in the woods on flatter ground in a tree-lined clearing just a short walk away. Maybe Denny had taken refuge there; perhaps it was a safe house provided for sly pigs just like him. Sneaking up on the building, Jupiter had a better look at it. It was in a poor state of repair, but the roof was more or less on, the front door was intact and it still had some glass in its window frames. Peering into the windows as he passed them, Jupiter saw only empty rooms, filled with leaf litter and bracken from the surrounding forest. If Denny was here, maybe he was round back where the ramshackle house met the trees; it would seem logical to hide out in the place with the most cover.

Jupiter strafed around the corner, heading for the back door, and trod on what felt like a bendy section of branch. He heard a loud snapping sound, then felt a warm, numb sensation at his ankle.

Looking down, he saw his leg in the jaws of a metal trap that was big enough to ensnare a bear. The trap's rusty metal teeth had penetrated his flesh, chomping right down to the marrow of his ankle bone. Blood gushed from the gaping wound and a rising scream filled his throat.

Someone appeared at his shoulder and knocked him unconscious before he could utter a sound. Falling, Jupiter was scooped up onto the shoulder of his assailant before he hit the ground.

The bear trap dangled from his ruined leg, heavy as a ball and chain, as the man carried Jupiter inside.

Chapter Twenty-Six

Tom cursed, hearing the computerized voicemail prompt once again, and slammed the receiver of his ancient hotel telephone onto its cradle so hard, the thing nearly flew off the nightstand. After showering away the blood, muck and sex of his adventures in the forest, he'd climbed into a clean set of clothes and phoned home.

Dialing his landline number using the old-fashioned dial on The Firs' prewar telephone had proven a chore, and for each of his three attempts the call had gone straight to voicemail. It was usually set for call monitoring, so it would at least ring a few times so Tom could check the caller ID before deciding to pick up or not.

I bet Ellie reset it, that interfering bitch, thought Tom, *she doesn't want me speaking to my own goddamn wife.*

Sighing, he picked up the receiver and dialed again. If Julia's sister didn't want him calling, he would at least make known his attempt to do so by leaving a message. He felt nervous and a little awkward as he listened to the automated message prompting him to "Please leave a message after the tone". What would he say, how should he say it? No time to think as the machine beeped in his ear.

"Oh, um, hi, baby, I just wanted to um, check in with you and ask how you are. I'm still in, um, Scotland...obviously. I, uh, lost my cell, so if you want to talk... I'll just get the number..."

He pulled open the draw beneath the nightstand, looking for the faded one-sheet brochure he remembered seeing in there when he first checked in. The drawer was empty.

"Wait a minute."

Tom placed the receiver on the nightstand and crossed to the desk in the corner of the room. His laptop was in sleep mode; little light flashing beneath the catch on the lid. He popped the catch and muttered words of encouragement as the device lumbered back into life. Clicking on his Douglass desktop file, he then opened the folder marked *Travel and Accommodations* and found the number.

"You still there?" he asked, absentmindedly forgetting he was talking to a machine. "Oh, of course not. Anyways, the number here is plus four-four as it's in the U.K. obviously..."

He was halfway through reciting the remainder of the numbers when the answer machine beeped shrilly in his ear; his time was up. Swearing under his breath, he clicked the phone off with his index finger, and was about to try calling a fifth time when there came a knock at the door.

"Who is it?" Tom hoped his tone would make it clear to whoever was knocking that he really wasn't in the mood for visitors—especially if they were called Dieter.

But the voice that answered him belonged to Holly.

"Mr. McCrae," she said, back to formalities, "the police are here. They'd like a word. Will I tell them you'll come down?"

"Sure," he answered. Then, after he heard her walking away; "Shit."

Tom tried to conceal his surprise upon seeing the same rotund police officer that had interviewed him at the airport, awaiting him in the lounge bar. Officer Travis was accompanied by a pencil-thin colleague, who was in the process of commandeering refreshments from old Mr. MacGregor at the bar. Holly was close by, wiping tables. The portly officer invited Tom to take a seat opposite him and waited for his junior to bring over a pint glass filled to the brim with cola and ice. Tom was used to seeing giant sodas in the malls and drive-thrus back home, but never before in a pint glass, in a pub. He tried not to stare as the fat man lifted the glass to his lips, soda bubbles dancing and popping beneath his stubby red nose.

"Second time this week, Mr...." The cop checked his notebook. "McCrae. Seems wherever there's trouble, you're not far away."

The skinny cop smirked, and Tom took an instant dislike to him. Tom hoped the interview would be over quickly; he longed for the quiet anonymity of his room.

"It's been an eventful couple days," Tom replied. "*Of,*" the cop corrected. "Couple *of* days, we say around here. But you're not from round here are you, sir, as I believe we ascertained in our last little chat at the airport?

"What exactly can I help you with, officer? I'm a little busy—I have a conference call scheduled."

"Conference call, eh? With whom?"

"With my employer back home."

"Oh, then we mustn't keep you, must we, Iver? Sounds important."

The skinny man, Iver, smirked again, his face taking on the aspect of a toothless old man's while working on a boiled sweet.

"Looks like you've been in the wars a bit," Travis indicated the network of scratches on Tom's skin. "Get those injuries in the fray, did we?"

"Actually, no. I was on a recce up at the Greyson's farm when I," Tom fidgeted with embarrassment, "well, I had a fall, got into a bit of a scrape with some Christmas trees."

"I see," Travis mused, looking suspicious and gesturing to Iver to take some notes in his little pad. "And when you got back from the farm, that's when you encountered your little band of enemies, was it?"

"The landlord's...wife was kind enough to give me a ride back here." Tom glanced awkwardly at Holly, who was stocking shelves with alcopop bottles and clean glasses. We heard a commotion and headed into the bar right away."

"And found your coworker beating up some locals?"

"Oh no, that wasn't it at all."

"But blows were exchanged."

"They were, but Dieter was hopelessly outnumbered. Anything he

179

did was purely in self-defense. Holly will back me up on that, I'm sure."

Tom hated to drag Holly into this, but it seemed Inspector Travis had taken a dislike to him and he needed all the help he could get. Glancing over at the bar again, he saw Holly disappear into the shadows of the public bar on the other side; a less than encouraging display of solidarity.

"Are you? Make a note of that, Iver; seems Mr. McCrae's story might require corroborating via our star witness."

Travis took a long gulp from his cola and belched, wiping his fat lips with the back of his hand.

"And about the other matter—the brakes on our car?" Tom ventured.

"Your man, Dieter—he phoned it in earlier. We were already on our way over here when we got the second call from Mr. MacGregor about the outbreak of violence."

"It took a long time for you guys to get here, if you don't mind me saying so?"

"Not at all," Travis replied, though his eyes told a different story. "Lot of local stations are all closed down, government cutbacks, you see. As a result, we are the nearest constabulary serving the Douglass area. Not much we can do about it, I'm afraid."

"But by the time you got here, the protesters were gone."

"Aye, we've got officers on the lookout for them—a double-decker bus is a pretty difficult thing to conceal..."

"So, our problem with the brakes, and this latest attack, you will look into them in case they are connected?"

"If that's an appropriate course of action, Mr. McCrae, we will indeed follow it."

Tom took a deep breath. *Appropriate?* Of course it was appropriate.

"Now, if you don't mind answering a couple of *my* questions," the fat man said.

"Of course." Tom eyed the carriage clock on the mantelpiece of the lounge bar.

"What exactly brings you to Douglass?"

"Business. As I told you back at the airport, I represent a company interested in developing a biofuels business here."

"That you did. And you suspect these environmental protesters are wise to your company's plans, is that it?"

"Seems logical, such groups have been known to get a little heavy handed in their approach."

"And you really think they'd go to the lengths of sabotaging your hire car in order to...save some trees?"

"People have the strangest beliefs." Tom thought again of the Jack Tree and the Jill Tree, and what Holly had said in passing, *"May my offering be made of flesh and blood, of hearth and home..."*

"Well, before we get too carried away with our conspiracy theories, I'd like to speak with your partner. I understand he'd had a fair bit to drink before it kicked off in here?"

The question was not for Tom, but more directed at MacGregor, who was maintaining a broody silence so thick you could have walked across it like a carpet. MacGregor grunted and turned his attention back to the tabloid newspaper he was pretending to read.

"It was his afternoon off," Tom ventured.

"You've made it perfectly clear you'd like to cover for your workmate," Travis said. "Admirable, in its way, I mean, I doubt I'd get anywhere near the same level of loyalty from the likes of Iver here. But if you could just let us question the man, that'd be very helpful."

The look on Travis's face was the opposite of the warmth of his words.

"I'll go get him," Tom offered. He was already poised to get up and leave the bar, eager to get away from the cops' vaguely sinister *Laurel and Hardy* double act.

"You do that, Mr. McCrae. And, Iver, another Coke if you'd be so kind. A half this time, or I'll be dying for a pish all the way back to the station."

As the skinny copper did his master's bidding, Tom slipped out of the bar and climbed the stairs to the guest rooms, the floorboards creaking with his footfalls as he went. He approached Dieter's door and knocked. Hearing no response, Tom put his ear to the door. Silence. He tried the handle, and the door opened. Dieter's suitcase lay open on the bed, half-packed, with clothes and other personal belongings scattered around it on the blanket.

"Dieter?" Tom called out, making his way across the room and to the en suite bathroom. The bathroom door was ajar, and it creaked even louder than the stairs as he pushed it open.

Dieter was nowhere to be found.

Chapter Twenty-Seven

Tom, Travis and Iver looked for Dieter everywhere, even venturing into the trees that bordered the parking lot to see if he'd maybe gone to walk off the booze and fallen asleep on a log somewhere. The glum cops also accompanied Tom to the local post office and general store to see if Dieter had popped in for a Snickers due to a case of drinker's munchies. The storekeeper, a stoic old lady named Mrs. Gillespie said she, "Hadnae seen hide nor hair of him". In fact no one that they asked in the village had seen him, he had simply vanished.

Iver suggested that the big man had staggered off drunk somewhere and passed out, joking that Dieter was behaving like more of a local than he might think. Brawling in the local pub then passing out in the woods were both traditional pursuits of Douglass loggers since time immemorial. Travis then reminded Iver to let him do the detective work, and Iver fell silent for the remainder of their search.

Tom reiterated that his company might want to file charges against the protestors and Officer Travis promised Tom to keep his concern about the severed brake cables on file. But he added that until they interviewed Dieter, they could not justify making any accusations against the protesters. Tom invited the police officers up to Greyson's farm so they could see the damage done to the car for themselves, but they fobbed him off with an "all in due course". Meantime, Tom was instructed to remain available for comment at The Firs. The revelation that he had also lost his mobile phone in the woods seemed to give Travis cause to eye him suspiciously one last time, before the rotund cop and his skinny sidekick finally left Douglass in a little hatchback police car that looked as though it had been culled from an Enid Blyton illustration.

With the policemen gone, Tom did one last circuit of the village, feeling incongruous with his scratched face and hands. At each house or cottage he passed, curtains twitched, their occupants peering out at him through surveillance slits in the gingham or lace; that feeling of being watched again. Let them look, thought Tom, maybe then they'll be on the lookout for Dieter. He wandered up past the houses to the oldest edge of the village, where the tumbledown ruins of what must have been the very first dwellings stood crumbling in the fields.

He stopped beneath a tall, wooden telegraph pole; an imposter standing among so many trees. A chill wind rose up and enveloped him, and he shivered. He remained where he was, rooted to the spot, breathing the cool, clean air. Douglass was a beautiful place, so quiet and still. In his mind's eye, a picture formed of Consortium bulldozers and mega-ton trucks roaring up and down the track where he was standing; massive worker drones helping to forge Douglass's new purpose as a center for biofuels. He felt a pang of guilt, feeling all of a sudden like he was the harbinger of such irrevocable change by the very act of being there, scoping out the risks and contractual complications for The Consortium Inc. At the spot where the fields met the village, he was between two seasons, and two worlds; autumn and the old, and winter and the new. He took a couple more breaths of that sweet, fresh air and headed back toward the pub, craving the warmth of the fireside.

The whisky proved just as warming as the fire, and Tom was on his third glass. He'd started off with a fifteen-year-old single malt that smelled of the forest floor and tasted like fire, before moving on to a mellow little number that was distilled, Holly told him, using local honey. This was by far his favorite; the first had warmed him up like a sweater taken straight from the radiator, but the second, the Dalwhinnie, had a more subtle, lasting warmth that grew in tingles from beneath the skin. Holly added a dash of soda water and slid the glass across the bar into his eager hand.

Tom was surprised when Holly had offered water with his whisky.

He'd long thought it was sacrilege to do so, especially in the country from where the stuff originated. She'd smiled, rolled her eyes and pointed out that if Tom went on a distillery tour, to any in the area, he'd be advised that whisky is already watered down to some extent during its creation. As they talked, Tom felt some of the tension from earlier dissipate between them, evaporated by the warm glow of the liquor. He was on his side of the bar, and she hers; they had reverted back to their roles of client and host, despite their fierce intimacy just a few hours earlier. Holly was easy company for sure, and Tom felt natural around her, like he could unwind. She'd made small talk about where he came from, his job, and had quizzed him on what a risk assessor who dealt with contractuals actually *did*. Whether or not she was genuinely interested, or merely fulfilling her part of the service industry bargain, was by the by to Tom. The ego-indulgence of talking about himself, his work, with this beautiful young woman was undeniably enjoyable. Holly's eyes twinkled as she asked what kind of risk assessment he would make of her. He chuckled, and almost toppled on his barstool. Leaning against the bar, feeling a little woozy, Tom asked if she could maybe add a dash more water to his drink. He had both answered and side-stepped her question in one.

"You've a way with people, Mr. McCrae," she said as she topped up his drink.

"I do?"

"I suppose that's why you're a successful businessman, your ability to lead a conversation?" She smiled at his puzzled look. "Must be a useful skill in meetings? I wonder who the real Tom McCrae is, though? I think I glimpsed part of him in the woods, beneath the Jill Tree..."

She leaned forward, and Tom saw an expanse of tender alabaster flesh beneath her blouse. She slid his drink across the bar and their fingers touched; the electricity passing between them once more.

"I'd like to see more of him, I think..."

Tom found the flattery in her words appealing, *arousing* even. He recalled how sweet her skin had smelled when they had made love in the forest, how hot her breath had felt against his neck. He took a sip

185

of his refilled drink, looked into her eyes.

"Are you happy out here, Holly? I mean truly?"

"You mean why did I marry a man more than twice my age?"

Sipping again, Tom nodded.

"My parents died when I was wee. Got myself into all sorts of trouble when I tried the city life. Wasn't cut out for it, you see. So I came home, to the hills. Tommy was good to me once, at a time when no one was good. He took me in."

"I can relate to that," Tom said, savoring the bite of whisky in his throat. "I was orphaned, when I was little." He swallowed, hard.

"So we're both waifs and strays." Holly smiled.

"And we're both married, Holly."

"True that, though it didn't seem to stop you in the woods."

"I guess not."

"Do you feel guilty about it? I didn't intend to make you feel bad, I just..."

"Do you? Feel guilt I mean? You clearly love your husband."

"That I do," she said. "But he...doesn't please me the way he used to."

Tom drained his glass and set it down on the bar, ready for another.

"I can relate to that, too," Tom replied, his voice dry.

As Holly topped him up, their conversation became more businesslike. She told him one drink never to water down was a fierce medicinal known as Laphroaig. Holly advised him the best time to drink that was when in the throes of a bad head cold, and to prove her point she took a bottle of the stuff from the shelf above the bar and uncorked it. Tom sniffed deep and found that it smelled medicinal in the truest sense of the word; like an expectorant that had been fermented in a peat bog for several centuries. Far too strong for him in the immediate; he'd stick with the honey malt for now. He was just savoring another sip when the phone rang behind the bar.

"For you," Holly said, covering the phone's mouthpiece with her hand.

"Huh?" He was miles away, adrift on a golden honeyed ocean. "Did they give a name?"

"A Mr. Mathers."

Saved by the bell, thought Tom. *Goddamn that bell.*

Tom sighed. "I'll take it in my room."

He hopped down from his barstool and headed for the door, then doubled back to pick up his whisky glass, sipping as he went—Dutch courage.

"How goes the war, Mr. McCrae?"

Over the phone, Tom could hear the unmistakable background noise of Mathers' favorite terrace café, up on the roof garden of Head Office. It was the executive's lunch location of choice.

"The war?"

"Reconnaissance, man. How goes it?"

"Ah, good, sir, in part but...not in, um, others."

"Speak up, man, damned difficult to hear you out here—have you been drinking?"

"Just with my, um, meal," Tom lied. "To get you up to speed, sir, I haven't been able to meet with the Greyson clan yet..."

"Clan," Mathers chuckled. "Very good."

"Yes, um, the elder statesman has proven quite difficult to pin down, but I am assured this weekend I'll be able to corner him. At a social function; my source tells me he's easier when lubricated."

More laughter erupted like a foghorn down the receiver. "Hence your dinnertime research into the local lubricants no doubt, very good, McCrae."

A bead of whisky-scented sweat trickled down Tom's temple. He wiped it away with the back of his hand, wishing he'd brought a cup of coffee up to his room instead of the Dalwhinnie.

"I have your memo in front of me here, Tom, and I see our Lord Lithgoe is on-side, very good. So once you've priced this Greyson fellow, we can soldier on, eh? Shaping up nicely, the Board will be pleased. Sharp instincts you have there, using the electricity hub as a base of ops, seeing as we own majority in that little outfit anyway. Good work."

"Thank you, sir."

"Now, any other potential flies in the ointment we should know about? No alarms, no surprises, my man..."

Tom's mind raced, as he thought of the cut brake lines, the dreadful scene in the bar with the protesters and the lunatic stalking him in the woods.

"Just a smallish fly in the ointment..."

"Yes?"

"There was a bit of an...incident, involving Dieter and some environmental protesters who seem to have gotten wind of why we're here."

There was a pause, and the line crackled from Mathers' end.

"Go on."

"He, um...well, there was a bit of a fight, in the bar at the place where we're staying."

"A fight? What, you mean like a bar brawl?"

"Exactly that, sir. After which, I really had no other option but to ask Dieter to return to the office."

"I see. But how are you going to get around, if you dismiss your driver?"

"Well, that's the other thing, sir—the car, I believe it was sabotaged." Another crackle on the line. Tom continued. "The brake lines were cut, myself and Dieter escaped unscathed, but still."

"And you think these protesters had something to do with it?"

"I do, sir. Local police have been informed, for all the good it will do."

"Ah, backwater cops, is it? Understood."

The line turned to static again, and Tom could just about discern Mathers issuing instructions to someone else before he returned to the call.

"Okay, McCrae, it seems from your report we have very little, logistically, to worry about. Work on this farmer guy, find his price, I'm sure I don't have to tell you to keep it reasonable but also to be aware that the Board will swallow it if it's the only variable putting the deal at risk. More pressing is the matter of the protesters; they can slow things up for us considerably if they get any press attention, which is the area in which these kids tend to excel. So the name of our game now is timing. Tick-tock, McCrae, the fire in which you and I burn and all that jazz. I'll move things along here, and you find your man and crush him, y'hear?"

"Loud and clear, sir."

"One more thing from our end, and it's really nothing to trouble yourself with, Tom—I mean I told them you're on assignment for as long as it takes and I call the shots on this stuff, but..."

A crackle on the line, like someone had picked up an extension; listening in.

"Are you still there, sir?"

"Still hearing me, McCrae?"

"Yes."

"Good, where was I? Oh yes, Internal might have a round or two of questions with you about the Monroe business."

"Monroe's...business in Douglass?"

"No, my man, not that. They just have a few loose ends to tie up on Monroe's untimely departure from the physical plane, so to speak. And as you were the last to see the man alive...as I said, nothing to worry about."

"Okay, sir, whatever questions they have I'll be glad to answer them, although I already said pretty much everything I could say in my statement to the police."

"I'm sure you did, McCrae. Very diligent, very thorough. Sure you'll do a good job."

"Thank you, sir." Tom didn't much like the way Mathers had thrown him this slight curveball about Internal sniffing around for an interview after the effect. But he had nothing to hide, after all. He had neglected to mention the man's last words during his brief chat with the cops at the office. *He's waiting...* If the confused ravings of a dying man were of use to Internal, then he'd share, of course—they could knock themselves out trying to find a deeper meaning in Monroe's words.

"What's that, McCrae?"

"Nothing, sir." Tom wasn't aware that he'd said anything aloud. It had been a long day. "Will there be anything else?"

"Put Dieter on the line, there's a good fellow. I want to hear what in the hell he has to say for himself."

"Another smallish fly, I'm afraid," Tom said.

"Oh?"

Tom took a deep breath and prepared himself to tell Mathers the part about Dieter's disappearing act. He took a slug of the honey malt; better than coffee after all.

A further ten-minute grilling, during which Tom's ear had started burning, and his call with Mathers was over. His superior had arrived at the same conclusion as Officer Travis; Dieter had no doubt slunk off somewhere to sleep off the effects of his ill-advised drinkathon and subsequent bare-knuckle fight. He had instructed Tom to have Dieter call the office as soon as he surfaced—the mysterious H.R. Department would step in and take care of the matter from there on in. Mathers had also arranged to have a new cell phone couriered to Tom at The Firs so he could be reached on the ground.

So much for my being off the grid, Tom thought as he lay back on his bed, still fully clothed. Still, it wasn't a bad thing for him to be contactable; he hadn't received a call back from Julia, nor did he expect one anytime soon, but at least with a replacement cell he could send her the token text message. In his heart of hearts, he wondered about his motivations for doing so, uncertain about whether he was genuinely concerned about Julia's wellbeing, or merely interested in pissing Ellie off. *Bit of both*, he chuckled inwardly. Setting the whisky glass down on the nightstand he rolled over onto his side and, curled up in a fetal position, descended into sleep.

Outside, the wind whispered through the trees and frost began to form on the windowpane. The first kiss of winter.

Chapter Twenty-Eight

Tom awoke to the sound of a sharp rapping. Head still muggy from the whiskies, he blinked away the fug from his eyes and sat up. It was still dark—the middle of the night. Stumbling from his bed, he stubbed his toe as he approached the door and, cursing, opened it.

No one there. He must have been dreaming.

He heard raised voices from down the hall. Holly and MacGregor were in the throes of an argument. Something smashed and Holly cried out. Had the old man hit her? Tom could not quite tell. Despite what had happened between them in the woods, or perhaps because of it, Tom decided it was not appropriate for him to get involved in a scene between husband and wife. Perhaps the old fellow had overhead their candid exchange at the bar earlier. Much as he gravely disapproved of MacGregor striking Holly, and he must have done the way she was now sobbing like a castigated child, Tom forced himself to retreat back into his room to mind his own business.

Then, he heard the same sharp rapping again. Impossibly, it was coming from the window behind him, but he was on the second floor. He stood in the doorway, eyeing the closed curtains with dread, and his every instinct told him to just leave the room, to head out into the hallway and raise the alarm.

More rapping ensued. He hissed through his teeth, and closed the door again. Crossing to the window, with fear rising in his belly, he tore back the curtains.

No one there.

Of course, anyone tapping on the glass up at that altitude would have to be a pretty accomplished free climber in order to do so. Tom rubbed his eyes, wondering what hellish time of the morning it was, when he caught a glimpse of something at the tree line beyond the windowpane.

Two pinpricks of searing red. Like angry eyes, watching.

He moved closer to the window, peering through the thin layer of seasonal frost that had formed there, gazing at the two vivid red eyes glinting between the dark, hulking tree trunks. A shiver passed down his spine as he peered out into the darkness, his rapid breaths making a little cloud of fog on the inside of the window.

Then, with a crash of lead, wood and glass, the window burst open—outward—and he felt something otherworldly close in around him like a freezing cloak of fear borne on the chill wind. His body felt weightless now, and he was lifted from the ground by an invisible force that held him fast. The shock of cold air as it swirled around his prone body made him gasp, and Tom was uprooted from the spot and dragged, kicking and silent screaming, outside like a newborn from the womb.

Down, down, to the trees.

His feet hit the ground running as he was deposited just beyond the tree line. He was puzzled as to why the forest floor felt so sharp and uncomfortable beneath his feet, then he remembered he had kicked off his shoes and socks before falling asleep on his bed. Barefoot in the forest, he tumbled through impenetrable night. He was in a white-hot fugue of panic, desperate to evade the omnipotent force that had taken him from his room and set him down on the forest floor. Here, he was as vulnerable as an insect in the forest's night garden; prey to the shadows that had haunted him his entire life. He ran on, his skin becoming gooseflesh beneath his clothes at the mournful call of an owl in the blackness above him. He ran until the breath had all but left his body, and he kept running until he could run no more.

Choking from exertion, Tom careered into a clearing; the noise of his intrusion startling sleeping wildlife in the trees. Dozens of pairs of unseen wings flapped and fluttered as the scared creatures made good their escape from this wheezing, sweating interloper.

Then, Tom realized his mistake.

Instead of running *away* from the shadow and threat gathering at his heels, he had allowed himself to be steered to this place. His pursuer had rounded on him and was now standing just a few meters away, long black body framed by a halo of rusty moonlight, as he leaned against the huge trunk of an immense tree.

"Show yourself," Tom demanded.

Even as he uttered the words, he knew their bravado was gossamer thin—he held no dominion here, and had no place issuing demands. But for the sake of his sanity he had to vanquish his fear, and so he took a shivering step forward, toward the shadowy figure. He winced at the sensation of something spiky, perhaps a holly leaf, piercing the underside of his right foot. Swallowing the pain, he took another step, and another, until he was at spitting distance from the tall shadow of the man-thing.

"Jack?" Tom said.

Deep within the frightened six-year-old boy's heart pounding in his thirty-six-year-old frame, he knew that was the tall man's name.

The shrill cry of a night bird came as answer, startling him to within an inch of his life. Trying to get his breathing back under control, Tom took another couple of steps forward, and what he saw made a mockery of his sense of perspective.

What he had thought to be the shadow of the man was in fact the shape of a second great tree. The man's forearm and fingers were in fact the smaller branches sprouting from that second tree; a tree he now recognized. In an instant, he realized where he was standing—in the hallowed grove beneath the Jack and Jill Trees. The cacophony of night rang out all around him, birds, foxes, and creature sounds he didn't have names for.

He turned around, glancing into the shadows, scared out of his wits. He was all alone in the dark, and yet utterly surrounded by the unknown and unseen. He backed up, imagining eyes everywhere—feeling that same sensation of being watched that he'd felt in the village earlier that day. But out there in the trees the feeling was amplified to such an extent that he felt it like a great weight bearing down on him. By day, the tall trees were things of beauty—age-old sentinels of the forest, homes to the birds that sang cheerily in the autumn sun—but at night, they had become like great columns, begging to crush him where he cowered.

He felt something touch his back, and he started. It was the trunk of the Jill Tree, the same rough, sinewy surface against which he and Holly had made love. Her warm hands were on him now, feeling their way across his chest, popping the buttons on his shirt and warming the surface of his skin.

"How?"

His voiced burned with questions.

"Shhh..."

Her breath at his ear, unmistakably sweet; sweeter than the honeyed malt he could still taste on his tongue through his fear and arousal.

She spun him around and into her. Her body was open wide, and already wet to the touch. Tom fell into her embrace and rocked with her urgent movements, feeling her lithe form undulate with him; a twin tide. Once again, the clothes fell from his body as they fucked, and he gave no resistance as she pulled his arms up and around until he was embracing the tree trunk.

But something was wrong.

First came the smell; rank and bitter like all the spoiled apples from Greyson's farm fermented across aeons. It was at once sweet, and disgusting, the very essence of putrefaction. Tom gagged, and he willed his manhood to wither inside Holly. But he was still hard as stone, and with his arms pinioned either side of the tree, he could do little but continue rocking and bucking with his mate. It was as though she were reeling him in; his arms held fast by the tree's branches somehow, the tender spot between his shoulder blades burning in agony as his back was stretched to breaking point.

Then, Holly was gone.

Her breath, just moments ago a lover's whisper in his ear, became a funeral moan—guttural and terrifying. Tom's bowels churned at the sound, his arms struggling against his bonds; no longer branches, but the hands of the Jack, holding him prone against the tree.

The rocking motion at his groin had become a rhythmic sucking, pulling him into the maw of what had once been Holly, and which was now something equally warm and wet, but *wrong* somehow.

Tom grimaced in pain as he tried to move his head in order to look down. He managed to twist his head to the right and, feeling the bark of the tree scrape his cheek, tucked his chin into his breastbone—

And the moment he did so, how he wished he hadn't.

Unable to control the rhythmic sucking at his groin, he was thrusting into the hole in the Jill Tree's trunk; the same one from which he had pulled a corn dolly in the calm light of day. In the dark secret of night, the hole had taken on a life of its own. It had opened up like a flower from its bud, a living vulva growing out of the tree trunk. The miasmic maw, into which Tom was being drawn ever more painfully, wore a mossy pudendum of soft pubic hair. The point where the mossy surface met the surrounding bark of the extremities of the orifice was indiscernible from human derma. Tom tried to stop thrusting, but each sucking motion grew more violent and powerful than the last. He felt like his back might fold in on itself, breaking him in two, enabling the tree to swallow him whole. His nerve endings screamed and, in spite of himself, he ejaculated into the sticky, insatiable organ at his groin.

Sobbing from pain, fear and exhaustion, Tom finally felt the pulsing motions subside and, slicked with drooling mucous, he fell away from the hellish cavity. Great loops of membranous fluid fell with him, tethering him wetly to the tree. As he fell, something else spilled from the red maw; dozens of tiny forms. They were like corn dolls, but alive somehow; hideous facsimiles of human life. Their heads, limbs and tiny torsos were battered and broken—apparently as a result of his thrusting. It was as though he had been skull-fucking death at the behest of this tree—deity's impossible sex organ. As they slid, in their collective hundreds now, from their rank womb the little creatures screamed. It was a terrible sound, like a thousand nails scraping against glass. Tom clutched his ears against the din, which was so piercing he felt he might pass out any moment. He clenched his eyes shut and screamed with them. All around, the night creatures joined the insane chorus; a whirlwind of agony—

Tom awoke, thrashing like a tiger in his bedclothes. He tumbled from the bed, still the middle of the night, still in semi-darkness. Rushing to the bathroom, he unclasped his belt with trembling hands, pulled down his pants and underclothes. Expecting to find blood and mucal filth there, he breathed a sigh of relief to find himself clean and dry.

Returning to the bedroom, Tom halted at a sudden *tap-tap* at the window. With a distinct sense of *deja-vu* he crossed to the curtains and tore them open. Nothing there. Was he still dreaming? He pinched his already scratched arm, hard enough to make a welt there. He was apparently awake. Feeling a little nauseous, he sloped back to the bed and crashed out. His feet were hurting. Sitting up to investigate, he found they were caked with dirt and leaf litter.

Lying on one side and curling up into a fetal position again, Tom tried to slow his racing mind, tried to make sense of what he had dreamed—or thought he had dreamed. Then he caught sight of a familiar shape lying on the nightstand next to the bed. He picked it up, examining it with incredulous eyes. The screen was covered in scratches and the casing smeared with dried mud, but it was unmistakably *his*.

His cell phone.

Chapter Twenty-Nine

"You found it then?" Holly said as she brought fresh toast and more coffee to Tom's breakfast table. "Your phone?"

Tom looked at her, eyes blank.

"Found it on the bar last night so I popped it up to your room."

"On the bar? How in the hell did it get there?"

"Someone must have found it. Honest folk in Douglass," Holly said, smiling, "Despite what others may say."

"Darnedest thing," Tom mused, checking for messages and finding none.

As his night terrors had given way to a crisp, clear day, the conundrum surrounding the reappearance of his mobile phone had proven to be the least of Tom's concerns. Dieter was still nowhere to be seen, his room had remained untouched, with his belongings still in there—undisturbed by human hands. With no local bus service in and out of the village, the only possible theory Tom had come up with was that Dieter had hitchhiked out of Douglass, still under the influence of one too many malts. But even if that were the case, it was still out of character for the big man not to have phoned The Firs to let Tom know he was okay. Or, if Dieter was bearing a grudge about having been summarily dismissed, at least to call Head Office to arrange a flight home. Neither, it seemed, had transpired thus far but there was little Tom could do about the situation. He had considered taking a hike through the woods again, in case he and the *Laurel and Hardy Show* cops had missed anything, but he felt sure they had scoured the surrounding area to the best of their combined abilities. Tom left his cell number with Holly, in case anyone called with news about his partner, and set about clearing the rather severe backlog of corporate paperwork that had mounted up since he'd last opened his laptop screen.

One of the emails required that he fact check a couple of the claims made in Monroe's original research spec for the biofuels plant proposal. He sifted through the subfolder on his desktop until he located the original field report Monroe had uploaded to the encrypted, shared network drive before he had taken his unceremonious nosedive off of the Executive Level. Scrolling through Monroe's PDF, containing the first recce photos and blueprints Tom had seen from Douglass before being assigned, he caught sight of something he had overlooked before. There, amidst a lot of very dry data about seasonal rainfall, slope gradients and risk of flooding, was a photo of a grove. Tom remembered the strange, chilly feeling the photo had stirred in him when he'd seen it the first time at his and Julia's apartment, in the kitchen.

He used the magnifying glass button on his PDF viewer to zoom in a little and his suspicions were confirmed; it was the same grove that had featured so prominently in his nightmare the night before. He shifted in his seat, feeling uncomfortable all of a sudden. Making sure he was not being watched by Holly, he zoomed in closer on the leafy scene. There, slightly left of center, were the huge Jack and Jill Trees, their shared roots identifiable at the bottom of the frame. But it was what stood *between* the trees that irked Tom. Jutting out from behind the Jack Tree was a shadow form—a figure. It had long talons for fingers, its face too dark to see in the shadows. Tom felt his pulse quicken. His mouth dry, he took another slug of hot coffee without even bothering to add any creamer, burning his tongue in the process. Zooming out, he rationalized that the figure could just be a trick of the light and shade, and that the talons were in fact the sharp branches of a smaller fir tree; perhaps even the wingtips of a bird caught and frozen in time within the frame.

Sudden laughter jolted him from his thoughts, and he glanced up at the window. Tom felt his stomach leap as a half-dozen bobbing heads passed by outside; their features horribly contorted through the uneven glass of the old leaded windows. He gripped his coffee cup tight, spilling the scalding contents onto his hand. Breathing heavily, he realized he was seeing a procession of manmade creations— *scarecrows*—as their makers carried them down the main thoroughfare into the village. Rising, he walked closer to the window and peered out. Villagers were carrying the scarecrows in an impromptu procession; some were slung over their shoulders, some in wheelbarrows. Some creations were so large, and so elaborate, that four people were needed to transport them down the street.

Neglecting the remainder of his breakfast, and his emails, Tom put his laptop to sleep and went in search of his jacket. He encountered MacGregor, making a rare appearance at the Reception desk at the foot of the stairs. The wiry old man was bent like a willow over the desk, repairing what looked like a fishing net covered in fake leaves of various shades of green and brown.

"You'll be off out to see the scarecrows then?" the old man muttered in that rising musical voice of his, without looking up from his work. His apparent argument with Holly the previous night, unless he had dreamt that too, must have cleared the air. These were the first words the landlord had uttered to Tom since the unfortunate incident with Dieter and the protestors.

"What's going on out there?" Tom asked.

His own voice sounded foolish to him somehow, excited as a schoolboy's.

"Samhain," MacGregor sighed, world-weary.

Tom climbed the stairs, two at a time.

Chapter Thirty

All around Tom, the sleepy little village of Douglass was in the process of transformation. He walked the main thoroughfare, marveling at the sudden explosion of life and color the length and breadth of the village. Pumpkins, turnips and squashes of every shape, size and hue lined doorways, windows, porches and walls. Makeshift stalls had sprung up outside several dwelling places; tables heaving with cakes, pastries, jarred preserves and other homemade produce for sale or to be raffled off. A large, hexagonal wooden tombola took pride of place on one such table next to a plastic-wrapped ham; apparently the grand prize in some wager to be had later in the day. And at every turn; the scarecrows.

Each household in the village had created one or more of the stiff figurines, and they were now being lashed to gateposts, assembled on front lawns and on the little patch of green outside the post office and general store. Some were cruder than others, either because they were fashioned by the clumsy hands of children, or concocted by the lascivious minds of adults. One or two scarecrows wore masks of celebrities, cut out from magazines. Tom was unfamiliar with the faces; perhaps they were television personalities known only within the British Isles. The children who had made these scarecrows had poked little eyeholes in the masks through which the straw stuffing that made up the football-sized heads was poking. The effect was a little disconcerting; even more so due to the fact that Tom did not recognize the faces on the masks. Another scarecrow, presumably some cheeky old granddad's masterpiece, was busy assaulting a blow-up sex doll from the rear. The locals and passing tourists seemed to find the risqué tableaux amusing, but Tom could not help but wonder if it was appropriate for a family gathering.

Tom walked on, past a sign on a gatepost that read *The Auld Abattoir*. The gate gave access to the garden of a retired butcher, which had become the recreation of times past when the house and outbuildings were in use as an abattoir and retail outlet for cuts of fresh local meat. Two butcher scarecrows, man and wife, stood proudly in their bloodstained aprons over a little flock of scare-sheep. Tom stopped still in his tracks when he saw the daddy scarecrow was holding a real-life meat cleaver aloft in one straw fist. The scare-sheep were crudely fashioned from rolls of chicken wire and yet more straw, dressed in real woolen skins with bright buttons for eyes. They were crouched low on the lawn, as if desperate to evade the swing of that butcher's cleaver, which looked like it could topple at any moment. Tom made a mental note to keep his distance from the bizarre, and potentially dangerous, scene.

Farther on, and the scarecrows on display continued. In pride of place on the post office green was a scarecrow on scare-horseback. The steed wore a mane of dried flowers, mounted on strands of trailing ivy, and the rider was dressed in a chain mail tabard of fairy lights that glimmered even in the daylight. Tom marveled at the effort that had clearly gone into the creation and stood agape as tourists and villagers took snapshots with their phones and digital cameras.

"Brilliant, aren't they?"

Tom had been so engrossed in admiring the rider and steed, he had not noticed Holly standing at his side. She was perspiring and out of breath, using the spectacle of the scarecrows as an excuse to take a breather. At her feet was a wooden barrel, big enough to contain at least a gallon of booze.

"Did you carry that all the way out here?"

"Rolled it."

"Where are you taking it?"

"To the yew tree in the churchyard. One of our many traditions."

"Need a hand?"

Holly smiled at him, still a little out of breath. She nodded and gave him a grateful smile.

"Come on, everybody, it's time to process to the churchyard," Holly announced.

Hoisting the sloshing barrel onto his shoulder, Tom walked with Holly up the lane, then right through the wide wooden gate and onto the track that led to the churchyard. A procession of villagers and tourists followed behind them, amongst the excited chatter of the few children in attendance.

"So why the barrel—and what's in here? Weighs a ton?" Tom asked, breathless.

"That's why I roll it usually," laughed Holly. "It's cider, made from the first apples of the summer. The Greysons make it, up at the farm. They keep the first barrel that they make aside until autumn, for the Samhain celebrations."

They reached another wooden gate at the end of the path. This second gate was older than the first, and warped with several seasons in the sun and rain. Lichen, the vivid yellow color of a sunburst, adorned the weathered stone gateposts either side. Holly led the way through the churchyard, toward a lone yew tree that stood at the perimeter of the gravestones, beyond two large, rectangular stone tombs. She gestured to Tom that the larger of the tombs was a good surface on which to set the barrel of cider down for now. He did so, trying not to damage the barrel by allowing it to slip from his sweaty hands. He knew now, in no uncertain terms, why Holly rolled the damned thing up to the churchyard. It would take an age for sure, but would mean a lot less perspiration.

"So," he asked, panting, "you all gather around a yew tree and drink this stuff?"

"Kind of." She smiled. "Look like you could do with a nip yourself, but we can't open it, not until everyone is here."

They waited for the others to catch up to them, a crowd of some forty people or more. Tom spied Joe Greyson at the back of the throng flanked by his two big-shouldered lads; Rory, the kid who had been working on the rental car, and the other his younger sibling. Tom wondered if one of the swarthy women walking nearby was Mrs. Greyson. He would have to find a sensitive way of wording that question if he was to get Greyson on-side during the Samhain revels as Holly had suggested. Holly was looking into the crowd, searching for someone in particular.

"What's wrong?" Tom asked.

"The old man, he's supposed to be dressed as our Jack in the Green today to officially start the revels..."

Tom remembered the fishing net covered in fake leaves he'd seen MacGregor struggling with earlier; so it was his costume.

"He complains every year, but every year he wears it." Holly continued, lowering her voice to a conspiratorial whisper. "Old fool enjoys it really—loves it, in fact."

One of the older men from the village approached Holly, asking what was up with the delay. A young lad, in his early teens with fiery curls, was dispatched to The Firs to see what was keeping old man MacGregor. The old villager exchanged a few more words before Holly nodded in agreement with the man and turned to Tom.

"Would you mind cracking that open, Tom? We'd better get started. We still have the tombola to do; and the scarecrow judging."

Tom got to work on the cork. It was as big as a fist and had been wedged into the barrel by stronger hands than his.

"Fergus, this is Mr. McCrae, our guest from the United States. Give him a wee hand with that cork before he does himself a damage..."

The old man smiled a partially toothless grin before stepping in with a penknife he had whipped from his back pocket. He said something unintelligible to Tom before getting to work on the cork as the crowd looked on. As it turned out, the delay was a useful one; old MacGregor was seen hurrying up the path as fast as his bony legs would carry him, accompanied by the boy.

There were hoots and whoops of delight as MacGregor made his entrance into the churchyard. He was dressed head to foot in the green leaves of his bizarre costume. His face was no longer visible, the net-like mesh beneath the leaves allowing him to see outside of his costume. Tom had never seen anything so bizarre. Well, not since the fornicating scarecrow he'd encountered back in the village. MacGregor looked like a walking Christmas Tree, minus the decorations.

The redheaded kid led the old man to the front of the throng. MacGregor leaned on the boy's shoulder awhile, huffing and puffing. When he finally got his breath back, he stood atop one of the rectangular tombs and made his address.

"Samhain is upon us, lassies and ladies, and as the veil grows thin between one world, and one season, and the next, we prepare to give thanks to our old friend the Jack in the Green!"

Right on cue, the cork popped from the barrel and the crowd cheered as one. Tom helped Fergus to right the barrel and avoid spilling its precious contents while the old villager knocked the faucet into the hole with the aid of a cube of loose rock marker from the foot of the tomb. Disposable plastic cups appeared as if from nowhere and Fergus got to work pouring enough measures to go around.

The landlord bellowed on. "We gather under the yew tree, symbol of life everlasting, as one season bleeds into the next. Just as each year the Holly King slays the Oak King, and vice versa, the yew branches fall. And up springs new life! The wood of the yew is said to have magical properties and the berries are poisonous. In times long gone, seers and mystics used the yew to see into the other world and bring back wisdom from those dear departed..."

MacGregor seemed to be enjoying his role as festival orator, hiding beneath his leafy canopy. His musical tones made a sweet lullaby of the words as they rolled from his tongue. Tom glanced at Holly as she watched her husband performing. She had love in her eyes, but could barely hide the yawn that was forming upon her lips. Tom wondered how much of an act she put on for the sake of appearances. He could not help but recall the arguments he had heard thus far via the thin walls at The Firs, and could not shake the suspicion that MacGregor had struck his wife during the last one. Holly was perhaps more like her elderly husband than she gave credit to. She was a performer, just as much as he was, putting on a front for the community at large.

His speech at an end, the landlord's arm appeared from a fold within his leafy garb. Fergus passed him a plastic cup, which MacGregor then held aloft in a toast to the crowd.

"Wassail!" he exclaimed.

"Wassail!" the crowd roared back at him.

Tom had no idea what "wassail" meant, but soon guessed the base meaning of the expression. The cider went down quickly. Tom followed suit and glugged down his cupful, welcoming the bittersweet opportunity to slake his thirst after having sweated all the way to the churchyard beneath the weight of the barrel.

His cup empty like everyone else's, Fergus muttered another unintelligible sentence and he and MacGregor lifted the barrel, holding it aloft. A number of menfolk moved to the front of the gathering; Joe Greyson and his boys among their number, and each gripped a corner of the barrel too. Then, with another cry of "Wassail!" the men swung and heaved the barrel at the trunk of the tree. It cracked open on impact, drenching the tree with foaming cider. Tom watched as the frothy bubbles fizzed and popped around the roots of the tree.

"The dead will be drunk tonight," the younger of Joe's lads said.

"Aye, and they'll not be the only ones who are dead drunk!" said the other.

Laughter rang out all around, and Tom added his voice to the mirth. Maybe it was simply the hit of the strong cider, but he felt now that he was blending in. He could see the camaraderie between the locals and tourists, promoted by the simple symbol and ritual of the tree and the shared alcohol. How many smiling faces the yew had witnessed during festivals, and how many sad ones during burials, Tom could only guess; it had to have stood here for at least a couple of centuries. At least as long as the church had been standing there, maybe longer. It felt good to be part of the revels, warm inside and ruddy-cheeked on a cold autumn day.

As the crowd began to disperse, MacGregor had one last announcement to make.

"May I remind you, lads and lassies, The Firs will be open for business in just an hour, so come sing your songs, fill your bellies and wet your whistles with us!"

Tom searched the dissipating throng for sight of Joe Greyson, and found him ruffling his lads' hair; giving them a pep talk not to get too drunk, no doubt. Seizing the moment, Tom strode towards them, lunging in with an outstretched hand.

"Mr. Greyson, Tom McCrae again..."

The atmosphere became frosty in an instant. The smiles fell from the faces of Joe and his boys, and they each regarded Tom with cold stares.

"Aye, I know who you are. Run along, boys," Joe finally said. His lads paused a moment, then headed off after the others, back into the village.

"If now isn't a good time... I mean, maybe I can buy you a drink?"

"It's never a good time, and I don't like to owe a stranger a favor."

"You wouldn't owe me a favor—just a drink," Tom said.

Joe ignored Tom's attempt at humor. "Do you reckon you can say your piece in, say five or ten minutes?"

"Sure."

"Then let's walk."

Chapter Thirty-One

Joe led the way through the graveyard and onto a little path that wended its way between the old headstones that jutted out of the ground like crooked teeth.

Tom followed him, taking two steps for every one of the farmer's.

As they passed parallel with the entrance to the church, Tom saw for the first time that it was boarded up.

"The church isn't in use anymore?"

"Not for a long time now. Stayed open for a wee while, for the odd village meeting, but folks have The Firs for that now."

Tom remembered. "Ah, Monroe's research notes said there's no pastor here at present."

"Last one ran off with a lassie from Edinburgh. She was married too; talk of the village that was."

"And none since then..." Tom wondered if it wasn't such a bad thing. The people of Douglass seemed to celebrate religion in a way that predated Christ and Christianity.

"Religions come and go. The people remain; they are what make a community, not men in collars, or fancy suits."

Tom wondered if Joe meant men like him. He let the barb pass.

"But your ancestors must be Scottish, name like McCrae?"

"I guess so," Tom replied.

"You mean you don't know?"

Tom had no desire to sound ignorant, but did not want to lie and get tripped up either; it struck him that to do so might be worse in the eyes of someone like Joe Greyson.

"I was born in the U.K., but I was orphaned when I was a little boy. Foster parents raised me on the West Coast, so that's always been home. California."

Tom was aware that California must sound like never-never land to an earthbound fellow like Greyson, who had presumably never set foot off the British Isles. Truth was that Tom had, once or twice, been tempted to trace his roots back to the U.K., using a genealogy service. He'd been especially tempted when he saw an online ad for such a service one night, while blazing drunk, after an argument with Julia. But he had found the whole process a little too corny in the cold, sober light of day. He had long since made his peace with the simplicity and anonymity that *not knowing* had afforded him.

"Is McCrae a common name over here?" Tom asked, eager to continue the small talk now the ice had been broken.

"Not so common, I wouldn't say so, no. There are a couple of McCraes here though."

"In the village? Really?"

"In this graveyard," Joe corrected. "I'll point them out on the way round. I used to know every single name on every single gravestone in this place. When I was younger, my pa used to bring me up here, get me to recite all the names and dates to him. He wasnae very good with reading. My mam taught me; said it would be useful later in life."

"Must be useful, running your own business?" There, Tom had said the "B" word; small talk over.

"It is, that, especially now my wife's gone. She used to do the books, handle all the accounts. It's been a steep learning curve since she passed."

"I'm sorry for your loss," Tom said.

"Are you?" Joe asked, his face unreadable. "Even though you didn't know her? You married, McCrae?"

Please don't ask me about me, Tom thought. The ring on his finger should have been indication enough.

"I am," he replied, guarded.

"Any kids?"

Tom wanted to say something about his and Julia's own loss, but the longer he took to find the words, the more his silence set in. He settled for a shake of his head. The farmer snorted, already judging Tom as a career-obsessed yuppie, no doubt, with no time for kids in his world of meetings and overseas flights. Maybe it was better for Tom to keep it that way, to avoid too much humanity to seep through any chink that might rupture his armor. Tom had to keep it businesslike; they were two men standing at a graveside, talking about the future.

"Your wife sounds like she was a...very hard-working person."

Joe shrugged. "Like an ox that one. If she were here today she'd have a fit about the state the filing is in, I'll say that much."

"A tough act to follow, huh?"

Joe stopped walking and bowed his head. Tom glanced in the direction of the farmer's gaze and saw an inscription on a nearby headstone; *Alice Greyson, beloved wife and mother, may she rest in peace.* The dates on the inscription told Tom she had passed on while in her early fifties. The gruff attitude of the farmer now had context for Tom; her dying so young had left an indelible mark.

"You know what she said to me, on her deathbed, Mr. McCrae?"

"Please, call me Tom."

"She said, 'Don't you ever sell up, Joe. Don't ever give up our land, don't sell out for our boys' sake, for the sake of a quiet life, nothing.' She made me promise."

Tom's heart sank. He stood stock-still, not knowing quite what to say. He knew that Joe knew that was the very reason he wanted to talk; that The Consortium deal depended on a takeover of all the forestry land, including Joe's plantation. To make that prospect palpable to a man who made a deathbed pact with his wife might be nigh-on impossible. But Tom had to try. Lithgoe's words echoed in his memory. *"Everyone has his price, Mr. McCrae."*

"So don't sell up," Tom said.

Joe looked taken aback; a rare chink in the armor. "You trying to be clever, McCrae?"

"Tom, and no," he replied. "It's just that not everything has to be done in absolutes. We buy; you sell, that's only one way of looking at it—and an archaic one at that."

"And another?"

"We build the business, you participate in it." Tom could not be sure if his concept was getting through, or if his words had gone completely over the farmer's head. Time to cut to the chase.

"You made a promise to Alice not to sell, but you and your lads need the security that your farm is going to turn a profit each season, year-in, year-out..."

Tom's use of Greyson's wife's first name was tactical. Even now he could see the man having a silent conversation with his dear departed. He pressed on.

"I've seen the profit-and-loss reports for your business..."

"How have you seen..."

"The Consortium is a multinational organization with offices in each and every city and major port across the globe, Mr. Greyson, and it sees everything. Now, bearing in mind the lousy summers you guys have been having, it's no surprise the pick-your-own fruit side of things has been sliding steadily these last few years. That and the fact that the supermarket giants are importing vast quantities from Brazil, South Africa, New Zealand. Your Christmas tree business does well, explaining why you and your boys have labored so extensively to expand the plantation and increase your yield over the last couple of winters. The spruces are on the up in more ways than one, and they've been *saving your bacon* as I believe the saying goes?"

Joe grunted. They started walking again, the path leading them past older, more decrepit headstones.

"But for the rest of the year, you guys are pretty fucked. Give it a half-decade or so and you might have to go back on that promise to your beloved wife after all, unless..."

"Unless?"

Joe's voice had become a tired whisper that might snap in the wind any second.

"Unless you enter into an agreement with my employers—a

211

partnership of sorts, Mr. Greyson, you and your boys would have jobs for life as part of the new biofuels outfit. And you could continue to expand your Christmas tree business alongside if your heart was still in it."

"Jobs for life, you say, but doing what?"

"Processing, mainly. When I was up at your place I saw huge, empty polytunnels where I'm guessing you used to nurse saplings? Apple trees and the like?"

Again, Joe grunted.

"Dead space, Mr. Greyson. And the fruit groves that aren't pulling their weight—if they were cleared, your farm could become the processing center for the end result wood pellets my company will be producing in their thousands. In their *millions*. So you wouldn't be selling up at all, but rather you would elevate your own business to unimagined heights, with guaranteed jobs for your boys and huge fringe benefits for the community you so clearly love."

The farmer had fallen silent, his great shoulders powering him on as they strolled among the dead ancestors of his fellows.

"Think about it," Tom concluded.

Joe Greyson sighed a great sigh. It was rather like the sound a shire horse might make.

"You're a smart cunt, McCrae," he said.

"*Tom*, and don't ever call me smart."

Joe halted and pointed at a grouping of grave markers near some windswept rowan trees.

"Your namesakes are over there, I think."

The farmer turned and started walking away.

"You'll think it over?" Tom called after him.

Joe kept walking, denying him an answer. Tom shrugged and walked on, towards the graves. He had made his best play. Now he had planted the seed, he would have to hope it would germinate. A shame he had not had the chance to water it in with a couple of drinks at The Firs; perhaps Joe would have been more compliant then.

As Tom approached the graves, he had to take a detour around the larger of the rowan trees. He circled it and noticed something lying on the ground beneath one of the headstones. At first he thought it was a collection of brown sacks, perhaps filled with leaf litter from the graveyard. As he got closer he realized it was a person, lying there on the scrubby grass. He thought it might be Fergus, lying there drunk after one-too-many wassails, due to its bony limbs and unkempt appearance.

Only when he was standing over it, did Tom realize he was looking at a scarecrow, lying there with its upper body propped up against the headstone. *Aleister McCrae* and *Morag McCrae* read the weathered inscription. There was no accompanying dedication; no birth or death dates and Tom could only imagine his namesakes had been too poor to afford a longer inscription from the stonemason's chisel. He found it odd that someone would leave a scarecrow lying on this particular grave. Tom looked over his shoulder in the direction of the gate. Greyson was long gone. Had the scarecrow been left here as some kind of prank? Maybe the farmer and his boys set this little show up to make fun of the stranger in their midst. Tom had to admit he didn't like the sight of the thing lying there beneath a headstone with his surname on it.

He was about to do an about-turn and hightail it out of the cemetery, when something struck him about the raggedy scarecrow; something familiar.

Crouching, Tom was already pleading for it not to be true but, as he pulled back the scarecrow's jacket to reveal the shirt beneath, his dreadful suspicion was confirmed.

The effigy lying beneath the headstone was wearing Dieter's clothes.

They were stained with blood.

Tom grabbed the scarecrow and lifted it from the grave. As he did so, more blood was revealed. This time, the blood had been used to scrawl a word on the headstone, beneath the old inscription. There, written in dripping crimson letters was a name:

JACK.

Chapter Thirty-Two

Tom walked through the village like a ghost, carrying the stiff body of the scarecrow under his arm. He could feel Dieter's blood on his fingers, still a little damp in places on the scarecrow's shirt and jacket, the same sensation he had experienced after cradling Monroe as he bled out on the polished floor at Head Office. Dieter's tie flapped in the breeze as Tom made his way along the main thoroughfare, forcing the Scarecrow Day revelers to step aside as he barreled on through. They barely seemed to notice the scarecrow he was carrying was wearing the bloodied garments of his colleague, yet he was hardly surprised given the macabre nature of some of the locals' straw creations. He passed the Auld Abattoir again, and saw the butcher-scarecrow's cleaver, still being held aloft, as it glinted in the golden afternoon light. Tom felt a wave of nausea at the possibility that Dieter was dead and lying in a ditch somewhere. Perhaps he had been killed just moments after Tom had dismissed him. It troubled Tom that the last words Dieter may have heard from another human being might have been his own angry remonstrations. *He might be alive,* Tom reminded himself. *This might be fake blood and the last laugh might be on me.* First things first; find whoever was responsible for this little prank, quiz them about Dieter's whereabouts, then get the Feds involved; whatever was necessary.

Powering his way up the lane and into The Firs, Tom dragged the scarecrow's sorry carcass all the way inside to the restaurant bar and slammed it down on a table beneath the startled eyes of the afternoon drinkers.

"Who did this?" Tom demanded, his eyes darting from face-to-face, looking for a telltale glimmer of guilt—anything that could give him someplace to start his accusations.

"Who would do a thing like this? These clothes—they were my buddy's. It's a sick damn joke, that's for sure, and when I find the person responsible..."

Something about the gathering in the pub struck Tom; it was deathly quiet, even before he had marched in with his macabre find from the graveyard, and not a soul was drinking. He looked to the bar, expecting to find old MacGregor looking back at him from his usual spot. Instead, he saw Holly, her face slicked with smudged eyeliner tears.

"Probably the same person who attacked my poor Tommy," she said.

Her voice was raw with anguish.

"Step aside," Tom said, and he pushed his way through the mute patrons.

Leaning over the bar, he saw MacGregor, being attended to by Fergus and a couple of concerned regulars. The old man's head had an angry red gash in it. He was out cold, and bleeding heavily. Lying next to him was the Jack in the Green costume. He was clutching on to it for dear life.

Tom looked into Holly's eyes, and she his. As they shared a silent moment, Tom knew she was thinking exactly what he was thinking.

Cosmo did this.

The paramedics came and went. Having stitched MacGregor's wound and treated him for concussion, they instructed Holly to make sure he had plenty of bed rest but told her to make sure he was alert, fed and watered between naps.

Tom phoned Travis from the telephone at Reception and left a message about his gory discovery in the graveyard. The officer on the line sounded like she did not know what to make of his story, but promised to pass it on just as soon as Travis returned from his rounds. Tom reiterated the urgency of the matter before hanging up.

He returned to the downstairs bar/restaurant, surrounded by

hangers-on eager to hear more about what had happened to the poor landlord. The scarecrow, dressed in Dieter's blood-slicked clothing, still lay on the table where he had left it. The locals did not pay it much heed; their collective focus on the gossip surrounding MacGregor and his head wound.

When Holly eventually came back downstairs, she announced she was closing up until further notice so she could better care for her husband. The locals left, some rather reluctantly Tom noted, apparently disappointed not to have further details about the assault to gossip about behind their twitching net curtains.

Holly told Tom he could, of course, stay but asked if he would mind helping himself to some sandwiches for his evening meal as she wouldn't have time to open the kitchen. Tom said he didn't mind at all. They talked awhile, and Holly intimated that MacGregor must have surprised someone in the kitchen as that was where he had been found, bleeding from his head wound. A bloodstained rolling pin was found on the floor next to him. Holly theorized that Cosmo had come into the pub to steal some food, as he had been caught in the act on more than one occasion before. Tom asked her if the vagrant had a known history of violent acts prior to the attack on her husband that afternoon, but Holly could neither confirm nor deny it.

Seeing how tired and stressed she was, Tom made his excuses and went upstairs to his room, taking a couple of plastic-wrapped sandwiches with him. The alternative was to remain in the bar and try to comfort her—and he did not want his advances to be misunderstood. His day had been trying enough without having the further grief of someone else's distraught wife weighing on his conscience. So he bailed, as politely as he could, and took the Dieter-scarecrow with him, unsure of what else to do with it.

Tom laid the scarecrow across the end of his bed and closed the door properly behind him. He crossed to the window and looked out at the tree line, a dark row of swaying sentinels welcoming the coming dusk. Peering into the gaps and hollows, he wondered if dark eyes were looking back at him, watching him unseen from the forest.

He closed the curtains and frowned at the scarecrow lying crucified on his bed. Tom picked the thing up and carried it to the bathroom, having no desire to look upon it a moment longer but aware he needed to keep a hold of it as evidence. As he leaned the scarecrow's head into his shoulder, he felt a weight thump against his chest. Leaning the scarecrow up against the bathroom doorway, he slipped his hand into the inside pocket of Dieter's bloodstained gray jacket. His fingers hit pay dirt and he pulled Dieter's wallet from the pocket. Rifling through its contents, Tom satisfied himself that nothing major was missing; all of the bankcard slots were occupied by gold or silver plastic, and there were a few dollar bills and Scottish fivers tucked into the cash compartment. That ruled out an opportunist mugging. Whoever had taken the trouble of removing Dieter's clothing had zero interest in his wallet; they would have felt the weight of it the same way Tom had when taking the jacket off of his body.

The fact that Dieter had not been robbed did little to assuage Tom's unease at the whole affair. The single word scrawled in blood on the headstone was still giving him the jitters. *JACK*. Whatever the macabre warning might mean, Tom was none the wiser about Dieter's whereabouts, or if the big man was alive or dead.

He rummaged in his pockets for the piece of paper that had Travis's number on it and called once again, using the ancient telephone on his nightstand. The same young officer from earlier answered and apologized; Travis was still out on police business. Tom asked her for Travis's cell phone number, but she politely told him that she had already left voicemail for Travis asking him to call Tom at the earliest opportunity. Trying, and failing, not to sound too terse Tom rang off and then dialed the number for Mathers at Head Office. The CEO, too, was out—lunching, no doubt on the Executive Terrace. Tom left another message with Mathers' P.A., and replaced the phone handset in its cradle.

He sat on the edge of the bed, staring at the phone; still no word from Julia, not a peep. He retrieved his cell phone and thumbed it to life, inspecting the scratches on its smooth, shiny surface. Each scratch was inlaid with dark mud from the woods, especially visible on the little furrows across the phone's glowing screen. It was as though the device had been subject to some ritual scarification during its mysterious travels; from his pocket to the forest floor, then back to his room while he slept. Acting on impulse now, he speed dialed Julia's cell. It was a little after midday back home, maybe he would get lucky and Ellie might be preparing lunch or out getting supplies—that way Julia might actually answer the phone for once.

He listened to the international dial tone of long, single pulses and, expecting the voicemail prompt to kick in any moment, was about to hang up when the call connected.

"Julia? You there?" His voice entered the crackling silence like a scared child venturing into a darkened room.He heard a heavy sigh, then, "You've got a goddamned nerve calling her."

The voice was Ellie's. Tom was in no mood for Julia's sister and her histrionics.

"Just put my wife on the line, I'd like to speak with her please."

"Oh, you gave that privilege up a long while ago, asshole."

Asshole? That was a little strong even for a ball breaker like Ellie.

"Just... Let me speak to Julia. I want to know she's okay."

Ellie made a noise that fell between a guffaw and snort.

"Oh, that's good of you, Tom, real good of you."

The line turned muffled. Ellie had placed her hand over the mouthpiece. He heard her speak, as though underwater, and caught a few words.

"It's him...do you want me to?"

More muffled noises, then Ellie's voice returned, loud and clear.

"My sister doesn't want to speak with you, not now, not ever."

Tom snorted. *More B.S.*

"Hey, if that's really the case, then I want to hear it from her not you."

Ellie ignored his attempted demand.

"She is off those awful meds you put her on, and back to her senses."

"Then that's good, right? I'm coming home soon, we can..."

Ellie cut him off, her voice strained with emotion.

"She told me everything, Tom, so it's useless pretending anymore. We already met with the lawyers and they'll have a restraining order in place before you can even clear customs."

Tom's stomach churned.

"What the hell is all this about? I want to speak to my wife."

He hadn't meant to raise his voice, but Ellie had that effect on him at the best of times.

"Just put her on, Ellie, or so help me, I'll..."

"You'll what? Assault me, too? Send me obscene texts? Just darn well try it, buster, and I'll send you to jail myself."

"Who assaulted anyone? What's this about texts?" Tom felt cold all of a sudden, his arms becoming nests of erect hairs. "For God's sake, Ellie, talk to me!"

"There is nothing more to talk about. Julia is filing for divorce, Tom. Get that into your thick skull right now. And you can forget ever seeing the baby, either, you relinquished that privilege too—a long time ago."

"Ellie, you're not making any sense. Baby? What baby? Our child died, I was there the night it happened."

"Oh, you sure were, you freak."

Ellie paused, composing herself for the killer punch.

"She's pregnant, Tom, and you are to stay the hell away from her, you hear me?"

Tom gasped. "Pregnant? But that's...that's wonderful. Are they...are they both okay?"

Both. Tom hadn't dared dream he could use that expression again; hadn't dared hope for the chance to start over with a new life that he and Julia had created.

"Ellie? You still there?"

"Oh, you are some piece of work, Tom McCrae," Ellie spat.

Tom could almost taste her bile through the echoing phone line.

"Mother and baby are going to be just fine, just so long as you stay the hell away from them."

The line went dead as Ellie hung up. Tom fumbled with the phone keys, dialing and re-dialing Julia's cell, then her landline. Her cell connected to an automated message saying the number was temporarily unavailable, and the landline—*his* landline—just rang and rang, indicating that Ellie had unplugged the phone from the wall. His mind whirled with the news of Julia's pregnancy, and the apparent fact that she now wanted a divorce based on Ellie's weird accusations against him. Recalling she'd said something about text messages, Tom navigated to the message menu on his smart phone, his thumb leaving a slick of adrenal sweat on the surface of the screen. Cursing his slippery digits, he found the folder labeled *Sent* and opened it.

Cycling through the list of messages, his heart sank. There were messages sent during the time he'd lost his phone, the timestamps listing them as delivered during the middle of the night, U.K. time. He opened one at random and found it contained a series of violent expletives, like stream of consciousness Tourette's Syndrome. The message had been sent to Julia at 3 a.m. the night of his tryst with Holly. Scrolling down the list to earlier messages, he spied one with a photo attachment. His heart filled with dread at the prospect of opening the message. Chest pounding, he thumbed the message header and the sweat that was covering his skin turned ice cold as his body temperature plummeted.

There, on the screen, was a photo of him and Holly, stark naked and entwined in each other's limbs against the trunk of the Jill Tree. The photo had been taken from a distance of some fifty feet or so, but the image was real. Tom and his betrayal; frozen in time by some unseen observer. This message, too, had been sent to Julia in the early hours of the morning. Tom scrolled down and saw a caption below the photograph.

JACK THE LAD.

The phone slid from his fingers and hit the carpet, and Tom started to weep.

Chapter Thirty-Three

Overnight, autumn turned to winter over Douglass. As the new day dawned, the little village looked fogbound, shrouded in drab gray daylight filtered through dense clouds that looked ripe to burst with thick snowflakes any moment. A bitter northeasterly wind picked up and did not stop, freezing pond water and topping each gatepost and roof tile with a layer of silver frost, the length and breadth of the village, with each gust.

Tom McCrae startled from his nightmare of talon hands and screaming trees. He opened his eyes at the shrill ring of the old telephone on the nightstand. Reaching out, still half-asleep, he answered.

"How goes the war, McCrae?"

Mathers.

What in the hell time is it anyway?

Tom wiped sleep from his eyes and checked; 6 a.m. local time. The boss was pulling a late shift, it seemed.

"You got my message, sir?" Tom wished he had a coffee in his free hand, craving the artificially enhanced clarity that caffeine might bring.

"Yes, terrible business by the sound of things. But you've held the fort admirably. And good to hear you met with Greyson, outlined our deal spec to him—that's why I'm calling, Tom..."

"But my message, about Dieter, his clothes—you guys are going to follow up on that? I found his wallet, God only knows what happened to him..."

"Why goodness me, we're going to follow up on it. You betcha,

Tom. Don't you worry about that. Such terror tactics are not to be taken lightly, and I can hear in your voice they got you good and rattled." Mathers cleared his throat. "But it's time now to ramp things up, fight fire with fire so to speak."

"Ramp things up?"

"Yes indeed. We've had a breakthrough. Your contracts department and our legal division bashed heads with the venture capitalist think tank on the seventh floor and they made, well, something of a discovery. Part of the power station land borders with the Greyson tract, but here's the good part; several acres on the other side went awry the last time the farmer renewed the lease. Must have been an oversight on his part..."

An oversight made just after his wife died, thought Tom. He felt a little sorry for the farmer; left to process paperwork he could scarcely understand following the loss of Alice, his rock.

"Little clutch of acreage just lying there in limbo, waiting for someone to reach out and grab 'em. So his bust is our boon," Mathers went on. "We've been able to secure the land via the power company. Our new plant will eat right into the Greyson estate and there isn't a damn thing he can do about it. The guys up on seven predict he'll sell up and move on within eighteen months, given the disruption and the noise pollution. Between you and me, I think they're running a book on it, and when those guys bet on something... Well, generally, it happens."

"I see," Tom said. It was all he *could* say. If every man had his price, Joe Greyson had just had his tender denied; without even having the chance to pitch it first.

"So, long story short, we've stepped up our timeline," Mathers said. "A team is on its way to you now, they should be with you early afternoon. Prep work is to start before nightfall. Any questions?"

"Ah, just a couple. What kind of team? What kind of prep?"

"Logging team, McCrae. First job to do is to improve access to the site. Power infrastructure, building foundations next. It's all down to your division's excellent research, Tom. You know the rest."

Tom did know the rest; he had helped build the schematic. The trees would come down, personnel would be shipped in, and the village as the locals knew it would be changed forever. An entire community superseded by heavy industry.

"You're probably eager to get home?"

Mathers' question hung in the cool air of Tom's room like a storm cloud.

In a way he was keen to return home, but he also dreaded what awaited him there. The prime suspects were recriminations, writs from lawyers, divorce papers—and the gnawing, hollow feeling that he would never be allowed to spend time with his child after he, or she, was born.

"If you can hang on a little while longer," Mathers continued. "Make sure the team has everything it needs to get started."

Tom mumbled his agreement, put the phone down and headed for the shower.

He had work to do.

Showered, and dressed in his suit, which included the last of his clean shirts, Tom grabbed his laptop bag and headed out the door for breakfast. As he walked the narrow corridor, he almost collided with Holly as she exited her room. She closed the door quietly, with a barely audible click of the handle and put a finger to her lips, gesturing for Tom to keep quiet until they were away from the door.

Downstairs, Holly prepared a fresh pot of coffee for her sole customer and filled him in on the latest regarding her husband's condition. He had woken during the night and said a few words, which included the confirmation of Holly's suspicions; Cosmo had indeed assaulted her Tommy in the kitchen. The old landlord had startled the vagrant, who was in the process of stealing some food from the monolithic refrigerator set against the rear wall. Cosmo had grabbed the rolling pin from the work counter before MacGregor could react. Holly told Tom she was going to call the police just as soon as she was done giving Tom his breakfast.

Tom then asked her if she thought it possible Cosmo was also responsible for the Dieter-scarecrow, and she said now that he had attacked her husband she wouldn't rule anything out.

"Who knows what he's been getting up to in those woods all this time," she mused. "I mean, I always thought of him as harmless enough, but he might be totally *doo-bloody-lalley* for all we know."

Tom ran his fingers across the scarified surface of his smart phone, inside his pocket. He had left out the part about the photo of him and Holly coupling against the tree. Maybe that was one of the things Cosmo had been getting up to in the woods. Tom's mind raced with conspiracy theories; the Greyson family had put Cosmo up to it, trying to get dirt on Tom so they could blackmail him, or launch a smear campaign in the press. Feeling hot all of a sudden, Tom loosened his collar and asked Holly for some water. She smiled at him, and he thought he'd detected a glimmer of pity in those big eyes of hers.

She was in on it, Tom thought, panicking a little now, *she was in on it all along.* It was a setup; the Greysons, Cosmo, her—all working together to bring him down. If a scandal like this hit the press, he would lose his job for sure. The Consortium had experienced its little scandals at the hands of investigative journalists in the past. Such affairs always ended with some poor sap taking the fall and being packed off to some retirement home in Florida. Tom felt sick. He had fallen for the oldest trick in the book. Maybe Dieter had worked it out, gotten wind of their plan; he had his ear to the local grapevine after all, there in the pub, mingling with the locals. They had gotten rid of him before he could warn Tom of his suspicions.

His paranoid thoughts weighing heavy on his mind, Tom did not notice Holly returning with a jug of water and a glass. He almost jumped out of his skin when she set it down in front of him. He grabbed the glass, filled it himself and gulped down water—all the while avoiding eye contact with Holly.

"I know you know what I'm going to ask you," she said, "and I don't want you to feel awkward about it, but please consider it would be of a great help to me, and the local people..."

Tom had no choice but to look her in the face now. As he did so, he noticed something draped across her arm. Something green.

"My Tommy has to be in his bed at least a week, so the doctor said. District nurse is coming today to check on him and change his dressings. I wouldn't ask, but we did say we needed to find a way for you to blend in. What better way than this?"

She took the green thing from the crook of her arm and unfolded it, dangling it in front of Tom. It was MacGregor's Jack in the Green costume.

"You...want me to wear that?" Tom asked, something close to fear in his voice.

"They like you, the local folk, you know that? Despite what you're here for, so many of them have said how nice you seem. Polite, quiet, not how they expected..." Her voice trailed off.

"Not how they expected an American?" Tom finished.

"To be truthful, aye."

She grinned. It was good to see her smile again; she looked fragile, and beautiful. Despite his conspiracy theories, Tom could not be sure he wouldn't make the same mistake with Holly all over again, given half a chance.

"You'd be the first McCrae in an age to wear The Green according to the old folk, and they're too canny to miss a beat," she said. "And if you want to show Joe Greyson your community spirit... Well, I don't know of a better way than this."

"What do I have to do, if I wear it?"

"Lead the procession, day after Samhain's the day the Jack comes out to play."

Tom thought of the name, etched in blood on the tombstone. He swallowed. His glass was empty, and his mouth was dry.

"Just try it for size," Holly said.

Before Tom could reply, she tugged it on over his head.

Chapter Thirty-Four

Outside, the village was gripped in the chill of a bank of freezing fog that had rolled in like a spectral tide. The inclement weather had done nothing to discourage the locals from continuing their festivities, however, and the main street was filled with even more people than the day before.

Tom followed Holly up to the post office and general store, feeling ridiculous clad in MacGregor's costume and peering out through the leafy eyeholes at the faces smiling back at him. They walked as far as the green, where locals and tourists alike were gathering.

Fergus, dressed in a horse costume, complete with long neck and snapping jaw, cantered over to Tom's side. Pulling a wire attached to the jaw of his costume, Fergus played at biting Holly on the neck. She giggled and pushed the snapping horse's mouth away. Fergus then neighed his welcome to Tom, the horse like sound descending into wheezing coughs. Tom guessed Fergus had been playing the mare all morning, and perhaps only now the freezing air was getting to the old man's lungs. He was a bag of bones, and none too warmly dressed.

"Good on you," Fergus spluttered. "You wear The Green well, laddie, like you were born into it."

Tom nodded, aware that his gesture simply made him look more like a tree, bobbing in the wind. Fergus sidled closer.

"Only a canny wee man could pry that costume from the tight fist of old Tommy MacGregor," he whispered. "Feet under the table at The Firs, what else you going to take that's his?"

The old man was peering out of a gap in the horse's neck, straight at Holly. He chuckled lasciviously, his throat once again giving way to great wheezing coughs.

Choke on it, you skinny old bastard, Tom thought.

He was beginning to regret ever allowing Holly to force him into his ridiculous garb, let alone out in public.

Holly cleared her throat, and made an announcement. "Now we're just waiting on a few stragglers, then we'll all process up to the ancient trees. There'll be mulled wine awaiting when we get back."

Murmurs of approval rippled through the shivering crowd. Then, with the roar of an engine, the stragglers arrived. Peering through the eyeholes in his costume, Tom saw Joe Greyson, sitting proudly atop a huge tractor, both his sons in the cab by his side. As the massive vehicle trundled towards them, Tom saw it was towing an open-topped trailer as big as a bus. The trailer was stacked with hay bales from his barn, and crammed into every available inch of space were dozens of people. The crowd looked on as Joe parked up a short distance from the post office. His lads hopped out of the vehicle and dashed round to the rear of the trailer, unclipping the rear gate. One by one, the passengers disembarked, helping each other down onto the street.

Tom recognized the faces of the newcomers. Each and every one was a protestor from the violent clash at the airport. The last to clamber down from the trailer, like royalty, were Bill and the woman in the flowing skirts.

"What's all this, Joe? Who are all these people?" Holly sounded worried, and rightly so. Tom had witnessed first-hand the mayhem these protestors could create with their mere presence.

"They're here for the procession," Joe said. "Only it's less of a procession now and more of a protest."

"Against what?" Holly asked.

Joe looked straight at Tom. Even with his face hidden inside his costume, Tom felt vulnerable. He could feel Greyson's sharp hatred penetrating the canopy of green encasing him.

"Company men just arrived. They're setting up near the power plant. They've got a generator truck, dozens of vehicles—more traffic than Douglass has seen in many a long year."

"What are they doing up there?"

"Ask him," Joe said, pointing at Tom. "And while you're at it, ask him why they brought chainsaws."

Tom felt the crowd shift its collective focus on him. It was like being caught in the all-seeing glare of a lighthouse. He took a shuffling step back, heel catching the webbing at the bottom of his costume.

"I'm sorry," Tom said. "But it appears plans are moving quicker than anybody expected."

Collective dismay rang out from the villagers, a great worried crowd facing Tom, where moments ago there had been happy revelers ready for a day's walking.

"What about your offer, McCrae? I suppose that was all smoke and mirrors too?"

"Far from it, Joe..."

The farmer snorted.

"You've got to believe me, I made that offer in good faith. My...my superiors rode roughshod over that, and I'm sorry. I'm just..."

"Just doing your job, is that it, Tom?"

It was Holly. She had tears in her eyes.

"How can you let them cut the trees? They're older than any of us."

Her voice was heavy with sadness.

"New life will grow in their stead, new opportunities for Douglass; for your community."

Tom tried to sound convincing, but could see the crowd was already against him. Rory, looking furious, broke ranks and strode up to Tom, towering over him.

"Take that off," he yelled. "You have no right to wear it!"

The lad tore at Tom's costume, ripping the eyeholes open to form a hole the size of a bowling ball. Tom's head was exposed to the freezing air and he felt suddenly naked and afraid for his life. Rory clenched his massive fist, still clutching the costume in his other. Tom staggered backwards, avoiding the blow in part but still feeling the impact of the boy's knuckles on his chin. He fell to the ground, mouth filling with the salt-metal tang of blood, and scrambled backwards on his hands and feet. The ground felt cold and hard beneath him. Getting to his feet, Tom made for a break in the throng and ran.

He dashed through the surprised ranks of locals, tourists and protestors and emerged on the other side near to Joe's tractor. For a crazed instant, he considered jumping up into the cab and driving away—but even if the keys were still in the ignition, he couldn't drive. Skirting the front of the behemoth of a vehicle, he ran alongside its trailer and out onto the road. Someone cried out behind him, maybe Holly, and he saw a car hurtling towards him. He froze, his forward momentum reversing through his body until he tilted backwards on his heels and toppled onto his ass. The car skidded to a halt, narrowly avoiding hitting him.

Tom looked up and saw Officer Travis looking out the passenger window, directly at him.

Chapter Thirty-Five

"Officer, you've got to help me, these people want my blood."

"Calm down, Mr. McCrae, just come with us, you'll be all right now."

Tom's eyes darted in the direction of the driver's door. Iver was climbing out of the vehicle, slow and stealthy like a long, pale snake. Even in the foggy gloom, Tom spied the glint of a pair of handcuffs in Iver's hands.

"What do you want with me?"

Tom glanced over his shoulder. The Greysons and their protestors were closing in behind him; a small army of malcontents.

"Just a few questions, Mr. McCrae. Your employer contacted us with a matter of grave importance."

"You found Dieter? Where is he? Is he okay?"

"I'm afraid the investigation regarding your colleague is ongoing, Mr. McCrae. Our questions are regarding another of your colleagues...a Mr. Monroe."

"Monroe? What the fuck are you talking about?"

"Someone reported seeing you up on the mezzanine floor of your office with Mr. Monroe, just seconds before he took a tumble off the balcony."

"No, I...I was up there alone, after a meeting. I never even spoke to him until..."

Tom's aching brain reeled. Mathers had wanted him to stay put in the village so the cops could pick him up, take him in. The bastard had never intended for Tom to meet with the logging detail. Was this going to be it; the frame-up job to protect the good name of the company? He knew his corporate masters were ruthless; such tactics were their stock-in-trade. But trying to pin Monroe's suicide on him somehow? That marked a new low. All because of the scandalous snapshot of him and Holly in the woods. All because he had been so weak; easy game.

"I have to ask you to come quietly, and anything you say to us may be taken down as evidence against you..."

Iver had almost sidled his way around the front of the car. Tom could feel the sheer weight of numbers bearing down on him, like a giant breath at the back of his neck. Travis was creeping nearer to him, his open hands held out in supplication.

Tom looked around, frantic. He was trapped like a lab rat in a maze. He crouched low, aimed his shoulder at Travis and barreled toward him, knocking the policeman off his feet and into Iver. The two were a tangle of limbs next to their aged police car. Tom sprang onto the hood of the vehicle, then its roof. Feeling the metal bodywork buckle beneath his feet, Tom leaped off the other side of the vehicle and sprinted for the forest.

As he crashed into the cover of the trees, he heard a chorus of outraged voices behind him. Without pausing for breath, he ran on, his cloak of moss green camouflaging him from his pursuers.

But for how long, he could not be sure.

The freezing fog that, even now, was turning the sweat that covered Tom's body to ice gave him the advantage he needed. Every sound was swallowed up by the fog's dense blanket and visibility had been reduced to barely a few feet. Tom's pursuers were still out there, hunting him, but the fog had disorientated them into smaller groups. As he pushed on through the forest, Tom could hear their muffled cries as protestors and villagers alike tried to navigate their passage through the trees behind him. He was grateful, too, for MacGregor's ridiculous costume. If it came to it and his trackers got too close, he would simply lie down in the leaf litter and pray for them to pass without noticing him. He had to keep moving to avoid testing that theory—such a dangerous ruse would have to be his very last resort.

Running for what felt like an age had caused his leg muscles to start burning. His entire body surged with the adrenaline heat of his fear and the chill bite of the weather that seeped into his every pore. Tom's pulse pounded out of synch with his desire to flee and he felt his rib cage might burst under the stress being visited upon it by his struggling heart and lungs. He did not dare stop, but instead slowed his pace more out of necessity than design. Panting, he felt the freezing-cold damp air scratching his raw throat with each breath. Careering through the trees, now unable to keep much more than a limping pace, he heard a new sound like the buzzing of giant insects. The chill mist distorted the sound into a muffled drone. As the wind changed direction, it sounded for a moment like the noise was emanating from the confines of a great hive. The wind dropped, making the fog vapor swirl—and the sound clarified.

Chainsaws.

The logging team was somewhere up ahead. Tom clenched his fists until his fingernails almost drew blood from his palms and ran on, toward the sound.

Chapter Thirty-Six

The unholy cacophony of chainsaws rang out across the ancient woodland. Tom saw shafts of yellow light up ahead, slicing through the patches of darkness between the trees. Work lights, erected by the logging teamsters so they could better perform their function in the gloom of the freezing fog.

Springy bracken, twigs and soft earth gave way to the crunch of gravel and Tom realized he was now wandering the path leading the way to Electricity Substation D-5. As he neared the dark shapes of the railings, their half-dead captive trees on the other side, Tom halted in his tracks. Someone—or something—had flitted across the path no more than ten feet from where he stood. Rooted to the spot, he heard voices and saw a couple more shapes cross from the trees to the substation's perimeter fence.

Tom crept back to the side of the path and into the tree cover. He needed to get closer to see what he was up against. He took a few steps farther, behind the trees, parallel with the path. A twig snapped beneath his foot and he froze in his tracks. One of the figures turned and looked around. From his vantage point, he could now recognize Bill's face. With him were a couple of the heavier-set protesters; muscle he had brought along with him. The rat-faced protester looked straight at Tom. His heart pounded and he felt sure he had been spotted. But then Bill looked away and Tom exhaled a quiet, nervous breath. The Jack costume had camouflaged him well and he had gone undetected, for now. No chance but to stay absolutely still and wait for the protesters to do whatever they were doing before he could move on.

Peering through the mist and gloom, Tom saw one of the protesters clamber up onto the shoulders of the other. Anchoring himself using the railings, the man at the top then reached down with one hand to grab a hold of Bill and help him up.

Bill then walked up the railings, almost horizontal by the time he got to the top. With a lot of grunting, and a little cursing, the two other men helped push Bill forwards until the very top of the fence was level with his waist. Bill slipped out of his jacket and used it to cushion the sharp, lethal points of the railings. Over he clambered, sliding and then jumping to the ground on the other side. His cohorts stood waiting for him, separated from Bill by the railings.

Tom listened intently for a clue as to what was happening on the other side of the fence. He didn't have to wait long. There was a hammer-like banging sound, followed by a crash. Bill must have broken into the main power complex. Even at this distance Tom could feel the hum of electricity in the ground beneath his feet. Bill was certifiably insane to go in there; he risked being fried alive any moment.

The next sound Tom heard was a whoop of victory, and then he saw flames rising from within the compound. Bill had set a fire. With more whoops of celebration, he saw Bill return to the perimeter fence. His men pushed their arms through the railings, folding them on the other side to form crude human steps. Bill grabbed the railings and started to pull himself up, his feet now resting on the arms of the guy at the bottom.

Then another figure appeared from the swirling gloom. It was a tall man, dressed in a long coat. Tom could not see his face for the figure had his back to him but, even before he spied the axe in the man's hand, he knew in the yawning pit of his stomach that it was his stalker.

Without warning, the figure swung his axe into the lower spine of the man at the bottom of the human ladder. The man howled in agony and dropped to his knees, toppling the other who was stood on his shoulders. As the second of Bill's helpers hit the ground, their attacker lifted the axe again and sank its heavy blade into the center of his skull. Tom saw Bill's jaw drop as he looked on at his fallen comrades in abject horror. The figure regarded him for a moment, as though measuring the level of threat posed by Bill.

But Bill was now trapped behind the high railings, with the fire that he had just started growing into an inferno behind him. The axe-wielding figure lingered for a moment then took off down the path in the direction of the logging team.

Tom watched, wide-eyed and unable to move from fear of being spotted by the axman. But as the fire grew, Tom knew he had to help. He lumbered from the tree cover, his leafy costume snagging on branches as he went. Tom glanced in the direction of the attacker and saw only swirling smoke. He dashed over to the high railings.

Desperate, Bill was trying to clamber up the fence but his feet had no purchase on the slippery metal surface now his helpers had been slain.

"Climb up on this!"

Tom pointed at the yellow *Warning: Danger of Death* sign affixed to the railings. If Bill could get a foothold on the sign, he might be able to clamber the rest of the way with Tom's help.

Bill backed up as far as the smoke and flames would allow him and took a running jump at the railings. Holding on for dear life, he clambered up, crying out as the metal railings bit into the palms of his hands. His feet found the top of the sign and he rested for a moment, peering up at the top of the fence. He still had a way to go.

"Help me!"

Tom ran to where Bill was clinging on. The warning sign was at waist height. If he could clamber onto it on the other side, the same way Bill had, maybe he could help him with a leg up the same way his now-dead colleagues had. He had to try; the flames in the main building were growing fiercer by the second.

Clutching the railings, Tom pulled himself up and swung his body sideways until he got a foothold on the sign. There was a sharp cracking sound. The combined weight of two men had ripped the sign from the railings.

Tom fell too. He hit the ground with a painful jolt to his tailbone and the world before him exploded. Brick, metal and glass erupted in a ball of flame as the substation complex went up like a roman candle. Bill fell from the fence and toppled backwards into the fire and chaos that were of his own making. The angry orange light from the fire flickered through the mist. Bill's agonized screams amidst the inferno were so loud they almost drowned out the sound of the chainsaws that still echoed on throughout the forest. Tom approached the railings again but the heat was so intense he could feel it burning the hairs from his face.

Bill's screams ended, cut off by a fury of flames.

As the fire grew before Tom's eyes, he found his legs again and ran down the path the same way the figure had gone. He could not fathom the actions of Bill and his two henchmen; what kind of environmental protester would set a fire at a substation in the midst of dense woodland? Whatever the motivation, their reckless actions had cost them their lives—two at the sharp axe blade of their killer, and one by his own hand.

As he neared the end of the path, Tom could see the beams of the overhead work lights, yellow as sunlight. Somewhere up ahead, there was a crashing sound as a tall fir tree toppled. The teamsters were cutting their way through the trees lining the little access road no doubt, in order to extend it all the way up to the power substation. Tom glanced behind him at the flicker of flames, diffused by the mist and smoke. It could be that the loggers could not yet see the fire through the glare of the work lights—each of which was pumping out twenty kilowatts of artificial daylight. Tom had to warn them. Even on a damp day, the threat of a forest fire loomed like a shadow. Pushing on through the trees, he focused on the loudest chainsaw sound he could hear and aimed for it. Then, two things happened. The first was that the work lights dipped all of a sudden, then went out completely, plunging the woods into near darkness. The second was that the chainsaws stopped. One by one, their engines ceased, giving way to an increasing and eerie silence after all the hellish noise.

Tom could hear his heart beating in his eardrums. He ran on, slower now due to the gloom, and heard the first of the screams before he had even broken the tree line. With every stopped chainsaw, a new scream rose up on the misty air. Each cry was a raw, aching sound, telegraphing agony through the canopy of trees like a warning. Clutching his hands to his ears, Tom stumbled on, tripping over roots and fallen branches and tumbling into a clearing. The low hum of a chainsaw growled like a tiger. Searching out the source of the noise, Tom could just about make out the shape of a man lying on the forest floor. Creeping closer, Tom could see the man was clutching his leg. His foot was ankle deep in a large metal trap. Rusted, angry jaws had closed around the man's leg. Arterial blood was spurting from the wound like red wine from a broken barrel. The man, a logger dressed in a fluorescent yellow tabard over muddy work clothes, was trying to reach the chainsaw lying next to him. He looked petrified, and hadn't even noticed Tom standing nearby, dressed in his suit of green leaves. The man's twitching fingers gripped the handle of the chainsaw and he pulled it toward him, lifting it now with both hands.

No!

Tom tried to cry out, to try and intervene—to stop the logger from performing the desperate act he knew he was about to perform. But no sound would come from Tom's throat. The man revved the chainsaw and drove it into his trapped leg, slicing through the already shattered and twisted bone all the way through into the blood-drenched ground beneath. The leaves on Tom's costume were spattered with the man's blood which, now that his leg had been severed, was spurting out thick and fast. The logger dropped the chainsaw to the ground and tried to drag himself across the forest floor.

It was then that Tom realized he was not the only witness to this unspeakable *Grand Guignol*. Just a few feet away stood Cosmo, axe in hand. He stood, impervious, watching the desperate man—he couldn't be older than twenty-five—dragging his dead limb away from the trap. Sobbing in pain, the logger looked like he would pass out any moment. Cosmo stepped forward, clearly intent on denying his victim any such release. He towered over the tortured logger, swinging the axe, low this time, until the blade was embedded in the poor man's crotch. The logger roared like thunder, unable to process the agonies being visited on his already ravaged body. With another swing, and another, the looming vagrant used the axe to open up his victim from bottom to top, only stopping when his blade had ploughed a furrow of flesh right through to the sternum.

Tom gagged, tasting the bitter acid bite of mulled wine scorching his throat. He tried not to regurgitate, clamping his hands over his mouth as he careered away from the scene on trembling legs. He half-ran, half-fell from the dreadful scene, following the incline of the forest floor as it led him down a steep bank then up again over loose earth and knotted roots onto higher ground. Then, somewhere amidst the firs and the fire that raged behind him, another explosion rocked the forest.

The remaining buildings at Electricity Substation D-5 went up, lighting the sky with a shower of white sparks and ochre flames. Tom saw the forest before him light up too, a vista as clear as on a summer's day. He was standing in the glade before the ancient Jack and Jill Trees.

The sight illuminated before him was an atrocity to behold. It was as though Tom had wandered into the fabric of his worst nightmare.

Chapter Thirty-Seven

Tom stood dumbstruck and took in the horror before him. It was as though all his recurring nightmares and his waking, rational life had somehow blurred—two universes combined; the veil between them torn open by the sheer madness of what he was witnessing.

All around him lay the bodies and body parts of the logging team. There were the remains of six or more men, maybe even as many as ten, it was hard to tell given how far and wide their limbs were scattered. The shocking viscera of the amputated limbs, smashed torsos and severed heads was punctuated by the occasional flash of a bright yellow florescent tabard here and there amidst the leaves and gore. Blood seeped from the body parts, turning the leaf-strewn ground around the ancient trees into a dark quagmire. Tom became aware of a wet dripping sound, like raindrops that had gathered on the leaves and branches overhead. He looked up and saw a crimson rain of blood dripping from the sodden leaves above, bright droplets dancing in the golden flicker of the fire. Clamping his hand to his mouth in a vain attempt not to gag, he saw the source of the torrent and realized with a growing sense of terror and despair that he had seen this before.

He recognized the way the lower branches were bowed beneath the weight of so many internal organs; a sight that had haunted his nightmares for over thirty years. The men who lay eviscerated at his feet had been torn open; their intestines and internal organs draped across the lower branches of the Jack and Jill Trees like bright red tinsel. An eyeball dangled sickly, attached to a tree branch by its stringy optic nerve, next to a section of scalp that flapped and bled in the wind.

Sacrilegious offerings to the ancient trees; grim gifts from a madman.

And there, at the foot of the tree stood that madman; leaning on his axe and admiring the ripe, red fruits of his labors.

Tom, unable to stop himself from vocalizing his fear, let out a whimper. At the sound, the man turned and looked at Tom with indifferent eyes. In the light of the sub-station fire, Tom could see him clearly now. He was broad shouldered and powerful framed, dressed in a large, filthy, hooded overcoat, with ragged combat fatigues beneath. This man who had been watching Tom, haunting his every step in the forest and beyond was no supernatural force; Tom felt sure of that now. He was just a man, and a vagrant at that.

"You have no right to wear The Green."

The man's voice was a rough as gravel; it sounded like his throat had been cracked apart by screaming. His thick Eastern European accent made him sound like a gypsy to Tom, giving his words an earthy, mystical quality.

"You're the second person who said that to me today—Cosmo, isn't it?"

The vagrant grunted and took a single, lumbering step forward.

"You have no right to be here, these woods are mine. No one hunts or ruts here but me. No one but me has the right to wear The Green."

Every fiber of Tom's being told him to back off, but he held his ground.

"Is that why you've been following me around, because I'm pissing on your patch? It was you who sabotaged our brakes, wasn't it?"

The axman just snorted.

"And you who took the incriminating snapshot of me and Holly..."

"It surprises you I can use a mobile phone camera? Because I wear rags? Because I sleep rough?"

"Not at all," Tom said. "But it does surprise me you had the wherewithal to MMS it to my wife."

"Picked the first name I saw in your sent messages. City people always think you're so superior, but you know nothing of real life, of

241

real struggle."

"Maybe I have no right to be here as you say," Tom said, trying to speak Cosmo's language. "But no one owns these woods. People buy and sell them, but no one really owns them, do they? They're too wild. They live on, whatever we try to do to them."

"What do you know about it?" Cosmo sneered. "You come here with the stink of pollution on your clothes—in your hair and skin—and you bring chainsaws to hack and cut the trees where they stand. Where they have stood for centuries. You don't know what it takes to earn the right to wear The Green."

Tom looked at the charnel scene around him, all those men, so brutally slain.

"Slaughtering innocent people? Is that what it takes?"

Cosmo lifted the axe.

"I am their true protector. And I am here to hack and cut the likes of *you* down."

"Like you did to Dieter? My partner, the one whose clothes you put on that ridiculous scarecrow, remember? That was a nice touch, Cosmo; the police were particularly interested in that little maneuver. In fact, they're on their way now, not long until they find you..."

"Then they'll find you dead, also," Cosmo growled.

Tom froze as the huge man lunged for him, swinging the axe up high. He was intent on smashing it into Tom's skull. The vagrant roared a berserker's cry. Seeing the flash of the blade against the gloomy sky, Tom prayed to gods he did not even believe in that he would be able to dodge the sudden attack.

Then, someone else came crashing out of the trees, screaming bloody blue murder. Holly crashed into Cosmo, clinging to his long coat for dear life and knocking him off course. The axe swung wide of Tom's head and into the ground. Slipping on the miasma of blood and ruin at his feet, Tom fell.

Cosmo's axe had cut right through the conjoined roots of the Jack and Jill Trees, separating them. Foul, black fluid spurted from the severed roots like congealing blood. The vagrant gasped, choking at the blasphemous sight. He looked bereft, like a child whose toys had been confiscated from him. Cosmo spun around, glaring at Holly with hate-filled eyes.

Wrestling free of her grasp, he jabbed the flat end of the axe right between her eyes.

Tom stood watching, aghast, as Holly's legs buckled beneath her. She fell, lifeless, to the ground amidst the detritus of dead bodies and the oozing roots of the ancient trees.

Heaving the axe so that he was holding it with two hands again, Cosmo advanced.

Tom scrambled to his feet, turned on his heels and ran.

Chapter Thirty-Eight

As he ran, Tom tried to wrestle himself free of Tommy MacGregor's costume. If he had no right to wear it, as Cosmo had said, then let the mad, murderous fool have it; especially if it would slow him and his axe down a bit. But it was no good, the webbing and fake leaves were all in a tangle around him. The only way he might stand a chance of extricating himself from the costume would require stopping still for a minute or two, maybe more. That was a delay he dare not risk with a crazed axman at his heels.

Tom pushed on, beyond the huge trees and their cousins and into a glade. He saw a structure at the heart of the clearing, a ramshackle house in the woods, overgrown with ivy, weeds and young trees both inside and out. The front door was open, hanging off its hinges. With renewed vigor, Tom broke into a full-fledged sprint for the open door.

He was within twenty feet of his target when he glanced down to avoid tripping on some fallen branches. As he did so, he saw another potential peril in his path; the serrated metal jaws of a huge trap, lying partially hidden in the carpet of leaves that covered the forest floor in the clearing. He was running too fast to stop in his tracks and so, powering forward with three wide strides, he leaped into the air and over the trap, landing safely on the other side of it to continue his mad dash for the door.

Behind him, Tom heard an almighty *snap.* Had he triggered the trap somehow during his flight? He risked slowing his pace a little in order to glance over his shoulder and saw Cosmo, standing and swaying slightly, his face a rictus of pain. The man's scream rang out next; a wolflike howl that echoed off the branches of the surrounding trees like hell and damnation. Cosmo had become ensnared by his own trap. He had been so intent on catching up to Tom that he had missed the metal jaws at his feet. Fighting to keep his balance, Cosmo lost the battle and toppled to the ground and was even now desperately trying to free his damaged leg from the trap.

Tom charged on towards the door, crossing the threshold and crashing inside the tumbledown house. He slammed the door behind him and turned around to inspect his surroundings.

And found that he was *home.*

Home in the context of all the nightmares of his thirty-six years.

The small foyer in which he was standing was as recognizable to him as the taste of bread. The staircase, leading up to the second storey in a gentle curve, was as familiar as an illustration from a bedtime story. Even though the floorboards were warped and covered in moss and litter from the forest outside he felt sure he was standing in the arena of his dreams.

He walked on into what had once been the living room of the dwelling and drew a sharp breath upon seeing the fireplace. It was the mirror image of the one from his nightmares. He shivered, half-expecting to see red eyes, hot and searing like coals, glaring at him from that darkest of dark places. He crossed to the corner of the room where he had crawled so many hundreds of times in his tortured dreams; the same spot where he felt the hot, wet caress of the human viscera decorating that infernal Christmas tree.

With shock and disbelief, he saw that a fir tree had taken root beneath the stagnant floorboards, erupting through them in a defiant display of life, in the exact same spot where the Christmas tree stood in his nightmares. Remembering the branches of the Jack and Jill Trees bowing under the weight of their dark fruit, Tom backed away from the tree, eager to be at a distance from it and the long shadow it cast on the floorboards. As the weight of all his childhood fears closed in on him, he felt that the walls of the ramshackle house might collapse at any moment.

Then he heard a pained murmur.

The muffled sound had come from *beneath* the house, and he was about to dismiss it as an aural manifestation of his own dread when he heard it again, louder and more intense this time. He walked in the direction of the sound, weathered floorboards creaking beneath his feet with each step. In answer to the creaking of the floor, he heard the sound again as it took on the aspect of a child's plaintive moan. Tom shuddered, recalling the pitiful, wretched sounds he had made each time that horrific nightmare had woken him from his restless sleep almost every night for the past thirty years. Was the sound a phantom, come to torture him to madness then a slow death in the venue of his worst fears? He stumbled backwards, his heels becoming entangled in something heavy, and soft. He looked down, nervous that he would find yet more body parts like Cosmo's exhibition of atrocities he had witnessed in the woods. Relieved, he saw his feet were tangled in a dusty old rug. He kicked the thing away, making a cloud of dust, and noticed something beneath the tattered weave of the rug; the edges of a hatch, laid into the floorboards.

He knelt and dragged the heavy rug fully to one side, revealing the hatch in its entirety. He glanced around for something with which to pry the hatch open and found a broken chair leg that had been sheared off to a point lying nearby under a musty armchair. Driving the pointy end of the stake into the narrow gap between the hatch and the surrounding floorboards, Tom pushed then lifted. He repeated the movement, each time getting the stake a little farther into the gap until he had the hatch open a full two inches or more. Holding the stake in place, he used his free hand to grab the edge of the hatch and swing it up and over until it clattered onto the creaking floorboards amidst a plume of dust and earth. Peering down into the opening, Tom saw the wooden rungs of a ladder descending into the gloom.

He swung his feet over the precipice and onto the first rung of the ladder down to hell.

Chapter Thirty-Nine

The sweet-sour stench of decay hit Tom's nostrils before he was even halfway down the ladder. He swallowed, willing the churning pit of his stomach to settle. The whimpers he had heard through the floorboards were louder and more urgent now. Someone down there needed help, and he was the only person who could help. Gripping the rough sides of the ladder, he continued his descent into the stinking gloom.

Drip, drip, drip.

Something was leaking down there. Tom prayed it was just water.

His right foot hit the floor, which felt solid like stone. Still holding on to the ladder with one hand, he reached out and felt along the wall to his right, searching for a light source. Finding nothing, he felt along the wall with his left. Christ, but the smell was bad down there, a sickly, ripe odor like rotting onions.

Bingo.

Tom felt the unmistakable shape of a switch beneath his searching fingers. He hesitated before pressing it, uncertain that he wanted to see what was down there in the stink and dark. Hearing another pained whimper, he flicked the switch and shut his eyes tight against the sudden glare. He opened his eyes again slowly, allowing them to adjust to the light, and turned. A single, bare light bulb dangled from the wooden beams above illuminating a stone-floored cellar some fifteen feet square. The meager space had been converted into something resembling a home. A small kitchen area had been set up in one corner, with a few pots and pans poking out of a large wooden container. A bucket sat next to the pans, and Tom saw the source of the dripping sound; water was leaking from the ceiling above into the bucket.

Tom made his way around the foot of the ladder and saw the source of the whimpers. The dreadlocked protester Tom had tangled with at the airport, then the pub, was strapped to a chair. Bound and gagged, the young man's face was a mess of bruises and livid cuts. His eyes wide with terror, the protester murmured frantically through the gag, struggling all the while against his bonds. Tom rushed over to him and wrestled the blood-soaked gag free from the poor man's mouth.

"You have to get me out of here, before he comes back! He's fucking mental, made me watch him...do it. Says he hears a voice, talks to some demon upstairs all the time, please he's crazy..."

The frantic young man looked in the direction of a chair standing next to a makeshift bed fashioned from wooden pallets in the opposite corner. Mildewed blankets were piled up over two large, long shapes— one on the bed, one on the chair. Tom crossed to the chair and leaned over it to take a closer look. It smelled worse over there.

"No! Don't look! Just get me out of here, man! Before he comes back, please!"

But Tom already had a hold of the blanket covering the shape on the chair. Clutching his hand to his mouth, he pulled the blanket away, and recoiled from what he saw beneath.

Strapped to the chair was Dieter, or what was left of him, his wrists bound with binding wire that had cut all the way down to the bone. How he must have struggled. The savage wounds that had been visited upon his flesh made Tom wish that Dieter had been dead already when they were inflicted. An angry head wound still oozed with drying brain matter. The rest of his body had been flayed, gouged and torn by hands that did not know tenderness, in turn guided by a mind that knew no mercy. As Tom pulled the blanket back farther, Dieter's lifeless, broken head lolled to one side and his dead mouth spewed maggots down his blood-smeared chest. Tom looked into the spaces where Dieter's eyes had been before they were gouged away, leaving red raw sockets that described the horror of his colleague's final moments.

Tom knew that the shape on the bed next to Dieter was another body. He knew it was the source of the unspeakable stench permeating every square inch of the cellar. Tom swallowed his fear; he had to *see* what was under the blanket, he had to *know* what had happened down there in that filthy cellar in a vain attempt to understand it. He crossed to the bed, crouched down and pulled back the topmost blanket, then the next. Peeling back the final blanket, he gagged at the smell.

The girl still wore a shock of white-blonde hair, but it was the only thing about her that looked alive. Her skin was a pallid gray-green color, and bore livid welts and bruises. She was dressed in a silk chemise, the hem of which was thick with dried fluids. Beneath the hem her legs ended at the thigh where they had been amputated and crudely cauterized. The concision had been clumsily executed and the wounds unsuccessfully sealed. They wept with foul-smelling yellow ooze that was alive with writhing maggots. She had been no more than twenty years old when she died, but that had been several months ago. Somewhere beneath the ruinous odor, Tom could make out the faint scent of perfume. He saw a perfume bottle standing next to makeup containers, all of which stood in a neat row on a little shelf above her side of the bed. Perversely, Cosmo had painted the corpse's nails with pink nail polish and had applied a layer of red lipstick to her dried and peeling lips.

Tom's eyes filled with tears of revulsion and he vomited stomach bile onto the damp stone floor. A ringing filled his ears, like the pealing of a bell, and he clamped his hands over them in an attempt to block the sound out. As the sound faded, he became aware of the protester's voice again, begging him to set him free and get him out of there. Hands shaking, Tom got to his feet and set about trying to free the young man from his bonds. His trembling fingers made the task difficult, but once Tom had managed to free one hand, the man helped him untie the other. Tom then freed one of the man's ankles while he worked on the other. The protester had barely the strength to stand up. He was bleeding profusely from an array of wounds that covered his torso and limbs; the beginnings of the torture that had marked Dieter's demise. Tom swung the man's arm around his neck and helped him across to the ladder. Pausing for breath, Tom leaned the protester up against the ladder.

"What's your name?"

"Jupiter..." the young guy started, then shook his head and said, "Oh fuck it, man, I'm Brian."

"Okay, Brian, here's what we're going to do. I can't carry you up there, the opening is too narrow, so you go first and I'll help you up as best I can. Can you do that?"

The protester nodded. Groaning from his collected agonies, he took the first couple of steps up the ladder, with Tom holding on to his legs as he helped him to the next rung, then the next. The welcome smell of the forest wafted down from above as Brian and Tom struggled up the ladder together, urging them on to the summit where they would be free of the hideous stink of rot and ruin.

Tom clambered from the hellhole after Brian, collapsing next to him on the tangled rug. Breathing heavily from his ascent, Tom kneeled on all fours for a moment, before standing up on still-trembling legs. His head spun with the sudden rush of blood to his brain, and he steadied himself against the old armchair before reaching down and helping Brian to his feet.

The dim daylight creeping into the derelict house through the unhinged front door was a beacon to both of them. Swinging Brian's arm around his neck once more, Tom helped him take a few faltering steps toward freedom. They were almost at the threshold when the daylight disappeared into shadow.

A heartbeat later Cosmo came crashing through the front door, his wild eyes brimming with murderous intent.

Cosmo's huge hands found Jupiter first, and he was on him like a rabid hound. The protester's arm was torn from Tom's neck as Cosmo lifted the young man from his feet like he was a puppet. The vagrant punched Brian square in the face, knocking him straight into Tom, who staggered back, trying to keep his footing.

With no option but to back off into the living room, Tom watched as Cosmo thundered across the floorboards and scooped up Brian's limp form. The big man grabbed Brian's head like it was a football and slammed it into the doorframe, splintering the rotting wood into great shards that fell to the floor. Again and again he slammed the defenseless protester's face into the wooden frame until the lad's features were an unrecognizable mess of blood and exposed bone.

Tom continued backing away, and tripped on a loose floorboard. He fell back, into the fireplace. Gathering his legs under him, Tom gripped his knees tight and watched in horror as Cosmo tore Brian apart in a murderous fury. The vagrant was rage personified, his fingers gouging his victim's extremities amidst orgiastic showers of blood.

Tom was that six-year-old boy again, looking on helplessly at the ravaged bodies of his parents. Only this time he was watching the unspeakable as it happened. And this time he was seeing it from the hiding place of its architect. Tom felt those red eyes upon him once more and the nape of his neck turned to gooseflesh as a chill breeze oozed down the chimney like a ghostly breath. Terrified, he forced himself to look upwards at the little circle of light at the top of the vertical tunnel. He expected to see that red-eyed demon, clawing its way down the inside of the chimney stack like a great, black, carnivorous spider.

But Tom's eyes found something else within the confines of the fireplace.

There, hidden on the inside of the keystone beneath the mantle were two words, etched in a childish hand:

JACK McCRAE.

Tom knew in an instant the handwriting was his own, but how could that be? That this was the house from his worst nightmares was now an absolute certainty to him. But what event could have placed him inside the very fireplace where his greatest fear lay in hiding?

The sudden thump of Brian's lifeless body dropping to the floorboards shook Tom from his revelation. Cosmo, his work done on the protestor's broken carcass, turned his attention back to the cowering form in the fireplace. The vagrant stooped and picked up the wooden stake from the floor next to the trap door.

Brandishing it like a dagger, Cosmo moved in for the kill.

Chapter Forty

Tom glanced up, feverish, wondering if he could somehow make his escape by climbing up the chimney. Cosmo jabbed with the stake, and Tom fled to one side to avoid the blow. The vagrant leaned back, readying himself for another lunge. There was no way Tom could escape upwards now; he would have to try to face Cosmo or be dragged to the same grisly fate that Brian had suffered in front of him.

As the huge man lunged again with the sharp end of the stake, Tom reached up on instinct and clawed at the sides of the chimney flue. A cascade of black soot billowed from the fireplace and into Cosmo's eyes. Tom grabbed handfuls of the stuff and, emerging from his hiding place, threw them into Cosmo's face, blinding him. The vagrant coughed and spluttered, clawing at his face to clear his vision of thick black soot.

Cosmo was still blocking Tom's path; no way could he risk pushing past him without being grabbed, even though the man was temporarily blinded. Tom looked to the fireplace for an answer—and found one. Leaning up against the tile surround of the fireplace was an old metal poker. Tom grabbed it and whirled around to defend himself. The whites of Cosmo's eyes glared from the soot and gore coating his face. The vagrant lunged again, low, trying to stab Tom in his stomach. Sidestepping the lunge, Tom raised the poker and brought it down, hard, onto the back of Cosmo's neck.

Tom's attacker's knees buckled under the force of the blow and he hit the deck, facedown. He was out cold. Tom stood over Cosmo's prone body; poker poised to deliver another blow should the man dare to get up again.

"Tom?"

The frail little voice was Holly's. Tom looked up and saw her leaning against the doorframe. She looked deathly pale, her head bleeding from the wound Cosmo had inflicted.

"I remember," Tom said.

The fire poker fell from his fingers and clattered to the floor beside Cosmo.

Tom clutched his skull, a tidal wave of memories flooding his senses.

"Morag and Aleister McCrae. They lived in the house in the woods. Trees all around. Winter came, they were snowed in. Their only son, stillborn. No doctor could come, no midwife present for the birth. They took his body to the Jill Tree. An offering—just like you said, Holly."

"But how do you..."

Holly groaned and put her hand to her head where Cosmo had struck her.

Tom rambled on, words spilling from his lips faster than he could scarce form them.

"He lived. Somehow he lived. A voice nurtured him and the rot and ruin into which they had thrust him *sustained* him. He feasted on death's blood and offal. And he grew, Holly, oh how he grew; into a feral child, fed by the forest's bounty of blood and bone and raw, dead things.

"He was schooled by whispers, ancient lessons borne on the breeze through the leaves on the trees. The voice taught him how to hunt, how to kill and feed. And the voice belonged to the Jack in the Green. *His true father.*"

Holly clutched the doorframe, too weak to move.

"And when he grew big enough," Tom continued, "he began to watch the parents that had abandoned him. He watched his father placing logs in the hearth. He saw them through their warm windows while he shivered in the cold. Watched them trimming their tree. Placing gifts beneath it. Gifts for their dead son. Gifts for him. But the Jack told him he could not have them yet. Not until he was ready."

"Tom, you're scaring me. Please..."

Tom crossed to Holly. She tried to back away from him but fell. He caught hold of her, wrapped her arm around his neck and lifted her into his arms.

"Hush now," he said. "I have something to show you. But first you must rest."

Cradling her like a lover, he carried her over to the beat-up old armchair.

Her concussed expression turned to one of dread as he continued walking, past the chair and over to the hatch opening in the floor. He set her down at its edge.

"Where are you taking me?" she asked, then squealed as Tom pushed her headlong into the cellar.

Her body hit the stone floor beneath with a thud and a breaking of bone.

Chapter Forty-One

Tom smiled, remembering the sound Julia's body had made when he pushed her down the stairs at their apartment. Such a delirious night; the night she had told him she was pregnant. She'd seemed so wary of him since the miscarriage, afraid of him, even. Doped up on those drugs of hers, she hadn't been able to tell anyone what had he had done. The fact that she'd come to her senses, that she'd gone and told Ellie, didn't bother him. Julia was pregnant again, proof positive of the natural order of things; and he knew exactly how to handle it.

Life, death, and rebirth.

He had to honor the sacred cycle just as his *real* daddy had taught him.

Peering down into the dark depths of the cellar, he remembered the look of shock on Monroe's face as he pushed him to his death from the balcony at Head Office. No one had seen him; he'd waited until Mathers' secretary had gone for a bathroom break before doing the deed. He saw himself cradling the dying man's head, sweet, sticky blood coating his fingers.

He's in the trees, he's waiting...

His own words, not Monroe's; the poor bastard had been too brain-damaged to speak while they waited for the medics to come. The photos that Monroe had included in his PDF report had somehow reawakened the Jack within Tom; he knew that now. Faced with the image of the Jack and Jill Trees where he had been reborn, that secret, raging fire within him had been rekindled. Just as Julia's news that she was pregnant had fanned the flames some months before.

That same angry fire had burst forth during his argument with

Dieter. Cosmo must have been watching, and waiting. The vagrant must have knocked Dieter unconscious then dragged his body away so he could perform his workings upon it in peace—like the runt of the litter taking leftovers. The scarecrow wearing Dieter's clothes had been Cosmo's warning to Tom. But Cosmo had no idea what he was dealing with. Tom's true self had been emerging all his adult life, through nightmares and murderous acts. In a way, Tom admired Cosmo. He knew the woodsman worshipped at the same altar as he, heard the same nurturing voice he had. If things were different, he could have been a worthy successor of the Jack's affections. Or a partner in savage crimes. But his true father only had eyes for Tom.

All paths had led Tom here, to the forest. He was fated to come back to Douglass, destined to reclaim his birthright. Each of his offerings had been made of flesh and blood, and had brought him closer to hearth and home.

Tom climbed down into the cool dark of the cellar.

He had work to do.

Chapter Forty-Two

Holly awoke with an acrid, burning taste in her throat, her head splitting from a deep, throbbing headache. She was on the beaten old armchair next to the trap door. Still wide open, the stink emanating from the hatch gave the room a persistent charnel odor. Groaning, Holly tried to raise her hand to her forehead but could not move her arms. She looked down and saw that Tom had tied her to the chair with thick rope.

She struggled against her bonds. As she did so, Holly realized she could not feel her legs. Looking down, she saw a spike of bone protruding from the flesh of her right leg. Her left leg was twisted beneath her in such a bizarre configuration it must have been broken in at least three places. Numbness and nausea swam in her blood and her head span. She began to shiver and shake; she was going into shock.

"Oh, but you're freezing," Tom said. "Let me get a fire going."

Holly watched Tom as he stepped over Cosmo's body, which still lay facedown in front of the hearthstone. He then set about gathering up some dead branches and twigs from the floor. Placing them in the fireplace, along with some dry moss for kindling, he felt around in his pockets.

"Silly me, I don't smoke. *Nae bother.*"

His accent had the beginnings of a Scottish brogue, like another voice was breaking through and usurping his own. She fought against the ropes, wincing at the way they burned into her skin as she struggled.

Tom rooted through Cosmo's pockets as casually as he might

search through a desk drawer. Smiling, he found a box of matches tucked into the breast pocket. He pulled a match from the box, struck it and set fire to the kindling, blowing gently to help the little flames catch the larger twigs and branches. The fire caught, and he beamed up at Holly.

"There you go, lassie, you'll be a wee bit warmer already."

But Holly was freezing cold from the shock of her injuries, and from mortal terror. The very blood in her veins had slowed with fear. Her heart pounded in her chest and her face was slicked with cold sweat.

She barely heard Tom's words, asking if she was all right, if she wanted him to throw another log on the fire. All she could hear were screams inside her head. Splintered sounds telling her to run from that place and never look back. But her legs were useless, and broken. She gripped the musty old armrests of the chair so hard her fingers had begun to burrow beneath the rotten fabric.

In front of her was a fir tree. About five feet high, it had taken root beneath the floorboards and had sprung up into the room. Every inch of its branches was covered in human remains; threads of glistening sinew and shreds of skin and dreadlocked hair. Bones sat on the firmer branches like macabre gifts. At the top of the tree, the traditional location for an angel or a star, a heart had been impaled on the vertical branch, its chambers ruptured by sharp green needles that poked out of the top of the organ like dozens of little scalpel blades.

Holly wrestled her disbelieving eyes from the grim sight of the tree and looked at Tom. He stood, casual as Christmas, leaning against the mantelpiece above the fireplace like he was going to break into a carol.

He was holding an axe.

Chapter Forty-Three

"When he reached the age of six, he was ready."

Tom spoke in that weird Scottish-American hybrid as he paced the room.

"He watched them from the window over there, and they saw him. They knew in an instant who he was, though they dared not believe it. He was half-naked and freezing cold, and they brought him inside, built up the fire, and filled his belly with hot broth and warm milk. They asked him questions, so many questions, but he remained mute just like the Jack had told him. After a few hours he yawned and stretched, right on cue and they carried him up to bed in his old room. He listened to them for a wee while, debating at first, then arguing, and eventually blaming each other for thinking him dead when he was born. Their accusations turned to tears of contrition and their voices grew softer as their emotions clarified. It was a miracle that their wee boy had returned to them. For that, they had to thank the Jack in the Green. Somehow, the energies in the forest had course corrected the cycle of life, death, and rebirth and their beautiful boy had been restored to them, safe and strong.

"They went up to bed, and he waited; just like he had waited in the shadows of tall trees all those years. He stole into their room that night and did as the Jack told him. Carrying with him his father's axe, he killed them where they slept. Their eyes opened at the moment of impact and they saw the true face of the son they had abandoned."

Tom swung the axe to punctuate his tale; with such force that Holly felt a breeze pass over her skin. She pressed her upper body into the damp, limp armchair feeling more vulnerable than ever.

"Moments later, he had scooped those same eyes from their sockets and skipped downstairs to trim the tree with them. He dragged their corpses downstairs and worked for hours, finding decorative uses for the most secret parts of their bodies as he dissected and discovered them."

He glanced at the crimson decorations that festooned the tree and smiled—lost in a boyhood memory.

"His work done, he sat down under the tree and opened all his presents. There were six; one for each year he had been dead to them. He did not know what to do with the alien objects before him; wooden toys that served no purpose for hunting, or killing. He tossed them on the fire and let them all burn down. As he slept among the remains of his dead parents, his true father sang him to sleep with a lullaby that whispered through the trees—the softest song, a killer's song—just as he had each night since the boy's rebirth.

"A few days later, a caller came knocking; a midwife from the village. The snow had stopped, but still lay in a great drift that propped the front door open. She entered, fearful of what she may find, but nothing prepared her for the horrors that awaited her in that room—*in this room.*

"And, cowering amidst the terrors, she found the boy. He was in the fireplace, *this fireplace,* curled up in the ashes of his burned toys. He sobbed and sucked his thumb and wet himself, just like his daddy told him to; *his real daddy.* So they would take him away someplace new, with new parents, where he could grow big and strong. But his real hearth and home would always be here in the forest, and his real father would always be the Jack in the Green."

Still holding the axe in one hand, Tom took the poker from the floor next to Cosmo's body. After a moment's quiet contemplation, he thrust it into the fire and the blood coating its tip hissed in the flames.

"Tom, listen to me, you've been through a lot, we both have..."

Holly's voice died within her as Tom turned to face her; a face she no longer recognized. She swallowed, hard, and tried to find the words that might stay his hand.

"Let's walk back to the village, hey, both of us together?"

Tom strolled towards her, still brandishing the hot poker, the cold axe.

"Or you can stay here if you want... Tom?"

Her voice trailed off again. She was terrified.

The glowing red tip of the poker was reflected in Tom's eyes like blood and fire.

"My name isn't Tom. It's *Jack*. They gave me his name when I died. And through him I was reborn. I scratched my name in the hearth, just as a great painter would sign his masterwork."

Tom lifted the axe and Holly cried out in terror, wishing she could be free of him and his madhouse. He slammed the axe blade down into her belly, tearing the scream from her throat. His blow had opened her up like a flower. Blood gushed from the gaping hole where her cradle of life had once been. With hunger in his eyes, he discarded the axe then thrust the hot poker into her stomach cavity. He licked his lips, savoring the wet hiss of hot metal against ripe flesh.

Holly felt herself falling, drifting out of the conscious world and into the next. Her belly felt like it was on fire. As her vision blurred, the last thing she saw was Tom; uncoiling her intestines and draping them around the fir tree alongside the other bloody remains that hung there. His eyes reflected red, raw madness.

They were filled with all the uninhibited glee of a child unwrapping his presents on Christmas morning.

Chapter Forty-Four

Jack McCrae crossed to Cosmo's prone body. The vagrant was unconscious, leg still seeping blood from the puncture wounds inflicted by the teeth of his own trap. Jack tossed the poker back into the fire with another sizzle of hot blood. He bent double and pulled the Jack in the Green costume down and over his head. He held it in his hands for a few moments. The webbing and leaves were slicked with blood and soot. Crouching to the floor, Jack set about pulling the costume over Cosmo's head and onto his body. If the vagrant wanted so desperately to wear The Green, then so be it. The costume's fibers, laced with DNA, would tell a damning tale to any who studied them.

Jack would make sure his statement was filled with the grisly details of Cosmo's crimes against humanity, climaxing with his heroic struggle to overcome the crazed murderer using only his wits and the rusted old poker from the hearth. The likes of Officer Travis would lap his story up, dreaming of a book tie-in and movie-of-the-week adaptation; not a bad pension plan for any long-suffering cop after several years' faithful service.

Stepping outside, Jack breathed in the cold night air with its myriad scents of fresh pine and old earth. It filled him up like the unconditional love of his true father, who whispered to him now in Mathers' voice.

"This is what you do, what you're built for. You're our secret weapon, Jack. Clear the area for us. I'm sure you'll do an excellent job."

There was time for one last ritual. One last offering for the Jack.

Epilogue

Dusk was falling over the forest by the time Jack McCrae reached the Jack and Jill Trees. He knelt at the conjoined roots, severed by Cosmo's axe blow. The parts that were cut oozed with a black fluid, like poison from a wound. It was as though the trees were bleeding.

Perhaps they are, he thought.

He held the roots together and felt them fuse, the dark sap acting like glue. The roots would heal. The knowledge was innate within them.

Just a few feet away lay the opening in the trunk of the Jill Tree. It too was slicked with grue from Cosmo's murderous rampage. Like an automaton, Jack set about his work, the voice of his true father urging him on as he scooped up severed limbs and handfuls of wet organs before stuffing them into the orifice in the Jill Tree.

Something primal was controlling him now, some hidden place within him that had been unlocked forever. He continued fetching and carrying, scooping and cramming, until the Jill Tree was bursting with death's totems. Fingers, coils of intestine, and locks of hair joined the rest of the fleshy detritus protruding from the hole in the trunk.

Jack stepped back to survey his handiwork, and remembered his nightmare from the night he made love with Holly, when he was still Tom. All those little corn dollies, raw and screaming in the death hole, tiny faces too innocent to process the pain of their death and rebirth.

His brothers and sisters.

Death and rebirth, the cycle of life, thought Jack. *May my offering be made of flesh and blood, of hearth and home.*

Jack clutched his collar, bracing himself against the icy wind, and set off on the long walk back into the village. Oh, but he was rather looking forward to spending Christmas with his wife and unborn child.

The only way he knew how.

About the Author

Frazer Lee's first novel, *The Lamplighters,* was a Bram Stoker Award Finalist. His short stories have appeared in anthologies including the acclaimed *Read By Dawn* series.

Also a screenwriter and filmmaker, Frazer's screen credits include the award-winning short horror movies *On Edge, Red Lines, Simone* and the horror/thriller feature film (and movie novelization) *Panic Button.*

Frazer resides with his family in leafy Buckinghamshire, England. When he's not getting lost in a forest he is working on new fiction and film projects.

Official Website: www.frazerlee.com

Blog: http://frazerlee.wordpress.com

Twitter: http://twitter.com/frazer_lee

Facebook: www.facebook.com/AuthorFrazerLee

Author's Note

At the time of writing, the beautiful countryside and ancient forests that, in part, inspired this book are under threat from plans to build a high-speed railway. Please visit http://stophs2.org for more information, thank you.

(Frazer Lee, Buckinghamshire, 2013)

Life on Meditrine Island is luxurious...but brief.

The Lamplighters
© 2011 Frazer Lee

Marla Neuborn has found the best post-grad job in the world—as a "Lamplighter" working on Meditrine Island, an exclusive idyllic paradise owned and operated by a consortium of billionaires. All Lamplighters have to do is tend to the mansions, cook and clean, and turn on lights to make it appear the owners are home. But the job comes with conditions. Marla will not know the exact location of the island, and she will have no contact with the outside world for the duration of her stay.

Once on the island, Marla quickly learns the billionaire lifestyle is not all it is made out to be. The chief of security rules Meditrine with an iron fist. His private police force patrols the shores night and day, and CCTV cameras watch the Lamplighters relentlessly. Soon Marla will also discover first-hand that the island hides a terrible secret. She'll meet the resident known as the Skin Mechanic. And she'll find out why so few Lamplighters ever leave the island alive.

Available now in ebook and print from Samhain Publishing.

Enjoy the following excerpt from The Lamplighters...

"It's the greatest job in the world."

Vera smiled as she said the words.

"All I have to do is turn on the damn lights, water the plants; a few chores..."

Static crackled in her ear — the phone line was lousy tonight.

"Are you still there?"

"Yes," came the reply, "but I can hardly hear you. There's a weird kind of... echo."

"It's Jessie's uplink," Vera chuckled, "We're not really allowed to call anyone from the island..."

"Sorry... how... calling me?"

Christ, the line was getting choppy. Vera pressed the cordless handset closer to her ear, then checked herself.

"As if that'll make any difference," she said. Probably talking to herself now.

The crackling grew louder. She could still hear her friend's voice, buried beneath layers of digital cacophony. A faint echo smothered by an avalanche of noise.

There was something else in the mix too; an ominous growling hum like the electricity pylons near her home. Berlin, so far away now. Even as she thought it, the hum grew; drowning out what little was left of her friend's staccato tones.

And with a click, silence.

"*Scheiße,*" she cursed, stabbing the redial button. The phone was completely dead. Hacking an outside line was a fine art, she appreciated that, but Jessie clearly needed some new software. And she'd be giving that little bag of smoke back too.

First things first. Vera put the handset in its cradle and headed for the kitchen. She walked over to the huge range in the centre of the room and ignited all four of the gas taps. Then, crouching on her haunches, she turned the oven on full blast. The expensive smoked glass oven door afforded her a look at her own reflection. Only a month on Meditrine Island and already she looked five years younger. Amazing. Gone were the dark grey shadows around her eyes - even her signature brittle dry hair had a new luster. Berlin could take care of itself, thanks very much. The island really was like a fountain of youth, she thought as she rose and crossed to the patio door.

Unclipping the latch, Vera had to use two hands to slide the glass behemoth open. Whoever owned this house had a serious heavy glass fetish. Stepping out into the night, her senses were flooded. The island's fresh air was like no other; an intoxicating blend of jasmine and ocean spray. When she went back to the city, she'd have to remember to bottle and sell it.

Click.

Her quiet moment was suddenly blasted with fifteen hundred watts of raw security lighting as she stepped in front of the infrared sensors. She cursed the light for blinding her as she picked up the watering can, blinking away the white-hot glare. The light had brought the mosquitoes a-calling too. They whizzed around her as she dashed back into the kitchen.

Vera filled the watering can with cool, clear water at the bath-sized sink. This was the least tedious of her tasks - the plants were going to drink their fill tonight. Amidst such fabulous wealth, such meticulous order, it felt good that a mere backpacker could decide the fate of items so precious to their millionaire owners.

Millionaires? Billionaires, more likely.

She remembered Jessie's sardonic voice from the first time they'd hung out together, gossiping about who owned these mansions; this island. But Vera didn't really care who the owners were. That they were paying her handsomely to do a few chores was all she cared about. And the most strenuous chore was watering the plants. Easy money. "The job's a doozy," Jessie had giggled. 'Doozy Jessie' been working on the island longer than Vera and seemed to be going a little stir crazy...

As the water rose closer to the brim of the watering can, the security lights clicked off suddenly. *Like everything else on the island they ran to a tight schedule,* thought Vera. As she did so, milliseconds before the light bulbs faded, Vera saw something outside.

A figure.

She blinked twice, slow and firm. The ghost imprint of the blinding bulbs still there, forming crescent shaped black holes in her mind's eye. Was there someone out there?

Vera blinked again, then swore furiously as liquid spilled onto her feet. Soaked, she closed the faucet and let the watering can rest in the sink unit. *Shouldn't have smoked that joint before coming up to the house,* she thought, sounding for all the world like her mother. Scatterbrain, she used to call Vera whenever she lost the power to function normally; everyday tasks becoming impossibly hilarious missions. She still wondered if her mother had known her daughter was stoned, or if she simply believed her child was missing a neuron or two million.

The old clumsiness was really kicking in now, as she left little pools of water on the tiled floor on her way to the patio. Putting the can down (yet more spills) she grabbed the door handle and pulled with all her might.

Swoosh.

The glass giant slid open easier this time. Vera bent down to pick up the can — then the smell hit her.

Something had invaded the envelope of jasmine and surf, corrupting the very night air with its presence. A hospital smell, harsh and synthetic, like the way her dentist smelled. She'd hated the dentist since she was a kid. Had he followed her here, to paradise, tracking her down after all these years to do all that work she had chickened out of? To tut and frown disapprovingly through his paper mask, noting her cannabis-stained enamel and ugly overbite?

She leaned out into the night air, her nostrils searching for the source of the stifling smell. It was mixed with something else now, like ripe leather.

Click.

He was standing right next to her, impossibly close. Vera's heart blasted into her mouth, choking her scream. The source of the smell regarded her idly, his black eyes like camera lenses. Cold. Unforgiving.

Before she could react, Vera heard a swooshing sound. The smell of rubber gloves perversely filled her nostrils, pushing all the way back into her throat as if someone really had jammed two fingers up her nose. The intruder's dark form was a monolith, burned into her eyes by the security lights.

Click.

Swoosh.

The bulbs faded once more. Vera's senses imploded as the sliding door crushed her skull against the alloy doorframe.

Crunch.

Swoosh, as the door slid back again.

Crunch.

Vera's body jerked uselessly then fell still; her brains spattered across the cool, thick glass.

It's all about the story...

Romance

HORROR

www.samhainpublishing.com

Lightning Source UK Ltd.
Milton Keynes UK
UKOW04f0812070813

214995UK00002B/42/P